A FLASH OF SILVER

ANAM CARA
BOOK 1

SILK AUBREY

TRADEMARK ACKNOWLEDGMENTS

Kevlar

PROLOGUE
KINNIA

I sprinted toward the jagged, silver rift a hundred feet ahead, ignoring the whir of machines gaining on me. The sword strapped to my hip smacked against my burning legs with every stride. Earth's barren landscape blurred past in monochromatic grays. I focused on the glimpse of color between the edges of the rift's tear in reality.

Thrae, my home, my only hope, shone through that tiny gap in the hellhole I'd been trapped in for almost five years. I gathered the last of my waning *energy* and forced speed into my legs. I had to get through the rift.

The sound of my frantic footfalls disappeared beneath the blanket of beeping and hydraulics that chased me with automated grace. Tech, terrifying nightmares of metal, cables, and parts I couldn't name, raced after me. They could be killed, but for each one destroyed, two more took their place. Something our doomed party hadn't understood until too late. We'd been so naïve. I destroyed everything I loved, everyone I loved, and—

I needed to keep running.

Hope and terror fueled my leap through the vertical opening, barely wider than my body. The burning edges crackled against my skin. I landed face-first on the ground. Rich soil filled my nose. The sounds of birds and life almost deafened me. Tears of joy stung my chapped face as I dug my fingers into the rich dirt.

Home.

The dead and drained world of horrors abandoned by the humans that once ruled it lay behind me. I trembled as relief mixed with the adrenaline still pumping through my veins. Leaves crunched. I whipped my head toward the sound. A dizzying mixture of hot oranges, bright pinks, and rich golds swam into focus. I had landed in a forest, and such brilliant colors only existed in fae territory.

"What in Fire?" a man blurted.

My heart ached. It had been so long since I'd heard a voice other than my own, but I hadn't survived this long by letting my guard down. I shoved up into a crouch and grasped my sword's hilt. The rift hung open behind me, its edges burning into the thick bark of an orange-colored tree. Hydraulics hissed out.

I could taste freedom. Not even the fae could stop me now.

"Some…one came out of the rift," the same man said.

I scanned the vivid forest for the speaker.

A new, deeper male voice rumbled out of the trees. "Nothing good comes out of rifts."

My patchwork suit of Kevlar and metal glinted in the bright sunlight. My pale skin had gotten so dry and dirty it looked more like scales. Tech didn't have hair, and I kept mine so short, the breeze chilled my scalp. I looked nothing like the girl I'd been when I got trapped on Earth five years ago. I looked like the monsters I'd just escaped.

Two large men stepped around trees and into view. Not men, fae. The shorter one, bald and muscular, barely reached my six feet. Pale scars, purple and white scales, and navy tattoos stretched across his almost lilac-colored chest. He wore only brown pants and boots. Instead of eyebrows, he had more of those swirling blue tattoos, and his ears fanned into five delicate, deeper purple points.

"Someone close the Fire-damned rift." The other, about my height, slid into a fighting stance and lifted his lanky arms. His palms glowed with a fire that built until even his slit-pupiled eyes burned molten gold. "Zel!"

He wore one side of his hair shaved to the skull like mine, but the other glistened with fiery gold locks down to his chin. His brown pants matched his partner's, though a simple cream tunic covered his chest.

I rose to standing and drew the sword I'd found in a partially collapsed building a few weeks after I escaped the first lab. A metal plaque next to its case had read, "Katana." The word meant nothing, but I'd committed it to memory anyway.

Hydraulics hissed from the rift, much closer now.

"Zelimir!" The golden one's gaze flickered between the rift, seconds away from pouring Tech into Thrae, and me.

The shirtless fae stalked forward. His gaze bore into me as he reached for the sheath on this back and withdrew a massive, bright red axe with black veins on its surface.

My heart leapt to my throat. I reached for my *energy* but found only hollowness. I'd used the last of it to get to through the rift. The well of power that existed beneath my skin buzzed as the reservoir refilled, but I didn't yet have enough for any fancy tricks.

The shirtless fae stepped toward me. My dry scream cut through the roar of near-overwhelming hydraulics, and I charged just as a silver leg emerged from the rift and buried itself in the ground.

He cursed and dove out of my way. A third fae appeared at the edge of my vision. I veered to the right and focused on not tripping on the rocky forest floor. The fae wilds occupied the southern lands, and human territory, the north.

I could only run.

1

KINNIA

I shifted the pack on my back and rested my hand on the hilt of my katana. The blade bumped my quiver, both belted to my left side to balance the array of weapons I'd accumulated in the nearly two and a half years since I'd jumped through that rift into the fae wilds.

Tweek, Grant, Tommy, and I walked in loose formation around the cart in the merchant caravan we'd been contracted to guard. The rumbling wheels had become background noise long ago. Colorful goods strapped in place by even more colorful ancient bungee cords lay hidden under layers of dirty canvas. Merchant carts stretched before and behind us as we plodded ever southward.

The cloth I tied around my mouth and nose to keep from breathing in the dust kicked up by the teams of horses and oxen had shifted downward once again on my sweat-soaked face, and I tugged it back up.

Grant spit a wad of phlegm onto the dry, cracked ground. I dodged around the greenish patch with practiced ease.

"What? Hour left 'til the *Cross Roads?*" His voice crumbled like the dirt underfoot.

I shrugged. A sour smell filled the air. Another of the short man's farts.

Our destination, a human town that dared survive on the edge of the fae wilds, spawned rumors all the way in the far north, where I'd spent most of the last two and a half years. No other human settlement had so many fae visitors. I didn't really want to come face-to-face with any fae, but everyone talked about what their presence did to the architecture and customs. Being a mercenary allowed me to see unique places often enough to keep me satisfied, and I doubted anywhere was more unique than the *Cross Roads*.

I rubbed the dusty leather covering my stomach and tried to steady myself. I hadn't traveled back to the edge of the wilds to sightsee. As it had every day for the last few months, a small ball of tension like I'd eaten something my stomach refused to digest urged me ever south. I flexed my hand. *Energy* trickled into my muscles like a cool river of power, then away again. Completely different from the ball.

Tweek twitched and scratched his elbow. "Can't be more than an hour." The thin man stood an inch below my six feet and, like all the mercenaries I'd met over the last few years, he wore a ragged mix of leather, chain, and ancient nylon. I didn't touch old-Earth materials, though, and chain only weighed me down, so I'd pinched and saved until I could piece together fully leather armor.

Tommy scoffed.

Grant spit again. "Fuk'n guard duty. Fuk'n *Cross Roads*. Any insight for us, Dick?"

They all called me Dick, though I'd introduced myself as Declan, since our first night together ended with me breaking Tweek's nose a few weeks ago. I snorted and returned my hand to my sword. The men were crass and blunt, but they didn't ask much of me. After a couple nights of drinking, I took them up on their offer to join their crew for this job.

"Yeah, ya fuckin' know-it-all." Tommy sneered. "Any insights?"

He had the straightest nose of any of us but me, which he brought up often, and his paranoid streak stretched a mile wide.

"First time I've been here." I shrugged. Not really a lie. Two and a half years ago, the *Cross Roads* had gone by in a blur.

I adjusted my cuirass. Looking the part of a man came easily. I had broad enough shoulders, well-defined muscles, and the stance of a swordsman. My hands were calloused and rough from use. My flop of black curls obscured enough of my face, and my relatively small breasts looked flat enough under my cinched leather cuirass that I rarely even had to bind them. A pretty man, maybe, but still male. Men tended to be faster and stronger than women, so when I tapped into my *energy*, no one blinked an eye. Except Tommy.

I glanced at Tommy to see his narrowed eyes locked on me. The stone sent a curl of fear up my spine. Had he detected my fib about the *Cross Roads*? No, the stone was just making me nervous.

Once again, I tried to press my *energy* into the heavy lump in my gut. Like oil and water, the two didn't mix. *Energy* poured back into my body, and I shivered. The stone couldn't be caused by something natural. Couldn't be my *energy*. I'd known for some time now that could only mean one thing. Magic. But magic only came from fae. Despite centuries on Thrae, humans never had any.

"Freak," my last foster parents had said when they kicked me out. *"No magic in this house."*

I touched my bow, nestled in two pieces on my opposite hip, followed by the sheath of one of the two daggers I kept strapped to the outside of my thigh. Their familiarity grounded me in the present. The stone hadn't hurt me. It didn't keep me from eating or affect my life at all. It simply drew me south. Toward magic. Toward fae.

I hadn't followed the magic on purpose. I hadn't followed it at all. But by chance or fate, the best jobs over the past few months had meandered steadily south. Now, the mountain pass that protected human lands lay behind us. Rocky, barren plains stretched to the east, but my gaze always drifted south. The fae wilds loomed closer with every step.

Memories of bright colors and creatures I had no name for sped through my mind in a haze of horror and hope, but as always, horror surged forward. The landscape around me turned gray, and I envisioned the ground littered with machined metal and splotches of blood. My hands shook. The scent of sweat and livestock filled my nose. Thrae, I was on Thrae, not Earth.

"Firs' time Dick?" Grant laughed. "Yo'v got th'look of yuth a'out you."

Tommy cackled. "Can you even piss standing up yet?"

I seized onto his words like an anchor in the storm, and the memories vanished. I shrugged, and he laughed again. I didn't know my exact age, but I'd guess mid-twenties. Like pretending to be a man, when people assumed young, they gave me less thought.

Tweek scratched his nose and grinned. "Bet ya never been with a woman, neither."

The three of them laughed, and I joined in at their expense. The air pressure abruptly dropped. Someone yelled at the back of the caravan, and I whirled toward the sound. Two signal flares exploded in the air behind us. *Trouble.*

Grant grunted, "Get run'n."

I dropped my pack and sprinted down the line of wagons with Tweek at my side. Grant and Tommy would hold position at our wagon.

"What the fuck?" a man shouted.

The hiss of hydraulics set my heart to a wild rhythm. *No.* Rifts didn't appear outside the wilds. I skidded to a stop at the end of the caravan. The scouts might not recognize the shimmering split in reality that lay thirty feet ahead, but I'd never forget the silver of a rift.

I leapt atop the last cart with the other archers, unhooked my bow from my hip, and snapped it into a single piece. Metallic EarthTech glinted in the hot sun as the first silver, multi-hinged leg stepped through and onto Thraen soil. All the mercs would die if I didn't teach them how to fight these machines.

Five more legs reached through the rift and pulled the eight-foot-tall Tech from Earth into Thrae. A bleached, armless human torso with black cables intertwined and plugged into what would have been its hips and stomach bounced as it burst into a run with inhuman speed. Its vaguely human face gave way to a clear plastic dome that housed its pulsing brain. Oddly angled silvery arms with sharp claws jutted out of its back. A SpiderTech.

And two more behind it.

Hatred churned in my stomach. "Aim for the eyes!"

I grabbed an arrow from the quiver at my hip, nocked it, drew back my bowstring, and loosed. My arrow sliced through the monstrosity's eye and lodged in its brain. The Tech faltered, then stumbled to its knees.

Other archers followed my lead. On the ground, mercenaries with swords drawn charged the SpiderTechs. Human screams soon mixed with the clash of metal. I shot my second arrow into the lead Tech's other eye. Not dead until you smell oil. Sparks flew as it collapsed into a pile of metal.

Rancid oil assaulted my nose. My hands shook as I reached for another arrow. I gritted my teeth. They were in my world now. Another SpiderTech knocked over a group of mercenaries. I took aim and loosed another arrow. The Tech lurched to the side, and my arrow went wide.

The rift remained still as death, but no more abominations emerged. I grabbed another arrow. Draw, aim, breathe, release. Pods of fighters surrounded the remaining monstrosities and kept them from the wagons. A few mercs had discovered the weakness of the cables, but only the Tech brought down by arrows stayed down.

Three figures on horseback burst from the line of trees at the edge of fae territory. Fae guards, the only ones who could close rifts. About time. We were fortunate only the pack of SpiderTech had been near enough to come through.

The stone in my gut hummed. I grabbed for another arrow but found my quiver empty. Shit. I unstrung my bow, holstered it, and leapt to the ground.

"Cables!" I hollered. "Climb the bastards—aim for eyes and brains."

Sparking cables dangled from the barely functional body of the nearest SpiderTech. I dodged between its skittering legs, then swung up onto its back and grabbed its cold, human torso. The monster's head whirred as it spun to try to get a visual on me. I yanked one of my daggers from its sheath and drove the blade into the SpiderTech's brain, just above the glittering metal plate bearing its designation. Oil coated my arm, and the thing shuddered.

I dove off and rolled. One to go. Against my better instincts, I sheathed the knife still covered in oil, drew my katana, and charged the remaining machine. I threw myself across the ground and skidded between two metallic legs with my katana stretched up over my head.

The blade sliced through the underside of the SpiderTech. Oil sprayed down on me, and I struggled not to choke. I twirled and hacked into the seam that joined legs to body. Two legs thudded to the ground. The thing groaned as it fought to stay upright.

My fellow mercenaries roared. They'd managed to stretch a length of rope out in front of the Tech and surged forward as it wobbled. The rope hit the thing's remaining joints and swiped its legs out from beneath it.

I dove to the side and under the rope as the Tech crashed to the ground, then rolled to my feet. Mercenaries sank blades into the monster's head until only a pulp of oil, gears, and gray matter decorated the dry ground. Tense silence replaced the clash of metal and the buzz of electronics. Tech and mercenary bodies littered the ground.

The three fae now stood in front of the rift. One watched the battle-field with his arms crossed, while the other two faced the shimmering crack in reality, their backs to me. The slimmer one leapt atop the other's shoulders. The sun glinted off the golden, almost fire-colored hair on one side of his head.

The bare, broad shoulders of the fae on the bottom dented slightly with the weight of his friend as the one atop began tracing large, colorful fae letters across the rift's opening. My gaze caught where his tapered waist disappeared into his beltline, and I yanked my attention upward to the delicate, fanned ears jutting out from each side of his head fluttering in the wind. Warmth gathered in my gut. Navy tattoos kissed along his sculpted, lilac-colored back, ran across his shoulders, and swirled down his spine. Recognition tugged at my memory. Then, I realized why.

Could they be the same fae who chased me out of the wilds? The slim one continued to write fae letters in the air, and my arms pebbled with goose bumps. I frowned. His movements increased in grace and speed. The fae he stood on grabbed his ankles, purple biceps flexing. A deep frown creased the brow of the fae facing me.

My breath caught as I looked at him. He had at least a foot on me, with broad shoulders that matched his stature. Small dots of moisture collected on his dark skin, and the long twists of copper hair that hung well past his shoulders were so shiny they looked metallic. He wore the same cream tunic and brown pants as his companions, but he'd rolled his sleeves up to his elbows. The fabric strained across his pecs.

His mouth thinned to a line as he scanned the battlefield. His purple gaze met mine. My skin zinged. I took an involuntary step forward as the stone in my gut trembled. A black blur burst from the trees.

I froze. A dire wolf, one of the rare Earth animals who escaped with humanity and evolved in the wilds. The giant of a fae spun and bolted for the animal. The wolf veered back toward the trees. The stone tingled before going still once more. I shivered and rubbed my arms.

"Dick!" Tweek shouted.

I jumped. Blood rushed to my cheeks so fast it hurt. A blob of rancid oil dripped from my hair and landed on my nose. Sweat and dirt coated every inch of me, and my katana slipped in my oil-slicked fingers.

The air pressure returned to normal as the two remaining fae finished writing the bright letters in the air, and the rift winked out of existence. The golden one dropped to the ground, and they disappeared into the forest where the other fae and the wolf had gone.

My gut twisted. They hadn't even helped us fight. I forced myself to turn my back on them. Tweek held up a few of my arrows, and I nodded. Everything was fair game after a battle. If I wanted any ammunition, I needed to start salvaging.

Thankfully, only a few people lay unmoving on the battlefield. I knelt next to a dead mercenary and, after a brief moment of silence, cut a rag from his shirt. I wiped oil off my katana, gave cleaning the dagger up as a lost cause without water to clean the rag, and searched the battlefield for my arrows. Only two unaccounted for. Not bad.

I tried to scrub the worst of the oil from myself with the dirty rag until a green flare lit the sky. Time to return to our assigned wagons. The caravan had to move on. As I walked back up the line, my brain spun. How had a rift formed so far outside the fae wilds? Rifts needed raw magic, and only fae made the land produce that.

"What's going on in that pretty head of yurs?" Grant asked.

I'd taken this job for the money and would be headed back north as fast as I could. No good could come out of getting involved in fae affairs.

Absently, I rubbed my stomach. The stone taunted me, hummed, and urged me south once more. I shivered as I retook my position.

"Aw, Dick, we gonna hafta rename you Twat?" Grant asked.

I'd been so caught up in my thoughts, my male façade had dropped. Worse, I'd let fear take over.

"I kinda like Twat better." I made a rude gesture toward Tommy with my fingers in front of my crotch.

With Grant's roaring laughter, the caravan lumbered forward like we'd simply taken a rest. The stone in my stomach bubbled as I began walking south once more.

WE ARRIVED AT THE *Cross Roads* JUST AS THE SUN SET. WITH new coin weighing down my pockets, I followed Grant through the walled town's colorful, bustling center and toward its less colorful, rowdier outskirts. Humans and half-fae crowded the streets. A man paused at a street vendor, and I had to bite my lip to keep from commenting on the bushy, deep red tail sticking out the back of his pants.

Grant whistled. "Fuk'n hell, ya really haven't been before."

A tall, thin woman with bark-like skin and a sway in her hips disappeared down a side street.

Tommy tripped on something and barely caught himself before he fell. "I gotta see what's under that skirt."

I turned a giggle into a chuckle as Tweek slapped him on the back.

We walked through a puff of warm air. My heartbeat quickened, and goose bumps peppered my arms. Magic. I'd experienced it on my flight through the wilds. Grant, Tommy, and Tweek just laughed and kept walking. I laughed with them.

Pockets of magic hummed around the town. Art and color filled every corner. Gardens much too green for the height of summer decorated organically round buildings. Roads dead-ended and curled in random patterns no human would possibly design. Leaves with bright-red veins and neon-orange edges clung to the sides of buildings and threatened to take over the road. Human and not-so-human lived side-by-side.

Instead of the drab leathers and dark shades of most human lands, the locals wore bright colors or, in some cases, no clothing at all. I stopped short as a gray, rocklike fae somersaulted past followed by a small, humanoid boy with gray skin and piercing blue eyes. He gave me a big grin and rolled after the rocklike fae.

Grant grunted. "Half-breed."

I snorted. Humans and fae always professed to dislike each other, but sex seemed to be the one thing they could agree upon.

We reached a ramshackle tavern on the edge of town bearing the sign, *The Boat House.* Grant creaked the door open into a poorly lit common room crowded with patrons, like every other tavern I'd stayed in since becoming a merc. The smell of hot stew made my stomach growl. We wound our way through the mismatched collection of tightly packed chairs and tables toward the bar. A human man with a scraggly beard glanced up as we approached.

He took in our travel-stained clothes and heavy packs. "I've got a few spots left in the barn, if you leave my stable boy alone. A silver each."

I winced. Expensive for just a spot in the hay, but with the caravan rolling in, the town would be packed. We grumbled but paid. Grant let out one of his foul farts before we left the bar.

The large, red barn against the town's metal-and-wood walls was impossible to miss, even in the fading evening light. Iron bars penned cattle and horses in stalls on each side. The iron surprised me. According to rumor, fae couldn't stand the stuff. I snorted. Not that you could trust rumor. Humans and fae hadn't gotten along since humans exploded onto Thrae with Tech hot on their heels. I'd heard epic ballads about native fae heroes and whispered warnings about wicked fae tricksters in equal measure. I certainly wouldn't be looking into the wilds for answers.

Tommy stepped inside and poked a pile of hay. When it didn't move, he tossed his pack down. "I'm claiming this spot."

"That looks big enough." Grant grinned and added his pack to the pile.

Tweek didn't say anything, but he threw his pack down as well. The three looked at me to join.

"Sorry." I pointed at the ladder leading up to the loft. "For a silver, I'm taking the king's suite."

Grant laughed. "Don't be piss'n off the side in the middle of th'night."

"If I do, I'll aim for you." I gave him the finger and headed for the ladder with a bounce in my step. Hopefully, I'd get a smidgen of privacy up there.

"I'm going back in for dinner," Tommy said.

I changed my middle finger to a thumbs-up, and the three of them laughed.

A small fort of hay bales and blankets, likely what the stable boy called home, occupied half the loft. I dropped my pack and spread my bedroll near the opposite wall, underneath one of the many skylights. At least the smell of bodies and animal shit would cover my own odor in here. After almost four weeks on the road with only a single set of clothes and few bathing options, I reeked.

I took a deep breath and lay back on my bedroll, watching the final colors of sunset dissolve into darkness. With a start, I realized the weight in my gut didn't feel as solid anymore, more like a ball than a stone. It pulsed softly, as if ready for something. Shivers ran up my spine at memory of the fae's purple eyes, and the jolt that ran through me when he looked at me. I could no longer avoid the truth. The stone had to be magic.

And wherever magic went, Tech followed.

2

————

TEYR

I INSPECTED THE LAYER OF DIRT COVERING MY FINGERS IN the evening light with a frown. Our horses' fast walk ate up the ground between us and the *Cross Roads*. After closing the rift in human lands, Shade had a proper dire wolf freakout, howling and running in circles and refusing to relax. Zelimir made us scour the border for hours in case Shade sensed an impending rift the rest of us couldn't. Unsurprisingly, we'd turned up nothing. One rift on the human side could be explained by this strange little town and the magic it radiated. A second would be virtually impossible. And anyway, we all knew Zel's extensive search was just an attempt to avoid the fact that we had found our new fifth mate among the merchant caravan.

A zing of excitement tingled down my spine. I reached forward and scratched my Andalusian's palomino neck. The best thing humans ever did was give us horses. The beasts weren't native to Thrae, but a few snuck through the rifts in the big upheaval. They made getting around much easier. But perhaps I just felt particularly pleased with everything human this evening.

"I mean, at least the humans at the rift were halfway competent, right?" I said. "Doesn't that make the *Cross Roads* more exciting?"

Bash, on his Friesian next to me, grunted.

I sighed. I wouldn't be getting another word out of my part-dragon mate any time soon. He'd been grumpy since we realized the discovery of our new fifth meant we'd have to properly enter human territory. Maybe I'd have better luck with Zel. His long, copper twists bounced against his back with every step of his massive, bay Shire horse, the only beast big enough to cart his titan body.

"I mean, our new mate was hiding amongst the humans in the caravan, so that's definitely exciting." I grabbed my waterskin and poured some over my hands, then rubbed them together. The soot and dirt only moved around and gathered on the leather of my horse's reins. I needed a bath.

Zelimir scowled. "We shouldn't be getting a new fifth. This doesn't happen. Anam Caras don't heal themselves."

My heart squeezed, and I closed my eyes to say a prayer to Fire for our lost mate, Light. Six years ago, he had shot me a cocky grin and promised drinks that night as we waded into battle against a massive Tech horde. His death had almost broken us, and his absence left a hole in our Anam Cara, our soul bond, that remained as hot and jagged as any rift. We'd been incomplete and underpowered.

Until today.

I took a deep breath. Even the dirty air around the human town tasted sweet with the sparkle of a new fifth on the horizon. When I had drawn the runes to close the rift, magic had sprung easily to my fingers. Not nearly as strong as the magic had been with Light—we hadn't connected to our new fifth, or found him, technically—but the runes flowed with a liquid grace I'd almost forgotten. We could be whole again.

"History doesn't matter." I grinned. "We're getting a new mate."

"History is where we find our truths." Zelimir patted his saddlebag filled with thick tomes he'd taken with him when he'd abdicated the titan throne to join our Cara. "This is unnatural."

"Just because it never happened before doesn't make it unnatural. Caras were new once." I glared at my commander's back. Spoilsport.

He shook his head but didn't respond. I huffed and began braiding my horse's mane. We approached the gates of the *Cross Roads* as the last of the lackluster sunset dripped out of the sky. Zelimir exchanged a few words with the guards before they let us pass.

Bash's shoulders tensed the moment we entered the walls, and he furrowed his tattooed eyebrows. I sent him a wave of calm support through our Cara and felt Zel do the same. Something about humans set his teeth on edge, and I figured it had to do with the past he refused to talk about.

As always, it fell to me to bring the mood up. I bounced in my saddle. "So, what's the plan, Zelly?"

My commander tensed at the nickname, and I grinned.

"We find the fae and correct this error before it goes too far," he replied flatly.

I frowned. "But what if—"

"I'm not arguing with you, Teyr." Zelimir ran a hand through his twists. "Until we meet him, we can only speculate."

I shrugged elaborately, but he didn't look back at me. "Fine. I'm still excited."

Zelimir grunted and stopped in front of a long, low pub with a battered sign that read, *The Boat House*. Firelight spilled from its windows, and the sound of music and laughter drifted through the air. Our new mate sat inside, just the barest wisp of possibility.

"And I'm not excited." Zel dismounted. "The gate guard said most of the mercenaries ended up here." He eyed the pub warily. "My Cara leans in this direction as well."

I wiggled my eyebrows at him and dismounted as well. "Can't we make ourselves presentable first?" I rubbed a hand down my grubby arm.

Bash gestured toward the pub and jumped to the ground. "Humans are filthy."

We dropped our reins. Our battle-trained mounts needed no further instructions to wait for us.

"Our new fifth will notice." I ran my fingers through the flame of a torch on the outside of the building until its low heat warmed my fingers. "Even if he's among humans, he still has fae sensibilities."

Bash grunted. He never liked when I stuck my hands in fire, even after seventy-five years of knowing only the worst flames would burn an ember like me. I hoped our new fifth would be a better conversationalist than my current mates.

Zelimir shrugged. "Let's go in and find out."

I cut in front of my looming, grumpy mates with a wide smile, still feeling the warmth of the human flame. The music grew louder as I pushed open the door on screaming hinges. Every human in the place whipped toward us and froze. The music cut off on a sour note. We threaded our way through the mostly male patrons toward the bar. Hay and dirt crunched beneath my boots. A human woman carrying a tray of mugs hurried past us.

By the time we reached the bar, the music had picked back up, and conversation rolled off the low roof. I'd never spent time with humans, but I'd heard stories of excitement, bravery, and adventure that all began in human taverns. My heart raced. I wanted to thump my fist against the bar and demand a drink with that same exuberance, but the dirt and grease covering the lumpy wooden countertop stopped me.

I caught the barkeep's gaze. "We're looking for a fae mercenary."

"A fae mercenary?" The barkeep scoffed. "No such thing."

I tilted my head to the side and eyed my commander. *Pulses* traveled across our Cara, rippling the core of magic that lived in my gut with our unspoken language. Zelimir had no doubt our fifth sat somewhere in the tavern. My Cara hummed with the same feeling. Although we couldn't pinpoint him, he shared the tavern with us.

"Anything's possible." I met the barman's gaze with a smile.

He scowled. "This is a human-only establishment."

"So, you have some sort of magic that tests that?" I smiled brighter.

The barman pursed his lips. He eyed my pointed ears, then gave my much more visibly fae mates a longer look. A set of old iron swords behind the bar glinted in the low light. I struggled to keep smiling.

With a grunt, he threw his dirty rag down on the bar. "I don't want no trouble."

"Then three of your finest ales." I forced my smile bigger before finally letting it drop as he grabbed three mugs from below the bar.

Zelimir retrieved a handful of coins while I peered at the clientele.

No colorful hair. No tails. I couldn't make out pointed ears from here, but they didn't seem likely. Most of the men had similar builds and wore travel-stained armor. Every single one had a weapon within reach.

I turned back to the bar. My commander didn't have a single weapon on him. His standard Cara uniform disguised his princely upbringing, but he looked even larger than his seven feet, perched on a bar stool that groaned under his bulk. Although Bash had his double-headed cherry-stone axe holstered on his back and wore a shirt, his fanned ears and dragon scales gave him away before someone could even notice the purple tint to his skin.

The barkeep thumped three mugs of dishwater-brown liquid on the counter. I swallowed hard and looked at my ashen commander. Bash cursed under his breath, picked up a dirty tankard, and took a deep pull. I clasped my hands behind my back to ensure I didn't touch anything. No fae would ever choose to be here. Shock reverberated through me.

Our fifth had to be human.

I reached for my earlier excitement, but it had burned up amidst the sour looks, cacophony of noise, and piss-smelling ale. Humans didn't join Caras. They couldn't hear the call.

Bash's unease mixed with my own in our Cara. Purple and white scales crawled up his torso, onto his face, and slithered back down in an abortive version of the full-dragon transformation his mixed blood kept from him.

Zelimir clapped Bash's shoulder. A wave of my commander's calm and determination washed over us, but even his emotions carried a hint of uncertainty. Bash rolled his shoulders and crossed his arms. With his demons, a human as our fifth had to be his worst nightmare. It just might be mine as well.

Our new mate was a dirty, human man. He would expect to join with me, an ember, a fae blessed by Fire itself. My bond with my mates only made me stronger. A human couldn't come close to matching me. Matching us. As if to mock me, my Cara pushed my attention toward a table in the back as the group of human men there threw their heads back in raucous laughter.

3

ZELIMIR

Once we had enough information, I led us out of *The Boat House*. I'd stayed in town a few times over the years and knew a quieter inn with a reputation for colorful decor and fae-friendly faces.

Silence wrapped around us until we sat in a suite, clean, fed, and listening to the faint sounds of the town's nightlife drifting up through the windows. Not even Teyr had spoken for the last hour. My Cara hummed with a collective discomfort my mates didn't bother to keep out of the bond.

A human mate.

I massaged my herbal moisturizer into my last copper twist. "We have to tell the Lower Council."

Bash, my second-in-command, grunted agreement from where he sat cross-legged on his bed.

"Fuck." Teyr threw himself back onto one of the other four beds in the Cara-specific suite I'd requested out of habit.

I shook my head and opened one of the saddlebags piled on the fifth bed. Bash had learned a handful of human curse words from his regiment during the civil war, mostly older fae who'd fought alongside humans against Tech back when both were new, and all of us had picked them up, to my chagrin. I fished through the saddlebag for one of the two communication bowls we, like all Anam Caras, carried until the runes etched into the foggy glass surface grated against my fingers. Despite my strength, the palm-sized bowl sat heavily in my hand. I'd found Councilor Drax's bowl, the one that would allow us to speak to our old mentor alone, instead of the whole Lower Council. I should locate the other. All five of the powerful fae in charge of Anam Caras would want to hear this. Instead, I sat on the floor at the little table under the window with Councilor Drax's bowl. Fate had made my choice.

"Fine." Teyr stood, grabbed the mortar and pestle from Bash's saddlebag, and untied a small pouch from his belt.

He joined me on the floor, then began silently measuring out exact portions of the herbs needed to make the connection from the pouch and grinding them. We could use a pre-mixed blend, but the ember usually claimed he liked the ritual while chattering the whole time.

"No comment?" Normally, I wanted to throttle him for his constant stream of conversation, but the air felt dead without it.

Teyr slammed the mortar and pestle down on the table. "It's the same mixture every time."

I inhaled a breath to snap back but caught myself. He struggled with this as much as I did. Not only did we have an impossible fifth, but a human one. I clenched my fist. As commander, I had to keep us strong, keep us together. I'd let Light die. I'd lost Shade to his grief. Now, this. The stink of *The Boat House* curled around me, despite my shower.

"Well, are we just going to sit here?" Teyr demanded.

I scowled before dumping the herbs into the bowl and running my finger along the rim of the bowl to activate the connection. Moments later, a tiny, flickering image of our mentor from our Academy days, Councilor Drax, floated above the herbs.

"Zelimir. I wasn't expecting any communication." His bright pink eyes glowed to match the pink swirls accentuating his dark purple skin.

"My Cara has called out to a new fifth, and he's human." My gut twisted. The words sounded worse out loud.

A moment of tense, thick silence passed. I swallowed against a lump in my throat.

Councilor Drax leaned forward, attempting to study me through the magical interference. "You're sure?"

"Yes," I said. "We've yet to identify him, but we observed his general location, and there were no fae present."

Councilor Drax nodded and leaned back. "Give me a moment. The Lower Council needs to hear this."

My twisted gut looped over itself a few more times. He may as well have called in the Upper Council, who hadn't handled Cara matters directly in over two centuries. Teyr reached over and wrapped an arm around my waist, filling me with his strength and support. I *pulsed* my thanks but pulled out of his hold and closed off my emotions. The Lower Council couldn't see our weakness.

One by one, the four other Lower Councilors flickered into view. The surface of the little bowl crowded with ghostly figures.

"It's late. This better be important." Councilor Gnuq's balding head and wiry-furred lower half somehow still looked greasy in translucent form.

"You're at the *Cross Roads* after closing a rift in...human territory." Councilor Xerxes cocked his long, birdlike head to the side, mimicking the golden-winged bhelrian he could shift into.

Did the spymaster already know?

Councilor Odhrán pressed his nearly circular body forward, his over-long pointed ears quivering. "Come now, let the commander speak."

I gritted my teeth. "My Cara called out to another. I don't need to tell you the history. Something must be wrong, because the—" The words caught in my throat. I swallowed and pushed forward. "The fifth is human, a parasite. He cannot possibly fight at our side."

"A new fifth isn't even possible." Councilor Ambrocio's long beard drooped out of range of the projection, accentuating his ancient, wrin-kled face. "And if it were, something like that wouldn't grace a Cara who'd lost their fifth mere years ago with less than a century between them."

I struggled not to grimace. I didn't need to be reminded how green we were.

"If Commander Zelimir says it's true, it is." Councilor Drax frowned at the others. "What is your next move?"

I ran my hand through my hair. "Get rid of him. This is unnatural."

Teyr stiffened. Bash *pulsed* his support.

"And you're absolutely sure he's not fae?" Councilor Odhrán asked.

"The Cara led us to a pub full of rough-and-tumble men with little love for magic and even less respect. We've narrowed it down to four. Grant, Tommy, Tweek, and Dick." Teyr ticked off his fingers.

"Did any of them seem promising?" Councilor Odhrán leaned even closer.

"Doubtful." Teyr snorted.

The ember's vehemence surprised me.

"They're mercenaries, dirty and foul-mouthed," he said. "Grant spent most of the evening harassing the servers. Tweek drugged himself and melted into a pile of his own drool. Tommy and Dick seemed harmless enough. Dick might not even look so bad under all those layers of dirt."

I sent Teyr a sharp *pulse*, and he stopped abruptly.

The five councilors turned their attention from us and whispered amongst themselves. I clenched and unclenched my fists. If I could get rid of the human, I could focus on saving what we had left.

Councilor Odhrán stepped forward, eclipsing the other figures. "Figure out which human it is and bring him to the Academy posthaste. Keep him isolated from you. Do not let your Anam Cara connect, though it will want to." He glanced over his shoulder at the others. "As long as you stay apart, we may be able to fix your Cara yet. We'll learn more when you arrive."

I nodded.

"The soul bond will doom you." Councilor Ambrocio's thin voice echoed from behind the short elf with a little of the weight of one of his prophecies. "Do not grow attached, no matter what the magic wants. The leech must go."

Councilor Odhrán stepped back to reveal all the councilors once more.

"That won't be a problem." I smiled bitterly. "He's just a human."

Councilor Gnuq chuckled, and his image disappeared. Councilor Xerxes vanished without another word. He would contact his spy network immediately. The shifter needed information so quickly that he went hunting almost before the information even existed. The Council would be watching us.

"Be safe and make haste." Councilor Odhrán's image winked out.

"Good luck, Zelimir," Councilor Drax said.

I nodded and smiled something that felt almost honest.

He glanced into the distance beyond the bowl, then back. "With a human, the colosseum's portals cannot be opened for you, so you will have to journey by foot."

I sucked in a breath. I'd counted on using the portals to cut down on our time with the human.

Councilor Drax looked at the ancient figure still floating on my bowl. "Ambrocio, have you forgotten how to cut off a communication bowl again?"

Councilor Ambrocio scowled and drew himself up. "I've forgotten more than you'll ever know, boy."

"I'll be there in a minute." Councilor Drax disappeared.

Councilor Ambrocio opened his mouth, and I swirled my finger through the herbs, dispersing his image. The ancient, prophetic councilor's wisdom could be invaluable, but right now, I didn't need more on my mind.

I leaned down and blew the herb mix out of the bowl, destroying anyone's ability to replicate the magic, then turned to my second. Bash nodded firmly. With a sigh, I met Teyr's golden gaze.

"You're sure this is the right call?" Teyr flexed his fingers. "When I closed the rift, magic I've not felt since Light flowed though me." He bit his bottom lip. "We could be whole again."

"We're not broken." I wrapped an arm Teyr's shoulders and pulled him against my chest. "We don't need anyone to heal us. We just need time."

Teyr nodded against my tunic.

"How do we go about this?" Bash asked.

I released Teyr and returned to my saddlebags to retrieve a map. "We'll need a route that keeps away from aggressive fae, and a way to keep the human in the dark."

Teyr smiled. "Everyone wants a job that pays well."

4

———

KINNIA

Feather-light touches drifted across my body, conjuring sparks of pleasure. Someone ran their large hands up my side while they teased my nipples with their mouth, warm like a pocket of magic. Moisture pooled between my legs as I arched and opened my eyes. Purple eyes and a dark, muscled chest filled my vision. Copper twists hung from his head and danced across my breasts. He slid his warm hands across my stomach, toward my aching sex. I closed my eyes in anticipation, but the touch never came.

I opened my eyes to a world of murky gray. The ghost of dark skin and copper twists melted into cinnamon freckles and a mop of brownish-red hair. Alex, sitting across a flickering campfire from me with a teasing grin.

Silver flashed across his neck. Time slowed to a crawl as blood leaked down his chest. His head toppled backwards and disappeared behind the flames. Something cold and metallic bit into my stomach.

A cable. The Tech had caught me again.

I woke with a start, breathing hard. Cold dawn light seeped in through the skylight and kissed the loft. The smell of manure and hay filled my nose. The browns and reds of the barn swirled in my tear-streaked vision.

This is Thrae, not Earth, I reminded myself.

My heartbeat slowed, and I managed to take a deep breath. The last time I had a nightmare, I stabbed Grant. I needed to get myself under control before I accidentally struck the stableboy.

The remains of a hangover made my head throb slightly. I tried to sit up, but my blankets seemed to have gotten much heavier in the night. The blankets sucked in a heaving breath, then released it with a snore. Carefully, I picked up the katana I left by my pillow, then tried to slide out from beneath the weight.

The snoring stopped. A paw the size of my hand landed on my chest. The animal shifted, and a furry head floated into view. My breath caught as I stared into the muzzle of a giant, black dire wolf.

The beast stared back at me with mismatched eyes, the left brilliant white, the right, inky darkness, a sure sign of an Earth animal that had spent too many centuries on Thrae. I tried to look non-threatening. I'd heard stories of dire wolves, one of the rare Thrae-evolved creatures who still wandered into human territory, and seen their bloody work. If this beast wanted me dead, I'd already be dead.

The wolf pressed its cold, black nose against mine, then licked my cheek. It thumped its tail against my legs. A nervous laugh bubbled past my lips, and its tail thumped hard enough to raise bruises. The wolf behaved more like a dog than a killer. Alex, the rest of our family, and I had taken care of a street dog for a few months, until winter came. Called her Sylvie, fed her scraps. Harry even taught her to almost fetch. And Sylvie liked one thing best in the world.

Slowly, I set my katana back on the hay beside me, then dug my fingers into the thick fur behind one of the wolf's dark blue ears. He pressed his head into my hand and closed his eyes as I scratched.

"Where did you come from, little...wolf?" I snorted, then grimaced when the throbbing in my head increased with the action.

Little fit it as well as *normal* fit me. The dire wolf had to be tall enough to reach at least my hip.

The fuzzy-edged ball of magic fluttered and swelled to fill my gut like I'd eaten too much bread, then compressed back into...something else. Not a ball. Not a stone.

A complex, woven knot I couldn't imagine untangling.

All my knowledge of dire wolves melted away, and I pushed the beast off my chest. He slid obligingly off, which was almost scarier than the magic in my gut. A few strings detached themselves from the knot, and my pulse raced. I tried to sink *energy* into the magic. Anything to keep it contained. Like every other time I'd tried, my *energy* bounced right off.

I jolted upright and yanked my tunic up to stare at my stomach, half afraid the magic had swollen the flesh, but it remained flat and pale. My whole body twinged. An intangible string reached for something deep within me and seemed to take hold. Another stretched forward, and the others floated loosely. A warm tingling filled my muscles.

The wolf bared his fangs in what might have been a doggy smile. Blood rushed to my head, and the room swayed around me. The few loose threads of power flickered with excitement. Cold flooded through me as the warmth faded, and the dizzy spell with it. Some kind of magic just happened to me. But what?

The wolf rolled over and looked at me expectantly with his stomach exposed—definitely a boy. And at this distance, I could make out patches of navy blue in his black fur, another signature for Earth animals turned Thraen. He barked twice, and the sound echoed in the early morning quiet. I dropped my shirt with shaking hands and rubbed his stomach, as much to keep him quiet as to steady myself. I should've done something about the magic last night, but instead, I'd wasted my pay on bad beer and put off my problems for later. Well, later might've just become too late.

The dire wolf's ribs stood out under my fingers as I rubbed his soft side. He wagged his tail. I snorted. He seemed healthy, if hungry. Motion in my peripheral vision caught my attention. I turned and cursed while throwing an arm over my unbound breasts. Whenever possible, I slept without cuirass or binding to give my ribs a break, and I'd thought last night would be safe.

The stable boy peeked out from behind a wall of hay bales, his eyes wide as he took in the dire wolf.

I wrinkled my nose. "So, not yours."

He shook his head and disappeared back behind his wall. I reached under my tunic and tightened the binding's knot to flatten my chest. My breasts protested, and the skin around my sides pinched, but I'd grown used to the pain the last few years. At least I only had to commission extra-long tunics to avoid any questions below the waist.

The wolf whined. I scratched his head before crawling backward and standing. We eyed each other. His tongue lolled from the side of his mouth. Usually, the routine of arming myself centered me. Today, my head still throbbed, and my hands shook as I fastened my leather cuirass, laced up my gauntlets, and tugged my greaves over my leggings. Even belting my weapons to my hips didn't help with the dire wolf still staring at me and the magic roiling in my gut.

I needed some fae to remove the magic, and a job to take me back north. I fished out my coin purse and waterskin, left the rest of my pack and bedroll, and climbed down the ladder. When I reached the bottom, a soft whine issued over the side. I looked up.

The dire wolf balked and scrambled back from the edge. His legs trembled as he approached the ladder and he whined again. I bit my bottom lip to keep from laughing and waking the barn full of mercs. For a killing machine, he was awfully cute.

"How'd you get up there?" I asked.

The wolf huffed as if it were obvious. I shook my head. I couldn't leave him up there to maul the stableboy. I climbed halfway up the ladder and held out my arms. When he remained frozen, I climbed a few rungs higher and gathered him to my chest with a grunt. He weighed more than his boniness implied. I pushed *energy* into my arms and awkwardly descended the ladder. When his paws landed firmly on the ground once more, the wolf shook out his fur and chased his tail.

This time, I did laugh. "Don't spook the livestock."

"Shut up," Tommy mumbled.

I grinned and snuck through the stables with the wolf at my heels. The knot of magic purred happily in my gut. My smile melted away.

The first rays of sun brightened the world when I stepped out, and the small hangover throbbing in my temples made me wince. Someone in this town of half-breeds had to know how to get rid of magic. The trio of fae who'd lingered at the bar most of the night bloomed bright in my mind, but I pushed the thought away.

I retraced my steps toward the main gate, where I'd seen the merc guildhall. I could only get work there legally, and with the caravan rolling into town, there'd be more mercs than jobs for weeks. I needed to be first in line. A few people hurried along the curving roads, gazes trained straight ahead. The smell of fresh bread wafted from a bakery. A fur-covered woman batted at a tassel, momentarily distracted from setting up her stall.

Of course, no sign of the morning bustle touched the offices next to the gates. I found locked doors at both offices with signs telling me they opened in a few hours. I couldn't even peek in the shuttered windows. That left me with the magic in my gut.

The dire wolf yawned, exposing sharp canines. A few people skittered away from us. Maybe he wasn't quite as cute as I'd originally thought. His white and black eyes crossed as I rubbed the little divot between them.

I pulled my hand back. "You can't come with me. You'll scare people."

The wolf let out a bark that rattled my bones and reminded me he could step over a small pony. For some reason, that didn't frighten me.

I shrugged. "I can't tell you what to do, but I need to run some errands, and I'll throw rocks at you if you keep me from doing them." I glanced around. "I'll...find you this evening, and we can play or something."

He tilted his head, surprising awareness in his eye, then turned and trotted away. I sighed. I didn't believe in coincidences, but the wolf did have uncanny timing.

Only a few shops opened this early in the morning, but eventually, I found a circular, blue wood building with its door propped open and a sign in the window that read, *Components, Curses, and Curatives*. The smell of burning herbs and something strange drifted out. I took a deep breath to steady myself. The place looked fae enough that I wouldn't walk in unless I had to. The knot fizzed happily. I had to.

I stepped inside and blinked as my eyes adjusted to the dark. Dark, looming shelves holding dusty jars covered most of the floor, making the spacious shop cramped.

"Hello?" I called.

"Back here," someone called.

It sounded like a helpful voice. Hopefully, they'd still be in a helpful mood when I explained. I picked my way through the shelves to a low, blue counter at the back. Behind it stood a curvaceous woman with long, red hair, dark skin, and pointed, wine-colored ears sticking off the top of her head. She grinned, and I swallowed. Fae help for fae problems.

"Um." I attempted a smile. "I need a curative. I think."

She leaned on the counter with a conspiratorial smile. "Problems in the bedroom?"

I flushed. "No! No. It's my stomach. And it's...magic."

She nodded and grabbed a vibrant quill. "You came to the right place. My name's Slavica, and I can help you with whatever magical problem you have. What's your name?"

The fae woman's businesslike demeanor comforted me a little, but I didn't want to give her anything more than I had to. "Dick."

She smiled slyly and scratched those fae letters on the wood of the counter. "Symptoms?"

I answered her list of questions as honestly as I could without mentioning my *energy* or my flight through the wilds when I'd first arrived on Thrae. Any brush with magic then would have manifested side effects much sooner, anyway. This had to be something new, and I would turn over almost any other secret to have it gone.

When the blue wood crowded with her notes, she looked up and met my gaze. "Okay, one last question: why do you want to get rid of the magic?"

I'd gotten so used to the rhythm of answering her that words spilled from my mouth before I could catch them. "It's magic. Nothing good comes from magic." I winced. Fae had a reputation for touchiness. "I mean, I'm sure your magic is good. Good things come from it, I bet. That's why I'm here—"

Slavica put up a hand with curved, pointed nails. "Honesty is the best policy, Dick. Thank you for this." She tapped the counter. "All you need's a paste. I can whip one up for you. Come back tomorrow. Payment upon delivery."

I nodded and thanked her.

"Oh," she said. "And one more thing." She rustled through a packed drawer and removed a glittering golden charm that looked like one of those fae letters I kept seeing. "A little freebie for new customers. More legend than magic, but there's no harm in it. Supposed to protect you from evil."

A little bigger than my thumbnail and threaded onto a bit of leather cord, the amulet looked more like cheap, painted metal than anything special. I took it delicately and pocketed it with a smile. Like all fae stuff, I'd heard half a dozen legends about their letters. The one I heard most was that Earth used to have the same letters, called them runes, and could talk to the planet like fae did centuries before they ever dreamed of Tech. I doubted it. I'd see my fair share of broken signs on Earth, and none of them had letters like this. Regardless, I could toss the amulet behind *The Boat House*, where Slavica hopefully wouldn't find it and decide to curse my paste. I made my escape into the morning sunlight.

It felt like I'd spent forever in that shop, but the clock in the square told me I still had almost an hour until the guildhall opened. I breathed in fresh air. Tomorrow, the magic in my gut would be gone for good. With a newfound lightness in my step, I headed to find somewhere to stretch off my hangover.

5

BASH

I had most mornings to myself. Teyr would sleep well into the afternoon if no one woke him and, although my commander didn't sleep much later than me, he preferred human coffee and fae history books to company. The morning after we discovered the flaw in our Cara was no different. I rose early and left the suite for my morning exercises.

The early morning sunlight brought me no peace. Being in this human town made my skin crawl. Even at this hour, they swarmed over streets and market stalls. The sooner we caught and destroyed the parasite, the better. My commander had declared we didn't need watches last night, that he trusted the innkeeper, but in a town crawling with humans, there could be no trust. I'd kept watch all night.

Luckily, like most human towns, the *Cross Roads* had a childishly basic layout. Our inn sat on the main road, which led directly to the main gate. Perhaps outside the walls I could actually clear my head enough to benefit from my morning workout.

There were too many fae here, smiling too comfortably. I nodded at an Anam Secca in their red pants and cream tunics, a five-fae fighting unit trained at the Academy without any magic holding them together, and barely restrained my snarl. They didn't belong here. I didn't belong here. I needed to get out.

Of course, just as the gate came into view, I spotted the human Dick, slinking away from an apothecary with a cowlick curling the hair on the back of his head. My Cara reached for him. I slowed, grinding my teeth. With how much he drank last night, he shouldn't even be awake yet, much less invading my morning routine. Much less muddying my Cara bond with his humanity.

On this quiet street, I couldn't deny the Cara drew me to him. I *pulsed* the situation to Zelimir, who responded with orders to stick to the human like a burr. He'd send Teyr to check the others just in case. I *pulsed* back my acknowledgment and tried to keep the edge of irritation to myself. Exercises would have to wait. I crept after the human.

He strode down an alleyway and gaped at a small garden of orange and pink twisting snakeberry trees between a few buildings. I scowled. Humans knew nothing.

Instead of continuing past the garden, Dick stopped in the center. He lifted his arms and circled them to warm up his shoulders while running in place to ready his legs. I slipped into the shadow of a nearby building to watch. Placing my back against the wall did something for my nerves, at least. I scrubbed my hands down the invisibly armored pants of my Cara uniform and reassured myself I could handle one human.

The man did a few more stretches before drawing a strange, thin sword from a sheath strapped to his hip and held the blade out in front of him. He slid one foot back, the other forward, and dropped into a messy stance that balanced his weight evenly, instead of keeping most of it on his back leg. I shook my head.

He lunged forward and jumped back before swinging his sword in a showy arc and slamming it into the ground. A powerful move, if you wanted to expose your entire weak side to attack. He released his sword and rolled forward. I grimaced. I'd never yet seen a good reason to give up your weapon in a fight, especially as the weaker combatant. This human needed every advantage he could get.

Dick rolled back to his feet, his lean body balanced and ready for the series of kicks and punches he released on an invisible opponent. His form looked reasonable, though he over-rotated his left shoulder.

After a high kick that showed an impressive amount of flexibility, he flipped backward and landed with his hands on the ground and feet in the air, one palm on the hilt of his sword. I leaned forward. He held the handstand for a moment, controlling his balance, then flipped back onto his feet with his sword in a half-decent guard position. My lips twitched. He had control. Nothing more.

After a few deep breaths, he began again, making the same mistakes. I closed my eyes. Humans always thought they knew best, and they never learned. The back of my neck prickled. I whirled, but the alley behind me remained empty. I turned back to Dick, who'd started a new drill.

I'd spent centuries tamping down useless instincts until only the finest honed edge remained. This human churned up bad habits, pointless fears. I seethed as he worked through drills until sweat poured down his face and his chest heaved.

Finally, he pulled the small waterskin off his hip and took a swig before slicking back his hair. I huffed. Pointless vanity. He looked in my direction. I froze. He couldn't see me in the depths of shadow, but I wanted little less than to be caught watching the man.

Could he feel me? He raked a hand through the hair he'd just fixed and stared at the darkness that hid me. That showed some self-awareness. Far too quickly, he shrugged and swung his sword in impressive looking but completely useless circles around his hips. I released a breath and scowled. Dirty, thoughtless, self-serving humans.

Dick did a final flip-kick combination that would have been impressive if he hadn't fumbled the landing. He turned his fall into a controlled roll and came to rest on his back. High, musical giggles reached my ear fans, and I stiffened. He had just failed. He should be frustrated, embarrassed. Not pleased. My Cara hummed happily, and I punched myself in the gut to shut it up.

The man stood and sheathed his sword before heading out of the garden past me.

I stared at the patch of flattened grass where he'd landed. He didn't have magic. He'd messed up during what seemed to be basic training. Even if I wanted our Cara whole again, this man would be nothing but a liability. I shoved off the wall.

Through my Cara, I felt Teyr start moving north, toward the alley. I *pulsed* to let him know Dick was incoming. Peals of humor echoed through my Cara. I cracked a smile before I realized Teyr laughed at my word choice. I scowled and stalked from the alley. The ember stopped on the far side of the cobblestone plaza. Teyr smirked and downed a mug of coffee he'd almost certainly taken from the inn. I grimaced, imagining the burn on my own throat if I tried to gulp hot coffee. Sleep still hung so heavy in his eyes I doubted he even noticed what he once described to me as a *"pleasant warmth."*

"Dick is definitely the one. At least he's sort of pretty." He stared at the human. "Something about this has to be fun."

I shook my head.

"His friends let him cut in line." Teyr cocked his head to one side. "I wonder if he's used to being taken care of."

I grunted. The ember seemed to be enjoying our damnation far too much this morning.

"Dick, it is." Teyr smiled to himself and looked at the nuisance. "I wonder what he looks like cleaned up. I've never bedded a human."

I growled.

Teyr held up his hands. "Just curious. I know it's a bad idea. We have to keep the Cara from connecting."

I scowled. "He's a mistake."

"I know." Teyr's shoulders fell. "We could be on our way already if we just grabbed him."

"Bad idea." I narrowed my eyes at my impulsive mate. "Zelimir has a plan. We wait."

"Maybe I'll just offer him the job." Teyr eyed the human. "That line's gotta be at least an hour long. That's an hour we could spend traveling away from this cesspit."

I turned away. He would do whatever he wanted, as always. Only

Light could talk him down. And I couldn't disagree that an hour less in this town held a certain appeal.

Teyr walked off. I *pulsed* a warning to Zelimir and settled into a defensive stance. No such thing as over-caution where humans were involved.

6

——

KINNIA

Tweek, Tommy, and I roared with laughter as Grant mimicked the curves of a woman's hips and spanked his own ass. The knot of magic in my stomach twitched. They all fell silent and looked at something behind me. I stopped laughing, set my hand on the hilt of my katana, and turned.

The fae with the red-gold hair from yesterday looked me up and down. The vertical, catlike pupils in his golden eyes burned with heat.

He glanced at my hand on my sword, and smiled a wide, fake smile. "That won't do you much good."

His voice, a velvety tenor, wrapped around me. The stupid magic knot purred. This close, the perfect planes and angles of his face made my breath catch. Plush lips, square chin, and those eyes…. The arrogant bastard lifted an eyebrow teasingly. He hadn't lifted a finger to help us yesterday, and he matched my height and build closely enough. I could take him.

I gripped the hilt of my blade and widened my stance in case I needed to strike. "Can I help you?"

The fae raised his hands in a placating gesture. "I'm here to offer you work."

I studied him. His thick pants hugged his legs like they were made for him, and his cream-colored tunic fit just as well. Gold glinted at his wrists and nimble fingers. He could pay.

"That's not how this works," I said. "All work goes through the guildhall. You need to pick a less conspicuous location if you're trying to avoid city fees."

The fae furrowed his brow, then stuck out a tanned hand. "Let's try this again. My name's Teyr."

No calluses on his smooth, clean palm. He didn't fight with weapons. I took a deep breath and got a whiff of pine and cardamom. His scent, along with the knot in my gut, nudged me forward.

I smirked and wiggled my dirty fingers in his face. "I'm Declan, but I don't think you want to shake my hand."

Teyr's shoulders fell. "Your name's not Dick?"

"Nope." I popped the 'p' at the end of the word and grinned at my friends.

Tweek gave me a dirty look. Tommy and Grant started laughing.

"Well, *Declan*," Teyr said. "How about we get a drink? I'm buying."

The line shuffled forward. Teyr kept pace with us, and the magic in my gut bubbled happily.

"I need to get on the list first." I waved at the line.

"You might not need to." A more honest smile peeked out of his fake grin.

My insides fluttered in a way that had nothing to do with magic knots. I turned toward the front of the building so I couldn't see his face and shrugged. "Better safe." I didn't tell him I wouldn't be taking any jobs the fae had on offer.

"Fine," he said after a long silence. "One of your nasty beers at *The Boat House* when you're through here,"

I narrowed my eyes. I'd put money on the fact they were at the nicest place available. "I can come to you."

Grant nodded. "Get some ale 'at's not wat'rd down."

Teyr drew himself up. "*The Boat House* will do."

They were staying somewhere I wouldn't be welcome. I had no idea why three fae needed a human.

I snorted. "If I'm not there by noon, I'm still in this shitass line. Feel free to leave."

"I said when you're through here." He might as well have been spitting acid.

I met his molten-gold eyes. Butterflies filled my stomach, and the stupid magic pressed me toward him. It took all my willpower to turn my back instead.

"I'll see you later." I waved in acknowledgment. If I turned back to him, I wouldn't be able to stick to my end of the bargain. I wanted to let him take me away.

He huffed unhappily, but tension melted out of the air as he stormed off.

"Shit," I muttered.

Tommy nodded. "What did you do to draw the attention of the fae?"

I shook my head. "No clue."

THE GUILD OPENED LATE AND MOVED SLOWLY. THE CLOCK chimed noon as I ducked into the office. A short, plump man in flowing brown robes that marked him as the guild master sat behind a wooden table in a small stone room with a pen poised over a leather-bound notebook.

"Name," the guild master said.

I stood a little straighter. "Declan Rattilla."

He stiffened and looked up. "Declan? Staying at *The Boat House?*"

I blinked. I'd never been asked where I was staying by a guild master before. "Uh, yeah?"

"Right." He looked back down at his notebook and scribbled something. "You'll get no work from me."

My mouth went dry. "What?"

He gave me a hard look. "No work. Leave."

My jaw dropped. I'd never been turned down for guild work before. I didn't even know they could do that. I leaned toward the pompous guild master. I could convince him, threaten him, whatever I needed to do. I needed to get out of this town.

He crossed his arms. "I'll call the guards."

For a heartbeat, I considered just punching him in the face and dealing with the consequences later, but a night in the town jail would definitely not get me work.

I rocked back on my heels. "Can you tell me why?"

The man shook his head and scratched his jowls. Two gold bands glinted on his wrist. He grinned slyly as they jingled. I clenched my fist. Someone paid him. Someone? I was pretty sure I'd seen those bracelets on one of the fae last night. I spun and stormed out of the office.

Tweek, Tommy, and Grant stared at me, but I ignored them and scanned the courtyard for Teyr. His shining hair and knowing smirk remained absent. I crossed my arms. Teyr—no, all three of those fae— wanted something from me bad enough to stalk me, but they'd chosen a public meeting location. A bead of sweat ran down my temple, and when I whisked it away, my finger came back dark with grime.

I needed time to think before walking into a trap, and not reeking to high heaven would do wonders for my mood. My friends called after me, but I didn't reply. I marched my dirty, angry ass to the nearest bathhouse and used my dwindling pay to purchase a bath and laundry service.

The bath turned out to be less a room and more a round tent over a tub with an open shower. Steam gathered against the low, cream ceiling, and a small wooden dressing table lined with a selection of soaps sat on the far side.

I took my anger out on my skin, scrubbing every inch until I turned red under the showerhead. Once my temper cooled, I settled into the tub and poured in a random bottle of soap. The smell of honey filled the steamy space as the water frothed. Tension I'd grown all too accustomed to drained from my muscles.

Coming face-to-face with the rift yesterday had brought my past screaming back, and the vivid dream I'd had last night was the first dream about my found family I'd had in almost a month. Alex had looked the same as he had when we first met, though then I'd looked up at him through two black eyes that marked me as a troublemaker. When

I'd pointed out my bad first impression, he'd only laughed that warm laugh of his and taken me to meet the rest of his family, the band of teenagers he'd collected while living on the streets. I'd been doing poorly on my own since my last foster mother kicked me out, so that family became mine too.

For the first time, I belonged somewhere. Alex gave me something to believe in. Elaine held my hand when I had nightmares and didn't tell anyone. David teased, but he always brought me back an orange when he took stuff from the market. One time, I got Harry, our youngest, to laugh so hard he shot milk out of his nose and up into his glasses. They'd never worried about my *energy*. Like Alex said, we all had quirks.

Tears stung my eyes, and I slid under the water to wash the tears away. I missed my family like a hole in my chest, but I wouldn't think of that last day. I couldn't.

When I emerged, I wiped water from my eyes and pushed my history back into the recesses of my mind. Whatever my time on Earth had taken from me, it had given me the skills that let me be Declan. Declan was hard, dangerous, and above all, careful. Declan needed to focus on the problem at hand.

One of the threads from the knot in my belly unspooled and trailed to the east, as if something pulled it along. The knot tingled contentedly. I frowned at my stomach, distorted by the ripples of the bath. The magic had found what it wanted, and it didn't seem any closer to going away.

Running seemed like my best bet, especially once I picked up that paste from Slavica. I never liked living off the land, but I'd made this trek before. And once I crossed the mountains into human lands, there would be no more fae around to keep me from getting work.

With a plan in place, I decided to enjoy the bath I'd paid so handsomely for. I stayed in the tub until the water grew tepid, then a little longer. When the knock telling me I'd run out of time came, I groaned but got out of the tub. My now-clean clothes sat in a basket outside the door, and I buried my face in the warm, soft fabric. Fresh-smelling clothes were much too rare for my liking. I took my time dressing and tousled my hair in every direction. Lastly, I used the cold bathwater to clean my weapons from the battle yesterday.

Time to face the fae.

As I exited the bathhouse, someone screamed. I whirled toward a group of scattering people as a mass of black fur barreled toward me. Only long-honed instincts kept me on my feet as over a hundred pounds of dire wolf muscle landed on my chest. His paws easily reached my shoulders. He licked my face.

Humans and fae gawked. The wolf dropped to all fours and rubbed himself against my thighs and hips. He made the sort of scene that got the guards called. I hurried him along. He ran circles around me, oblivious to the panic he'd created as he yipped excitedly.

I snorted. "We've got to find your owner."

7

———

ZELIMIR

I SAT IN *The Boat House*, LISTENING TO THE CHAIR underneath me complain every time I shifted. My mates and I had procured a corner table in the relative quiet of the mid-morning. My second wedged himself into the place where two walls met so he could keep a wary eye on the room. Teyr stalked toward the unlit fireplace, then spun on his heel and headed back over a creaky board in the floor. His pacing had been slowly driving me insane.

I ran a hand through my hair and crossed my arms. I'd cut off the human's ability to get work. Bash had taken his things from the barn and tucked them between himself and the wall. The man had no choice but to come to us. Teyr crossed the squeaky board again.

"Knock it off," I growled.

The ember stopped but didn't sit. He tapped his foot instead, which grated on my nerves even more. I rolled my shoulders and stared at the watered-down ale warming in its metal tankard on the table in front of me, just another reminder how far we'd traveled. Most metal took too much development so, in the wilds, we used pure metals like gold for decoration and replaced the rest with a plentiful red mineral called cherrystone.

Teyr put his hands on his hips. "It's almost one."

"We'll give it another half hour, and if he doesn't show"—I sighed —"we'll start looking."

Bash grunted. The oldest of us sat still as stone, except for his flickering eyes. Nothing escaped his notice. I relied on his medley of magic, befitting his mixed heritage. Everyone could pick out the dragon in him on sight, and he had many of the dragons' mental magics, but what other fae heritage he had remained unknown.

I took a sip of ale and winced. Watered-down human sludge. I pushed the strange metal tankard away, leaned back in my groaning seat, and trained my attention on the door.

An Anam Cara consisted of five fae. Aptly named twin brothers, Shade and Light, powerful divar mages connected to Thrae itself, had completed our quintet. Light could manipulate sunlight and instill joy in even the darkest of fae, while Shade raised undead armies and scattered darkness in his wake. Divar couldn't shift naturally, but the brothers had crafted a powerful spell to occasionally take on the forms of dire wolves to turn off their bizarre, ever-circling minds.

The tavern door swung open, and daylight streamed in. Declan. My Cara warmed with joy. I spent years schooling my force magic under my father, King Zephyr's, tutelage, and I clamped down on my Cara with the same intensity and precision. I would not allow faulty magic to mislead me. The man had no magic about him. Even the dull static I usually got off humans seemed muted.

Declan blinked his wide, blue eyes, adjusting to the dim light of the room. The patter of paws on the straw-covered wooden floor drew my attention down to Shade, who waltzed in practically between the human's legs.

My stomach sank. I hadn't seen Shade's fae face since Light died. We didn't even really know if he was still in there. I'd felt him drifting around town all day, but he always seemed to wander aimlessly. I didn't know he'd found the human. I didn't know if he'd felt the change at all, even after he refused to relax yesterday. He rubbed his face against Declan's leg, throwing off the man's confident stride. I knew he'd taken Light's death the hardest, but his easy affiliation with the human parasite stung like a betrayal.

Declan stumbled, regained his balance, and stopped in front of us with a scowl. "Give me my shit back."

I ignored the strange way his lilting, husky voice, higher than I anticipated, danced across my flesh, and lifted my hands into the air to show I didn't have his belongings. Teyr sat down with a grin.

Declan gritted his teeth.

"Told you it would work." Teyr put his hands behind his head and whistled. "Well, not-Dick, you clean up nicely."

The human seemed markedly cleaner, and his still-damp hair dangled in his eyes. I couldn't disagree with Teyr's assessment. A silence fell, broken only by Shade's whine. The human slid his fingers into his fur.

Bash gestured toward Shade. "Your dog?"

Teyr winced. I studied the human.

Declan frowned. "This is a dire wolf. I'd think fae would recognize the animal, considering it's your magic that bastardized a regular wolf into this."

Shade whined again and butted his head against Declan's leg. When Declan didn't acknowledge him, the dire wolf barked and rammed the man's knees. Declan sat in the empty chair instead of toppling over. Shade jumped up and draped himself across the human's lap. Declan cursed and tried to push the wolf off, but Shade licked his face. The human grinned, and some of his worry lines faded away.

I found a smile pulling at my own lips and quickly lifted my tankard. Thankfully, I remembered at the last moment not to drink. Declan grasped Shade by the scruff and forced him to the floor.

The pull of the Cara would affect us, but we couldn't encourage the magic. This human represented a threat to all Caras, to the very magic of Thrae itself. We needed to keep our distance until the Lower Council removed him. I needed to lead by example.

"Of course, he's not mine." Declan sighed. "He snuck into my bedroll last night and spent the day following me around."

Teyr leaned forward. "He climbed into bed with you? We found your stuff in a hayloft."

"I don't know how he got up there." Declan rested his hand on Shade's head. It looked like a comforting gesture, but I couldn't tell for whom. "I had to lift him down this morning." Declan snorted. "He's too well-trained to be wild, but I can't keep him—I can't afford to feed myself half the time."

Teyr recoiled. "Well-trained?"

Although I kept my expression neutral, I didn't disagree with the ember's skepticism. Shade was a menace.

"He's ours," I said finally. "He usually doesn't come into towns."

"Oh." Declan removed his fingers from Shade's fur.

I grimaced and *pulsed* accusation to the wolf for bonding with the mistake we needed to terminate. Shade didn't react. He hadn't for the last six years. His fae mind stayed locked inside the beast.

The human crossed his arms. "Well, you've stolen my stuff, blocked me from getting work, and had your wolf tail me all day." He looked at Teyr. "Do you need a job done, or was this just to screw with me?"

Teyr leaned forward, eyes bright.

I spoke before he could make an inane joke. "We need you to come into fae wilds with us and speak to our Lower Council."

Declan raised a brow. "What council? What for?"

Teyr clasped his hands on the table. "We have a Lower Council to oversee daily fae affairs. The Lower Council wants to talk to you about the attack you witnessed on the border."

The gold-plated lie rolled off Teyr's silver tongue.

"There were a bunch of people involved." Declan rubbed his chin. "Why me?"

Our lie grew thin here, but Teyr had prepared. "We watched you fight. You felled more SpiderTech than any human we've ever seen. You're competent, so the Council will trust your report."

"Uh-huh." Declan's eyes narrowed. "And this has nothing to do with the fae bullshit in my stomach that keeps pulling me toward you?"

Damn it. He could feel the Cara. Bash made a sound between a growl and a sigh.

"How do you know it's fae?" I asked.

Declan looked at me like I was stupid. "Do you know another magic? I'm not an idiot."

"Most humans are." I prodded the man for magic again. Nothing. He couldn't be fae.

"Copping a good feel?" Declan leaned back in his chair.

I pulled my magic back and scowled. I didn't need another complication. The small wooden chair groaned. It would be just my luck if the human craftsmanship gave out at this very moment. We seemed to have gotten stuck with the only half-intelligent human in Thrae. We wouldn't be able to keep him in the dark.

"We cannot divulge the details of our proposition until we're farther into the wilds."

"Sure thing." Declan chuckled.

He knew we were lying.

"Well, I've got somebody on this side of the border willing to fix this problem for me, so I'll pass," he said.

I gritted my teeth. I couldn't imagine what sort of ridiculous con artist would claim they could get rid of a Cara in this human town. Legend said even the Upper Council found the process difficult.

"They lied." Teyr shrugged.

"Doubtful." He pulled out a golden rune on a loop of leather. "Gave me this and everything."

I picked it up. Just like the human, it didn't have a shred of magic in it, not even static.

"That rune is useless garbage." I threw it back down. "And we need the report regardless."

Declan scoffed and stuffed the rune into his pocket. "For all I know, you guys called up that rift to force my hand."

From the way he looked at the rune before he tucked it away, I could tell we'd worried him at least. Time for the final push.

I placed my hands flat on the table. "Nobody 'calls' rifts. They're random. And nobody in this town has the power to get rid of this magic for you." I *pulsed* to Bash, who tossed a small coin pouch at the man.

Declan snagged it out of the air and peeked inside. His eyes widened.

"Ten gold just to accept the job," Teyr said. "One hundred gold at time of completion."

I couldn't tear my gaze from Declan's delicate features. He weighed the money pouch in one hand and dropped his other back onto Shade's head, absently scratching behind his dark blue ear. Shade rumbled a purring noise I didn't know he could make. The sight of them so happy made my vision go red. I stood, scruffed the wolf, and hauled him roughly away from Declan. Shade looked up at me with hurt in his eyes.

"It's a good deal." Teyr tried to pull Declan's attention from me. "And the only deal you'll get this side of the pass."

I turned away from the wolf and reminded myself it had to be this way.

Declan scowled. "If nobody here can help me get rid of this magic, can you?"

I nodded.

The man cracked his neck. "I don't really have a choice here. I mean, the gold is more than I could make in ten years, but this isn't even subtle coercion, it's kidnapping."

Teyr raised a brow. "Are you a child?"

Declan gave him a flat look.

"Are you holding a down payment in your hand?" Teyr leaned forward.

The human shook his head. "You threw it at me."

"Then I think we're settled." Teyr brushed his palms together as if removing dust.

Declan threw the bag of gold down on the table and clenched his fists. He closed his eyes and breathed slowly for a moment. My Cara reached for the man, wanting to help him, but I yanked it back. He had to come with us.

Declan opened his eyes and pressed his hands onto the table. "No more rifts, right?"

"No more rifts," Teyr said. "I'll get the horses."

We couldn't promise that. My Cara ached. I ignored the feeling.

Declan gritted his teeth when Bash brought the man's pack out from behind him. The human accepted it and ran a quick, private inventory before repacking the bag with his new gold. Of course, we'd already been through the contents. Nothing particularly outstanding or worrying.

"If you're to survive the trip, we should lay down a few ground rules," I said. "The wilds are a dangerous place. Don't accept any gifts, don't touch anyone, and most of all, don't make any deals."

The man rolled his eyes, and I bit back a sigh. Clearly, his parents had done him the disservice of passing on little fae lore. He would be trouble. I pointed toward the door. He stood, and I fell into step at his back. Neither he nor the gold would leave my sight until I had him on a horse, riding toward the Academy.

The man stopped just outside the door. I stopped in the doorway. He couldn't get back into the bar past me. A moment of tense silence passed. If he ran, I could pin him with my force magic before he got far enough to be a problem, but I didn't particularly want to be banned from the *Cross Roads*.

"I don't even know your names," he finally said.

Perhaps that would be better. But the councilors wanted him alive, so he needed to be able to call for us.

I pointed to my chest. "Zelimir. You know Teyr, and my second is Bash."

The dragon grunted behind me.

The human mouthed each name before pointing to Shade. "And the wolf?

I looked at Teyr, next to the three horses. "Shade."

Declan wrinkled his nose. "Not very creative for a black dog."

Shade whined mournfully. I almost laughed, but I managed to turn it into a grunt. I knew what needed to be done. These emotions would only distract me.

8

______

TEYR

My Andalusian glowed in the night as he clopped along the dirt road behind Bash's and Zelimir's steeds. Declan warmed my back as he finally relaxed against me. We'd promised him his own mount as soon as we were able to get one, but for now, he had to ride double. Zelly put him with me because our combined weight would strain my horse the least. I let out a tense breath. On the one hand, holding himself away from me as he had for the last half hour had to be uncomfortable. On the other, my mind kept drifting to his big, blue eyes and the fine point of his chin. He might be human, but clean....

I could already feel Zel's *pulse* of disapproval.

Declan pressed his hands into my sides. "I'm sorry."

My fae ears barely caught his quiet words. I flexed my abs—for professional reasons, of course—then said, "For what?"

Declan stiffened as if surprised I'd heard him. "I'm honestly not sure."

I barked a laugh. Declan's return chuckle rumbled against my back. It would be so easy to turn and kiss him. Zelimir's purple eyes flashed as he whipped around to pin me with a warning glare. I rolled my eyes. Declan, human, bad—no fun. Only two weeks to the Academy.

Zel urged his Shire horse into a canter. My horse picked up speed, happy to match pace with the beasts in the lead. I only knew humans from stories, and Declan had already given credence to some of them. His eyes lit up at the mere mention of gold. The night before, at *The Boat House*, he'd been dirty and drunk and consumed with himself.

But in front of the guild this morning had been different. The man had told me to piss off when I'd tried to pluck him out of the line of mercenaries. He'd stood his ground, despite my charm, and argued with me. He'd even smirked as he'd told me no. Told *me* no.

I rocked into the horse's rhythm, forcing Declan to adjust as well. He shifted his legs against mine. His honey-and-leather scent drifted into my nose. He smelled good. Really good. I'd enjoyed many lovers over the years, from curvy elves to bark-like treants, of every gender under the sun. Pleasure had to be one of the greatest parts of life, and I saw no reason to deny myself. But I'd not yet had the opportunity to sate my curiosity about humans, and Declan made me very curious.

I tamped down the urge. Closeness like that would only speed up the Cara connections, and I wanted Declan as a partner in bed, not in life.

When my mates and I had accepted the bond, our magic—our very essences—fused in a connection that ran deeper than anything I'd ever experienced. The Cara let me live in my mate's emotions. I loved to feel Zelimir's frustration with my antics and Bash's amusement behind his too-serious face. We experienced each other's heartbreaks and triumphs. It made everything I'd lost to get here almost worth it.

The Anam Cara had saved me, more than once.

Light had been my best friend, my lover, my partner-in-crime. After a death, Caras lived half-lives. They never repaired. If not for Bash and Zelimir, I'd still be a mess. Sharing pain lessened the burden. I wanted Declan's presence to mean something, change something. But Shade still darted through the woods ahead of us on four legs, as he had since Light died, and no human, however pretty, could replace Light.

I squeezed my reins. The leather creaked. Against my better judgment, I prodded Declan's essence. No magic. No static. Nothing.

"Why do you keep doing that?" Declan snapped.

"Because I want you to be something you're not."

I took a breath to say more, but Zelimir's anger whipped through my

Cara. I exhaled and *pulsed* apologies to my mates, Shade included. I had no idea if he understood, but I owed it to him anyway. Declan had nothing to add to our unit. I needed to limit my exposure.

THE MOON HUNG HIGH IN THE SKY WHEN WE REACHED THE first fae waystation. The handful of buildings squatted, ramshackle and quiet, too close to the border to be a true village. A few families and an inn survived off the business of Cara border patrols like us and the rare trader that dared venture between the fae wilds and the Cross Roads.

In the dark, the buildings looked like any human dwelling surrounded by trees. Light shone through a few windows, and a sign above the inn's door creaked in the light breeze. In the daylight, I knew the differences would be clear. Humans tore chunks out of the land to build with, but we knew Thrae better than that. These buildings, like all buildings in the wilds, had been grown right out of the ground with living material. This particular waystation specialized in trees with room-sized gaps in the trunks.

We stopped in front of the inn. Declan jumped down before I could offer him a hand. Backlit by a window, he spread his legs and reached for the ground with a groan, then eased back up to relax his muscles from our long ride. Blood rushed out of my brain.

"Been a while?" I smirked.

I didn't even need Zelimir's *pulse* to immediately regret my question. Every interaction would encourage the bond. But I'd never been good at keeping my mouth shut.

Declan squatted with one leg bent and the other extended. His big, blue eyes twinkled. "It has."

I forced myself to focus on my horse. My mates had already dismounted and begun leading their horses toward the stables. I swung down.

"Can we purchase horses here?" Declan asked hopefully.

I loosened the girth on my saddle as my imagination raced away with that groan. "Nope. Another day of riding double tomorrow, but there should be a horse at the end of that."

He sighed. "Well, as long as there's light at the end of the tunnel."

I glanced at him, unsure if I liked the relief in his voice. It couldn't have been that bad to ride double with me. Before indignation could get the better of me, a streak of black-and-navy fur bowled into Declan and sent him sprawling. Shade landed on his stomach and licked his face. A peal of laughter bubbled out of the human. The innocence in that laugh, the pure joy, took me aback. I led my horse away. With any luck, Declan would never learn about the necromancer trapped inside the wolf.

To my surprise, the two were still playing when I exited the stables. Shade asked us for attention pretty often, but I couldn't remember him ever playing like this. Zelimir and Bash had already gone inside. With a dramatic sigh, I broke Shade and Declan up, and we headed in. Declan panted, and Shade ran loops around us both.

When we entered the common room, Declan's eyes lit up. The space lay empty except for us and a half-elven innkeeper, but Declan stared like he'd never seen anything like it before. I shook myself. He probably hadn't.

"Showers in every room. Make sure you use them." Zelimir stared at Declan's dusty clothes and the slobber marks on his cheeks. "Fae bathe daily. Food will be available soon. We leave an hour after dawn."

"Do I get answers tonight?" Declan asked flatly.

Zelimir ran his hand across his long, copper twists. "Tomorrow."

Declan took a deep breath. "I'll go figure out that shower."

Zelimir nodded, his face impassive. A moment of awkward silence passed before the innkeeper got Declan's attention, and the two walked up the stairs and out of sight. Bash scruffed Shade as he lunged after the human. Only a growl from Zelimir kept me from following too.

"Come on, Zelly, I have needs," I said. "A look's not going to encourage the Cara."

"We'll find you a different human." Zelimir's gaze lingered on the stairs where Declan had disappeared.

Shade whined.

"We need to keep them apart," Bash relaxed his grip and pet Shade apologetically.

The wolf howled and sat.

"Yeah, good luck with that." I looked at Shade. "Telling Declan the truth might help. Tomorrow, we'll be far enough into the wilds that he can't run."

Zelimir frowned. "The damage might already be done. I should have prepared for Shade to latch on." He swallowed. "He's been so distant for so long. And you know how he…." Zel shook his head. "I just didn't really think he would accept a replacement for his brother."

I frowned and tried not to think about how closely that echoed my own opinions. Our usual table already had cherrystone utensils, and we sat. Bash took his favorite spot with his back to a wall, Zelimir took the head, and I sat wherever I damn well pleased. Tonight, that meant a seat with a view of the window. Watching the wilds settled my nerves.

Bash grunted. "Shade has no control as a wolf. Declan doesn't know better. It's up to us."

Zelimir's frown turned into a scowl. "How did Shade get into the hayloft? He couldn't have shifted back into a fae."

"After this long? Even asleep, we would've felt it." I shook my head. "But he's a massive dire wolf with a Thrae-touched fae trapped inside him. If he really wants to get somewhere, he does." I folded and unfolded my napkin. "I need someone else to take Declan tomorrow."

Zelimir crossed his arms. "You're the lightest of us. It makes the most sense he rides with you."

I tapped my feet and barely resisted the urge to pace. "I'm attracted to him. Humans are a novelty, and—"

"A novelty no one needs." Bash stood and stomped to the bar.

I let the grumpy dragon get out of earshot before I continued. "I can't hate him. He smells like honey and leather, and I could feel his human curves on my back."

Zel sighed. "You have a problem."

I wrinkled my nose. "My appreciation of flesh is not a problem."

"Not tonight, Teyr."

I ground my teeth. "Regardless, he's too friendly. We just need to rotate him."

Zelimir nodded slowly and shifted to stare out the window. He didn't dismiss me out of hand, at least. I coaxed Shade to my side. The dire wolf rested his big head on my thighs, his puppy-dog eyes drooping as he looked mournfully at the stairs. I stroked his back in sympathy. Bash returned with a round of laceblossom ales.

Zelimir picked up his bright red tankard. "He's a liability, and we're on Council orders. I don't want him unguarded." He took a sip and set the tankard down on the table with a very un-princely *thump*. "I don't trust humans. Even with a bag of gold waiting for them at the end. But Teyr makes a good point. We'll rotate the human, starting tomorrow."

Bash's gaze darkened, but he didn't disagree. He never did. He hated humans more than Zelimir and me combined, but the dragon remained unfalteringly loyal to our commander. Caras encouraged fae to trust each other, but when I disagreed with Zelimir, I happily gave him a piece of my mind.

Soon, the food arrived, and the chicken and fumewort stew warmed my stomach. I'd even started getting used to the human-raised poultry so many border inns used during the last six years.

As I polished off my bowl, I looked out the window at the dark forest. The two-week ride to the Academy would take us through parts of the wilds I hadn't seen since Light's death, and I found myself looking forward to the journey. Border patrol had gotten dull.

The shadowy brush shifted in a way that made my heart leap into overdrive. Someone stood out there, watching. The leaves rustled again. A wine-colored, four-legged urander scampered out with its long, poofy tail waving. I relaxed. We might be on a Thrae-changing mission, but paranoia wouldn't help anyone. Declan's full bowl of stew sat untouched on the table. If he starved, we'd never get to the Academy.

"Leave him be." Zelimir emphasized his order with a *pulse*.

I grabbed the bowl anyway and waved my uptight commander off with my free hand as I headed for the stairs. Zel had gotten two rooms, a Cara suite for us and a double, the smallest the inn had, with a much heavier lock the innkeeper promised to close from the outside, for

Declan. I made my way toward Declan's—the one Declan and I would share, I decided. Someone needed to keep an eye on him, after all. The stew sloshed as I shouldered open the door. Low snores emanated from the bed against the far wall. A small pile of weapons lay on the floor, and Declan's odd sword lay on the bed beside him. I set the bowl down on his dresser. Since Zelimir might actually kill me if he escaped, I grabbed the key hanging on the wall and locked the door.

My burst of rebellion started feeling ridiculous. I didn't want Declan any more than my mates. I just wanted…someone.

After a few laps around the room, I decided to ignore the sleeping human and go about my normal evening ritual. My long, hot shower didn't wake him. I changed into a loose shirt and found myself very near his bed. His damp hair wet the pillowcase, but the faint smell of horse still clung to him. Based on the lack of clothes laying around, Declan had chosen to sleep in his armor. He'd pulled all that clinging leather back on over his wet body.

I ran my hand down my clean shirt and crossed to the bed on the other side of the room. Zel wanted me up at dawn, and that meant I should have been asleep yesterday. I slid under the blankets and realized I'd already grown accustomed to Declan's snores. Like so many things about the man, they were surprisingly delicate. I wondered what he would look like if he ever relaxed. I'd only seen him smile for Shade. Perhaps….

The lock on our door clicked open. I jumped up, igniting my desire into fire on my fingertips. I knew I'd seen someone in those bushes outside. The door eased open, and Shade's black nose poked through. I laughed as he slipped inside and crawled into bed with Declan. How he got the door open, I'd never know, but if Zel had lost control of him, I didn't have a shot. I closed the door, settled back down, and let the familiar sound of twin snores lull me to sleep for the first time in a long time.

9

KINNIA

The first rays of sunlight streamed in through the perfectly circular window of the fae inn, and a dark, furry lump crowded half my slim cot. Once again, Shade had snuck into my bed without waking me. I frowned but scratched his silky ears. He thumped his tail against my leg. I wrapped my arms around him and gave him a quick squeeze before getting up.

Shade remained on the cot with his head on his paws. A snoring nest of blankets on the other bed with a smidgen of fiery hair peeking out told me I had a roommate. My face flamed. I'd left my cuirass on last night, not knowing what to expect in the wilds, but I hadn't bound my chest in any other way. The bindings compressed my lungs, making me pant for breath during even the briefest fights, so I avoided them whenever I thought I could get away with it. But if these fae were going to be sneaking in while I was asleep....

I belted on my arsenal as quietly as I could, tightened the bindings to crush my breasts to nonexistence, and turned to leave. A bowl of cold stew on the dresser at the foot of the bed reminded me I'd passed out without dinner last night. I muttered a begrudging *thanks* to Teyr, half because he couldn't hear me, and grabbed the bowl.

As I slipped into the hall with Shade trailing close behind, a ball of bright light flared to life over my left shoulder. It bounded after me as I walked toward the stairs. *Fae.* I rolled my eyes.

The light illuminated a hall I'd barely looked at last night. I skimmed my fingers across the flat, unbroken expanse of wood that made up the wall, like the one I'd seen downstairs. At the next perfectly circular window, I spotted tree bark curling in around the edges. I peeked out. The same bark spread down the outside wall to what looked like natural roots. Even the stairs jutted out of the wall like they were a natural extension of the tree. Elaine would've spent the rest of her life in this place, if she could. Before Alex, she slept in trees to keep safe at night, and she said nothing beat waking up to light filtering through leaves or flowers.

I devoured the leftovers in the empty common room and stretched out on a chair. A moment passed where I almost didn't regret taking this job.

"What do you think, Shade?" I asked.

He cocked his head at me as if he understood.

I grinned. "Well, I'm deep in fae territory with nothing to back me up but a few dozen Tech kills and my wits. Am I in completely over my head?"

He chuffed and nudged my thigh with his head.

"All right, fair enough. My wits have gotten me pretty far." I'd survived long years with little else. "Are you getting the feeling Zelimir and Bash hate me?"

Shade lifted his head and looked at me mournfully. Then, if I didn't know any better, I'd swear the wolf nodded. I leapt up, and he skittered back. I'd never understood why people talked to animals.

My sore muscles protested after yesterday's ride, but I headed out into the pale morning light and found a large, open space between the stables and the inn. Shade followed me. Judging by the sun, I had forty-five minutes to kill before another ass-breaking ride. With a deep breath, I began my morning stretches.

Soon, I flowed through the core attacks and defenses I used in almost every fight. My body slid from one position to the next with practiced ease. Necessity had been an effective teacher, though my breath started to race against the compression of the bindings. Fucking fae.

"Stay away from Teyr." Bash's deep, gravelly voice shattered my peace.

I whirled to find the scaled fae silhouetted by the rising sun. Shade lay to his left, his dark blue ear perked up as if listening.

"I don't know how to respond to that." I let my sword hang by my side.

"Humans do not belong in the wilds," he said.

I frowned. "Big talk from someone escorting me in."

The air crackled with tension. His stance widened. I started to raise my katana. He darted toward me, faster than I could track, and grabbed my wrist in one calloused hand.

"Oh, hell no." I'd spent years fighting larger opponents.

I stepped into his arm, twisted, and broke his hold. He stumbled back, off-balance. The momentum of the move carried me past him, but I whirled to face him.

Bash had already regained his balance. He gave me a onceover as he settled back into a fighting stance. Adrenaline danced through my veins despite the tightness in my chest. These fae needed to know I wouldn't blindly follow their lead.

"Seems to me I have to stay intact to give a report." I sheathed my sword. "Fists?"

Bash huffed but unbuckled the giant axe sheath on his back. I left my belt on. Outnumbered, I wouldn't be taking it off for almost anything. He slipped off yet another long-sleeved, cream tunic. His muscled, lilac chest left no doubt about his strength. I kept my gaze on his six-pack. Everything else connected to that spot. I could predict his every move, even through the tattoos.

Shade barked, and our match began.

Bash darted forward and slammed his foot into the outside of my thigh. My knee nearly buckled, but I steadied myself and got my arms up just in time to block a jab aimed at my face.

His shoulder twitched, a sure sign of a low left hook. I blocked, again. My forearms already smarted. With a cry, I thrust an uppercut into his square chin. He staggered back in what seemed more like surprise than pain. I caught my breath achingly. He leapt toward me with another kick at my leg.

Predictable. I jumped back, but his momentum carried him forward, and his elbow caught me in the shoulder. Pain bloomed, and I winced. My pulse thudded in my ears as I dropped to the ground to sweep his legs. I may as well have kicked a tree trunk. He didn't go down, but he wobbled just enough that his guard dropped.

I shot up and slammed a double-handed punch into his gut. He grunted and swung his fist around to clip the side of my head. My ears rang, but I had to press my advantage. I wrapped both my arms around one of his and kneed him where I hoped his balls were. His face hardly moved, and he launched his free fist toward my nose. I expected pain, but his bruising blow glanced off my cheek. The fae was holding back.

His mistake.

I slid back and left him an opening on my right side, panting visibly for the first time. He snorted, then surged forward to tackle me to the dirt. I drove my knee into his face. As he crumpled, I grabbed the hand he favored for his strikes and twisted his arm behind his back, as far up as I could manage, then tangled one of my legs around his. His shoulder muscles groaned against my grip. If he tried to step, I'd lay him down.

"Don't grab me." I kept him in the lock for an extra heartbeat, then released him.

My blood raced in my veins as adrenaline shot through my system. I danced back out of his reach and celebrated breathlessly. Shade barked excitedly. Bash straightened. For the first time since I'd met him, excitement brightened his gray eyes. I'd almost describe him as handsome.

I sucked in a breath. Was this fighting or foreplay? Bash's muscles rippled, and the stupid magic knot in my belly simmered. His gaze grew distant, and he looked behind me. I whirled.

Zelimir stood in the door of the stable with his horse's bridle in his hand and the same distant look on his face. His brow wrinkled with something like disgust. I blinked. The expression disappeared as soon as it came.

"You ride with me today." Zelimir ran his free hand along those almost waist-length copper twists and strode back into the stable.

I frowned. Shade wound around my legs and snuffled. He nearly knocked me over, but I steadied myself on his haunches with a laugh. Bash grunted and cracked his neck. His ass strained against his pants as he reached down to pick up his discarded shirt and axe.

Shade bumped my leg with his snout, and I banished the picture of Bash's muscled chest as he headed into the stable. My hormones needed to relax. These fae wanted something from me, and they were willing to lie about it. I couldn't let their good looks distract me.

I turned back toward the inn to grab my pack. Teyr appeared in the doorway, eyes still half-closed, and tossed my pack to me like it weighed nothing. I caught it with a grunt. He blew past me into the stable, looking like he wanted nothing more than to crawl back into bed.

Bash's words at the beginning of our fight came back to me. *"Stay away from Teyr."*

I grinned and called, "Your bodyguard did well defending your honor."

None of the fae answered. Shade whined, and I squatted to scratch behind his navy-blue ear, then his black one. He licked my nose. A shiver ran down my spine. I glanced around the empty courtyard but saw no one.

10

ZELIMIR

Declan clutched my waist as my Shire horse took an extra-large step to kick at an itch on his back leg. The human's honey-and-leather scent filled my nose. Teyr hadn't been exaggerating. I closed my eyes to enjoy the smell, then snapped them back open and focused on the road. Cara magic, not real interest. Cara magic I had to bring to heel.

"Sorry." Declan pushed himself back onto the precarious seat I'd made him out of my saddlebags.

I grunted and did my best to pretend he didn't exist. We'd been riding in silence for a few hours. Bash rode ahead, scouting our path, and Teyr trailed behind, muttering to his palomino. Standard procedure for border sweeps, just farther into the wilds.

Shade burst out of the forest on my left with something green and bleeding in his snout, and my horse skidded sideways. Declan yelped and wrapped his arms around me.

"Shade," I growled.

The wolf dropped his kill and raced back into the forest, howling. I *pulsed* to Teyr to stop and see if the dead animal was edible. My heart raced as Declan shifted his grip to my hips.

"Ah, sorry again." He regained his balance on the saddle, then slid once more into his seat and released me. "Your horse is just really wide. I need handles or something."

"He's a Shire horse." I patted his shoulder. The beast had carried me into and out of battle for a long time now. "Not as fast as a Friesian, but he's a trooper. He can walk for days and could easily carry two of me."

"I've only ridden a few times," Declan said. "Horses aren't cheap. But I guess all that's gonna change for me soon."

I grunted, grateful for the reminder of the man's greed.

Declan shifted against my back. "Am I sitting on books?"

"You are." I doubted the man could read.

Teyr resumed position at the back of the line with a freshly killed, bright green henesh hanging from his saddlebag. I nodded. The little woodland prey animal would make a wonderful stew for dinner, very earthy.

Declan shifted again. "What are you?"

I tensed. "I'm fae."

He snorted. "Obviously. What clan?"

"Some things are not for humans to know." I scowled. I should never have told him about my horse.

We fell into silence once more. The clop of hooves on hard ground and twitter of birds swelled. The forest around us looked different than forests in human territory I knew. Their dark greens and browns lingered this close to the border, but fae influence poked out in patches of vivid color. Green leaves tinged with purple on brown branches streaked with hints of vivid turquoise shaded us from the sun. Legend claimed that before the humans arrived, the whole world had been vibrant, that the color happened naturally in response to us. An orange flower unfurled and bloomed to my right.

Declan gasped. "How do they grow so fast?"

I swallowed a groan. Why couldn't he figure out I didn't want to talk to him? "Magic."

Declan swatted my shoulder. "I know that, but there has to be more to it."

Years of diplomatic training shed off me. This human had to learn his place. "Why do you insist on being a nuisance?"

He scoffed. "I figure I'm owed answers to a couple questions since you're kidnapping me into parts unknown with no exit plan."

"Owed?" I laughed in disbelief. "You must be joking. You're 'owed' the one hundred gold we promised you. No more, no less."

"Oh, come on," he said. "How hard is it to give a couple of yes or no answers? A few details?"

I massaged my scalp between my twists. Then, I smiled where he couldn't see. "All right. How about, for every question I answer, I take one gold off your pay?"

He'd never accept that.

"Works for me," he said.

I deflated. The human seemed to do a victory dance at my backside.

"What type of fae are you?" he asked. "And don't leave out the good parts."

I dropped the reins so as not to mislead the horse in my irritation. He knew the path to the Academy well enough. "We call ourselves titans. We're descendants of the old fae who walked this world when it was new. They disappeared millennia ago."

He hummed. "Titans? Like from Earth mythology?"

I shrugged. "Earth and Thrae mirror each other in many ways, although we didn't know that until *humans* created rifts."

"That was like six hundred years ago." Declan pressed a hand to my shoulder blade. "And I'm not the one who created them."

Tingles ran down my back. I shook him off. The human touched far too much.

"So, what kind of magic do you have?" he asked, clearly unaware of his effect on me.

I grunted. "Force. I can make anything out of raw will."

"That's kinda cool." He hummed. "Can you make a blanket if you're cold?"

"I can make anything I imagine, but I haven't tried that one." I snorted. "I've made swords, spears, hammers...gags."

Declan scoffed. I smiled.

The path narrowed, and the bright trees grew closer. Declan's hand appeared at the edge of my vision, reaching for a tall, dark green mushroom. I grabbed his wrist a little too hard, pulling him around me and half into my lap.

"That'll kill you in two seconds flat." My heart raced with worry, and I forced my voice to come out evenly. "I said, no touching. That goes double if it seems enticing."

He frowned up at me. Some emotion weighed down his bright blue eyes. I pushed him back behind me, and he slipped his arms around my waist to steady himself. My breath caught in my throat, and I shoved him off with a growl.

"We're going to take a break shortly," I said. "There's time for one last question, if you value your money so cheaply."

"Why is everything in the wilds so weird?" he asked without hesitation.

I shook my head. "Because magic is weird. Fae are the same. Some live thousands of years, some a few hours. We barely agree on anything, but when you can get us to work together...."

Bash came into view up ahead, kneeling at the clear pool where I'd planned to stop. He splashed water onto his lilac face. I smiled.

"If you can work together, then what?" Declan asked.

I couldn't force the smile off my face as I turned to him. "You're out of questions."

Teyr shot me a dirty look for breaking my own rules as he trotted past. I kicked my horse to catch up with him, forcing Declan to grab my waist a final time.

11

———

KINNIA

The moment Zelimir's massive horse slid to a stop, I released his waist and leapt off. I had to tuck and roll to keep from hurting myself on the landing.

"We'll rest for twenty minutes. Stretch your legs." Zelimir dismounted more smoothly, rattling the red fastenings on his saddle where I thought metal would normally be found. "Water and feed the horses as well," he ordered the others.

I needed to relieve myself, but I couldn't imagine where would be safe. Everything this deep in the wilds seemed to glow. Even the tree sap oozed bright red.

Teyr dismounted and grinned at me. "Stay away from anything gold or extra shiny. Leprechauns might be small, but they'll bite your dick off."

I stared at him. "Leprechauns are real?"

Teyr started laughing, and I wrinkled my nose. Of course, they weren't.

"Stay close," Zelimir said over Teyr's laughter.

I nodded and followed a narrow stream branching off from the small pool about twenty feet. Though I could still hear the fae, I made sure I'd left their line of sight before relieving myself. I rinsed my hands in the river, then splashed cool water over my face and neck.

Kneeling on the bank, I listened to the laughing water and birds I didn't recognize. Wind whispered through high, silvery grass behind me. I'd heard dozens of stories of people wandering into the wilds never to be seen again. I started to understand why. I could stay here forever. Maybe I'd dump these moody fae and just wander the wilds on my own. Zelimir's warnings seemed ridiculous.

A pile of jewel-toned rocks peeked above the water slightly upriver. I nestled my waterskin amongst them to fill and stretched out on the bank. A frog—or something like that—croaked nearby. For a moment, I let myself imagine my family resting on the bank with me. David would know the frog-thing's name and a dozen facts about it. Harry would copy the frog's croak louder and louder until David stopped talking or Alex stopped him. Elaine would coax all of us to pull off our shoes and stick our aching feet in the water.

I hardly noticed the rustling at first. When it grew louder, I assumed Shade had found me through the tall grass. After a moment passed without so much as a whimper, the hairs on the back of my neck stood at attention. I sat up. The grass quivered in a pattern snaking right toward me, and fast. My bow would be useless in close quarters, so I leapt to my feet and drew my katana.

Three gray-skinned fae barely taller than my knees sprang out of the bushes and skidded to a halt. They wore multicolored leather and furs, but square pieces of green metal I recognized from Earth glinted on their hips and necks. A twist of thin cables hung out of one's oily, pointed ear and disappeared behind his scrawny neck. He bared sharp teeth that contrasted his too-round head.

Goblins. I'd never seen one in real life, but I'd read about them. None of the books said anything about any fae using Earth materials. A howl that rattled my teeth and seared my ears came from behind them. The trio flinched, sprinted toward me, then continued past. I turned to watch them scatter on the other side of the river. They were running. Which meant....

I whipped back as a huge, mottled orange-and-blue beast prowled out of the bushes. Its slavering jaw hung open, exposing rows of wickedly sharp teeth. It growled low in its throat, and the ground shook. I met its malevolent green gaze.

The beast pounced. I launched myself toward the nearest tree, and it whirled midair to track my progress. With barely a second's hesitation, the creature landed and sprang again. I leapt onto the lowest branch, then climbed higher until I crouched above the beast. With my katana gripped in both hands, I positioned myself directly over the creature's head and stepped off the branch.

As I fell, it disappeared and reappeared a few feet away. I hit the ground hard, knees rattling with the impact, and my blade bit uselessly into the dirt. My breath gasped out of my lungs, and I couldn't get it back through the bindings. Curved, vicious claws appeared at the edge of my vision. I flung myself into a roll, losing my katana in the process. Green-white teeth snapped mere inches away. I jumped to my feet, just out of reach.

A burst of fire exploded against the beast's back. Its face twisted in rage and pain before it spun away from me. Something invisible slammed into its right side. At almost the same moment, a spear of pure purple slammed into the animal's left. The beast howled and charged but didn't get far before the attacks hit its left and right sides again. This time, the animal stumbled and, with a final ground-shaking cry, exploded into a mass of flowers.

I picked up one of the little yellow buds. I didn't recognize the flower, but the stem bent like normal, and the petals twitched as my hand shook. I sucked in a lungful of air, dropped the flower, and looked for my useless sword.

Zelimir walked up to me as I plucked my katana from a bush. Purple magic still crackled over his fingertips. "We're in the wilds now."

I shivered but looked up into his hard gaze anyway.

"Stay close was not a suggestion," he said, then stalked off.

I'd been barely twenty feet from the horses. My throat constricted as a wave of helplessness swept over me. I couldn't leave these fae. I couldn't survive the wilds on my own. Panic clawed its way up my chest. I'd gotten myself trapped again, but unlike Earth, nothing here was straightforward.

12

______

BASH

I clenched my fist and fought to breathe normally with the human behind me. My horse tripped on the flat path. I couldn't even ride properly with Declan on my saddle. His human warmth burned into my back. My stomach churned.

Zelimir had been right. We needed to rotate the man. Anything to keep Teyr from making the kind of mistake we couldn't come back from. The demons of my childhood in human territory didn't control me anymore.

I focused on the battle with the barghest. The animal should have been easy to defeat, but we'd been slow to react to Declan's fear. Declan didn't realize it, but we'd been forced to defend him by the terror that shot through our Cara bond. The human had stupidly tried to cleave the creature in half with his sword. My shoulder hadn't yet forgotten the man had some skills, but he had no idea what to do with them.

I rolled out my shoulders, trying to banish the unease of responding to him like a mate in trouble. Zelimir said we needed to protect the human through the wilds, get him to the Academy intact. We had to save him. Regardless of what my commander said, I wished we had let him die and dragged the corpse after us. His very presence weakened us.

My horse stumbled again. I gritted my teeth and inhaled slowly. My

Cara hummed, reminding me with roiling guilt that the first emotion I'd felt from the man had been fear. Caras shouldn't develop that way. My horse tripped a third time. Declan steadied himself by gripping my shoulder. I shrugged him off, but the place he touched seared.

He had full access to my unprotected back. A bead of sweat that had nothing to do with the temperature rolled down my temple and through my scales. Two and a half centuries had passed since my last brush with humanity. But that didn't matter. Even after all this time, I carried those years in the church too close to the surface. My arm twitched, and old scars jumped under layers of runic tattoos. Declan shifted slightly to the left. I leaned the other way.

Time dripped by. I rolled up my sleeves. Usually, the unconstrained feeling of shirtlessness eased my nerves, but now, my bare flesh would only make my vulnerabilities more obvious. Teyr and Zelimir sent waves of calm, but the emotion came through muted and watery. Light sifted down through the rainbow leaves like stained glass. Hints of brown on the trunks looked like bricks. I gritted my teeth. Declan couldn't continue to ride at my back.

"Front." My voice came out harsh and fast.

The man had been quiet, maybe lost in his near-death experience with the barghest earlier. I didn't want to care. But he stirred as if from reverie and slid down my horse's black flank when I stopped. I removed my foot from the stirrup to give him purchase. He stared up at my mount. My commander *pulsed* to ask what happened.

"Faster." I grabbed Declan's arm and hauled him up in front of me.

Declan was much lighter than I'd guessed. I almost threw him over the other side, but he caught himself on the pommel. At least I could keep an eye on him like this. I wrapped one arm in front of Declan and grabbed my reins. The other, I balled into a fist on my leg to keep from shoving him back off. It would be so easy. My Cara hummed, happy to have our fifth so close. I growled. Not our fifth.

Declan stiffened and leaned forward. His long, gray tunic shifted with the motion, exposing the place where his muscular shoulders met his long, graceful neck.

"Just relax." I rocked with my horse's long gait. "The barghest is gone now."

The comforting words left my lips before I could stop them. He didn't react. I flinched back. The Cara made me soft toward the human and drew out my protective dragon instincts. I considered shoving him off my horse again, but Zelimir's orders echoed in my mind. I wished, not for the first time, that I could turn off the bond.

Declan didn't relax. My horse struggled as the double weight on his back refused to sway in time with his steps. I released my fist and wrapped my other arm around the man's waist. Goose bumps broke out between my scales. I barely swallowed down sudden nausea.

The human pulled farther away. "It's not so much the barghest that has me worried right now."

"I don't care. You're hurting my horse." I tensed my arm across his stomach and readied for a fight.

Instead, he leaned back and matched my movements. He still didn't relax, but his pitiful effort helped.

Declan scratched behind my Friesian's ears. "Sorry, horsey."

I snorted and returned my arm to my leg.

The warmth and softness of his body against mine quickly grew distracting. Sitting, he barely reached my shoulders. With every sway, his hair grazed my chin. He smelled clean, like fresh water, leather, and…honey? I clenched my hands.

"There will always be more barghests," I said suddenly. "And things worse than that."

Declan missed or ignored the violence my tone threatened and said, "What could be worse than a barghest?"

Fury rocketed. The man sounded so casual as to be mocking. Declan might have forced himself into our Cara, but he had no power here. He needed to know that. I needed to make him understand. I called up some of my most disturbing memories—the worst Tech, chunks of human flesh grotesquely fused with cables and metal. I could tell the human exactly what he wanted to know.

As I opened my mouth, magic seared through my skull. The memories mixed throughout my past and poured into Declan's mind. I grabbed my head and tried to snatch them back, but the magic wouldn't answer.

The world around me vanished as Declan and I fell deeper into my terror. Mental images raced across my mind's eye.

Chunks of metal stream out of a rift faster than a horse can run.

A priest smiles as he lowers a slim knife to my chest.

Buzzing metal bugs whizz through the air, shooting lasers that melt through fae skin and bones.

I scream, begging for my teachers to stop the pain.

A massive Tech with arms made of thousands of moving pieces cuts through fae as even more monstrosities pour through the rift behind it.

Sharp teeth sank into the flesh around my ankle with a burst of pain. The link between Declan and I severed. I flinched backward, and my eyes snapped open. The vibrant colors of the wilds replaced the horrors in my memories.

My horse stood stock-still sideways on the trail. Teyr and Zelimir blocked our path. My commander glared at me. My Cara thrummed with Declan's fear, hurt, and anger. I had pinned him against my chest. His shaking hand gripped my restraining arm hard enough that his nails drew thin lines of my grayish blood. I released him, and he dove off the horse. My arm ached.

Fuck.

Shade whined. I winced. The wolf rubbed up against Declan, who didn't look at me or acknowledge him. The human just stared at the forest ahead in silence.

"I'll run alongside the horses." The man rolled his shoulders and pulled his pack from where it hung from my saddlebag.

Teyr *pulsed* repeated demands to know what happened. I silently cursed. I hadn't manifested a new magic in decades. Something about the human pulled new power out of my mixed blood, and I wielded it like a cudgel.

Declan opened his pack. His hands visibly shook as he disarmed himself to get rid of the extra weight. He hadn't even been born when I killed the human priests who'd imprisoned me.

Shade whined again, but the rest of us sat silently. Zelimir shared conflicted feelings with me. If the man feared us, he would keep his distance, but any emotion, good or bad, risked strengthening the bond. My regret joined my commander's. I had sworn I would never treat anyone the way my captors treated me. Yet, I had forced terror on a man who'd done me no harm.

The human pulled out his waterskin and slung it over his shoulder. I risked meeting his stony blue gaze. When we fought, his eyes had lit with joy and focus. Now, I couldn't find anything but blank disdain. My Cara whirled with a steady stream of human emotions. He put up a good front for the terror pouring into me.

"Look, you can ride with me," Teyr said.

Declan flattened his lips and looked into the trees. "I won't slow you down by walking."

Teyr scoffed. "We're still twenty miles off."

Declan stretched his legs. "If I need a break or can't keep up, we can reassess. Move out."

He didn't wait for a response before taking off down the road. Shade trotted after the human, but even he kept his distance.

"What did you do?" Teyr hissed as we swiveled our horses to follow.

My emotions, my magic, everything had fallen out of balance even worse than the early days of the civil war. I needed to meditate.

"How could the magic have made such a mistake to bring us him?" I whispered.

"I don't know." Zelimir frowned. "But the Council said they'd look into it when we arrive. With the uptick in rifts, we can't afford to become even more divided than we already are."

We nudged our horses into a trot and caught up with Declan. I swallowed a pang of guilt. His waterskin smacked against his shoulder with every step. He stared sullenly forward. I *pulsed* to Zelimir that I would scout ahead and galloped past the human. Anything to escape the familiar dullness I'd glimpsed in his eyes.

13

KINNIA

MY PANTING ALMOST DROWNED OUT MY POUNDING footsteps, but it didn't come close to drowning out my thoughts. The fae's gazes sat heavily on me, as they had for every moment of the last who-knew-how-many miles. I tried to run faster, harder, but I'd already pushed my body to its limits. Running had seemed like a great idea before I'd remembered I shouldn't use my *energy*. I could feel their magic, so my new "friends" would probably sense my *energy* through whatever stupid fae bond we shared.

One foot in front of the other.

Bash and Teyr rode in front of me, nearly out of sight through the trees, and Zelimir brought up the rear. The strings from the fae knot in my belly strained in their directions. The sweat pouring down my body chilled me.

I should have devoted my life to getting rid of this magic when the first couple tonics didn't work. Instead, I'd let it lead me south. I should have stuck around to at least try Slavica's paste. Instead, I'd bent to the trio's offer. Hell, I'd barely asked any questions. Would there even be a hundred gold once we got to this Council?

I tripped on a stone. My next few steps wobbled until I found my rhythm once more.

The memories Bash had forced into my mind reopened old wounds. The pressure of restraints as those humans bent over him reminded me too much of the times on Earth I'd been captured and woken up with cables in my skin. He couldn't impress me with Tech—I'd seen much worse in my almost five years on Earth—but I couldn't stop seeing the violence. Fighting metal monsters, I'd never seen that much blood spilled. Except—

Alex. Elaine. David. Harry. Their faces, bloody and broken, danced through my mind. I might be the only one who remembered their names. A tear slipped down my cheek. I wobbled, almost numb from fatigue, and stumbled on flat ground this time. Shade appeared from the woods and leaned into me, keeping me on my feet. I swiped the tear away and leaned off him. I needed to stop running, but I couldn't ride with the fae.

One foot in front of the other.

The ground disappeared under my strides. The horses' hooves thundered around me as the magical colors of the fae forest glowed with the beginning of sunset. I couldn't enjoy them anymore. I slowed enough to swallow the remaining contents of my waterskin, then pushed for speed once more. My toe caught a rock, and once again, only Shade kept me from eating dirt.

If Bash hadn't held back when we'd fought this morning at the fae inn, he could've beaten me to a pulp, despite my *energy*. The beams of magic that fried the barghest could take me out just as easily. I might not have their magic, and I might not have their knowledge, but when it came down to sheer will, they had nothing on me.

I just needed to think of my kidnappers like that mushroom from this morning. They looked beautiful, smelled like the best dessert, but if I wasn't careful, I would be dead the second I touched them.

The trees ahead looked oddly square. I blinked. The square trees resolved into rough, bark-covered buildings, and I nearly wept with relief. This had to be our stopping point. I lengthened my stride and slowed to a walk, stretching with each step. Shade pressed himself against my hip. I couldn't push him aside anymore.

Teyr reined in his horse alongside me. "Just a little farther."

"Yeah." I couldn't guess at the emotion in the wiry fae's voice. "I need to cool down. That's our stop?"

"It is," he said.

Silence dangled between us as I waited for an explanation. If I stopped walking, I would collapse. I leaned against Shade for support as I finally caught my breath. My heart rate started to slow.

"Does it have a name?" I asked.

"The Waltzing Willow." Teyr tapped his feet in the stirrups. "It's off the main road."

"Great. I'll find you there." I flexed my run-swollen hands. When he didn't leave, I frowned up at him. "Do you need something?"

He blinked. "You're shaking. You're about to collapse."

Of course. They sent the charmer. They wanted me to admit I'd pushed myself too far. "I've run twenty miles before, and I'll run it again. Piss off."

Teyr hesitated, his gaze going distant like he heard something I didn't, then nodded and nudged his horse into a canter. I pushed aside my anger and hurt. My *energy* swirled under my skin. I hadn't used it since meeting these fae, so the well of power sat comfortably full.

I'd only survived on Earth because of my *energy*. Using it less when I returned to Thrae had been a struggle, but people always seemed to notice. I'd been run out of one town for stopping a cart with my bare hands, and another for saving a woman from a larger attacker. I missed the easy buzz of power under my skin now more than ever.

Shade bumped my elbow with his nose, and I scratched him absently. The string in my gut hummed happily. I needed his warmth at my hip to cover the last few hundred feet, but I couldn't forget he was one of them. Not that the others seemed to believe that. They talked about him like an obstacle or not at all. I didn't know why they bothered to travel with him if they liked him so little. But if they didn't speak to him, they couldn't know if....

I met Shade's mismatched gaze and pushed *energy* into my muscles before I could lose my nerve. His tongue lolled out of his mouth, but he gave no sign anything changed.

Music and laughter exploded out of a huge, nestlike building a few doors down. I picked up my pace as much as I could. If the giant, magical, Earth-migrant wolf couldn't feel anything, it stood to reason the others couldn't either. I finally had an edge.

I reached the door of the inn and pushed through. A very unmanly yelp burst from my lips as I grabbed for the door and managed to cling to the side of the frame, dangling above a deep pond instead of the floor that should have been there.

Shade yipped and planted his butt on the surface of the water. I caught sight of the bar to my left and tables spread across the top of the pond. Magic.

Teyr rose from a table in the far corner where he sat with the others next to a set of wide, wooden stairs and walked toward me across the top of the pond. "What are you doing?"

"It's water," I said stupidly.

Teyr stopped next to me. "It's magic. There's a pond *under* the floor."

I knew it was magic. Fucking fae. Still, I clung to the door as two sparkling, golden fish swam beneath my feet. Teyr chuckled and jumped up and down a few times to demonstrate there was no danger. I lowered my feet onto the floor. Afternoon sunlight reflected off the water's surface, and I looked up through a clear ceiling at the sky. I returned my attention to the pond as a turtle-like creature with a glowing pink and purple shell drifted by on a rotting log.

In human territory, beauty tended to be hard-won. The wilds over-brimmed with it. I smiled. Then, I scowled. The stupid turtle was probably poisonous or something.

Teyr scruffed Shade and pulled him back to the table where the other two fae sat. Shade dropped to the floor and placed his head on his paws, gaze on me. Teyr pulled out a chair and looked meaningfully at me, but I ignored him. I needed to get away from these fae and figure out how to destroy this stupid knot in my gut.

I tried to storm across the floor, but instead, stumbled on wobbling legs to the bar. "I need a private room for the night."

The bartender, a petite, brown-skinned woman with chunky hair that looked to be made of stiff bark, glanced at my companions. I seethed. Of course, they'd already "handled" everything.

She frowned as she looked back at me. "Zelimir says that's all right."

I gritted my teeth. "Right. Can I have that now? Do you have laundry service?"

"You're lucky Zelimir pays well, human." She spit the word like an insult.

I crossed my arms, too tired and impatient to care.

"You can have whatever you like." She pursed her lips. "Leave your washing outside the door."

She led me to the stairs. Shade barked and rushed toward me. I steeled myself. I needed total privacy. And to stop craving the comfort of the wolf.

I squatted and scowled. "If you even try, I'll chase you out and break one of your paws, so you don't get a second shot."

Teyr choked on his drink. Bash smacked his mate's back. I stalked up the stairs after the woman. She gestured to a door at the end of a hallway too long to be contained by the walls of the building I'd seen, then spun on her heel and left. I rolled my eyes but continued to the room.

The door melted away at my touch, revealing an ovular room with a single bed, a low table, and a second, slightly open door that led to a bathroom. I stepped inside and, before I could worry about how to close a door that had dematerialized, it faded back into position behind me. One problem solved.

I stripped off my weapons, armor, clothes, and underwear. My breasts ached as I released them from the binding for the first time in two days. I'd had to loosen them at night a little to keep in shape to fight, but it was still more consistent binding than I'd tried in years. I rubbed them in apology for that and the weeks to come, then put the clothes outside before pulling on new underwear and sinking to the bed. I wanted to pace, to flee, to scream, but my muscles protested any movement. At least I could finally, finally breathe.

The fae knot bubbled in my gut, taunting me. I'd been in worse situations than this. No matter what came next, I would have clean clothes at the end of the day. I sat up on the wood floor and crossed my legs. I'd never had a chance to test the limits of my *energy*. Too much time spent hiding and scraping by. I took a deep breath and placed my hands on my bare stomach.

Last time I tried using my *energy* on the knot, nothing happened. But I didn't know what it was then. Now, I knew, and I wanted it gone. I gathered my *energy*, then pictured spears and lances and the beams the fae had used to destroy the barghest and loosed *energy* at the knot of magic. It bounced harmlessly off and knocked the breath out of me. I rocked back on my forearms, the only part of me that didn't hurt, and tried to steady myself.

I had one chance to get this right. The more *energy* I spent, the less I'd have tomorrow, and I'd be using it to make the trip easier from now on. Plus, the fae might notice the effect over time. If I couldn't touch the knot, maybe I could surround it. I sat up and put my hands back on my stomach. My leg muscles burned with fatigue.

Focus.

To keep the test simple, I envisioned *energy* surrounding the luminous tangle in my gut. The *energy* dragged itself around the knot of magic until it surrounded the knot. Then, achingly, I isolated that sphere of *energy* from the rest of the power buzzing in my body.

The *energy* in the sphere, the shield, shimmered with tension. I panted as my body shivered with the new sensation. I'd never cut any of my *energy* off from the rest before. But as I caught my breath, the thin shield held. The strings floated more slowly, as if underwater. Something more complex would certainly cut them off for good. I released the shield with a breath and whooped before clapping my hand over my mouth.

A new Declan would be born tonight, and I couldn't have any interruptions.

14

———————

ZELIMIR

I rubbed sleep from my eyes as I crossed the common room the following morning. My second stood sentry in the corner by our table. Shade crunched away at something beneath the table. I decided not to ask what. I reached the table, and Bash handed me a coffee.

I sipped the hot brew. "You were alone in your morning exertions?"

He grunted an affirmative. I warmed my hands around the mug. The human seemed to start his day with exercise, but it looked like the spar had been a one-off.

"The locals are curious about our...companion," Bash said. "The barkeep asked me if he was *the* human last night. The one in the Cara."

News had leaked from the Academy? I took my seat. I'd noticed the gazes trailing after us last night but assumed the blame lay on the presence of a human this deep in the wilds. I would have to stay on guard.

The Waltzing Willow's door banged open, and a satyr sauntered in. He carried no weapons and kept his gaze on the clear floor. Last night, I dreamed of Declan's face as he marveled at the floor of this place. Certainly, the Cara was trying to inspire positive feelings between us, but I'd spent my life around magic, and I couldn't remember it ever being that exciting. I wanted to see the world through his eyes.

"I can't help wondering." Teyr would never let me live down what I was about to ask. Worse, the idea I was mulling over gave me a warm feeling I liked. "Could we be missing something?"

Bash clenched his jaw. "He's human."

Perhaps the dragon had learned something yesterday. I ran my hand through my hair. "I disliked cutting off my conversation with him."

Bash grunted acknowledgment and opened his Cara. A mix of anger, regret, and determination filtered into me. I reciprocated the gesture and shared confusion so thick we could have eaten it for breakfast.

I'd never been as drawn to someone as I was Declan. Yes, the magic of the Cara pulled me to him, but Declan had something about him beyond our magic. He stood up to Teyr's charm and handled Bash's temper. Our short conversation showed curiosity and critical thinking humans rarely used. The man's arms wrapped around my waist left tingles in their wake.

I checked Declan's Cara to ensure he hadn't run in the night, then frowned. Our growing bond with the man seemed thinner. I'd been expecting the opposite, and the change didn't give me the relief I'd hoped for.

Teyr stumbled down the stairs and yawned as he dropped into the seat next to Bash. The dragon pushed a cup of coffee into his hands.

"Why do you get up so early?" Teyr grumbled.

I ignored his standard morning complaint. I'd never met someone more opposed to rising with the sun. "How is your Cara with the human, Teyr?"

The ember took a long swig of coffee. I could almost see the caffeine working its magic in him. An extra loud *crack* came from whatever Shade found to demolish.

Teyr smiled at his cup before sucking down another mouthful. "I'd no idea humans only owned one set of clothing. No wonder they smell."

"I asked you a question," I said.

"He was just a pile of sweaty rags when he walked in last night." Teyr wrinkled his nose.

I fisted the hand tucked under my arm.

"All I'm saying is"—Teyr took another sip—"between the barghest and the run, maybe the magic didn't make a mistake. And regardless, he doesn't deserve to be punished for something he has no control over."

I shook my head. "I don't care how attractive or impressive you think the human is, you have to stop saying that. We received direct orders from the Lower Council, which hasn't steered us wrong in the last hundred years. The magic did make a mistake."

"Being slightly skilled doesn't make him fae," Bash said.

Teyr harumphed. "You two are no fun."

I ran a hand through my twists. What either Council said became law for the Anam Caras. Thrae itself chose the Caras, but the Lower Council trained us and taught us the vows that truly bound us. They gave us the unity that made us strong.

"Just keep your distance." I met my second's gaze, then the ember's.

Teyr *pulsed* my order right back to me.

I frowned. "We don't know what the Lower Council knows. We must obey them. We cannot let the Cara solidify."

"Council this, Council that." Teyr rubbed his stomach. "Does anyone else feel something weird with the Cara?"

I clutched the edge of the table, driving wood splinters into my palm to keep from lunging forward and blackening the ember's eye.

"Morning," Declan said.

Teyr jumped and spilled his coffee on the table. I eyed the human. He looked much better this morning—well-rested. His bright blue eyes twinkled as he took in the magic of the room once more. I squashed a sudden desire to explain how it all worked.

Teyr sullenly set his cup next to the spilled coffee. "How can anyone be happy in the morning? Our Cara even hates this morning. It's all short and foggy."

Declan froze, then frowned as if reminding himself of something. Shade whimpered miserably, but the human ignored the wolf and took a seat at our table. He drew his shoulders back, veiled his expressions behind a wall of self-control, and folded his hands neatly on the table.

How many times had I done the same thing, hiding my true feelings so I could please my father? The world? Shade jammed his wet nose against my leg. I reached down and stroked the wolf.

Bash crossed his arms, eyes on Declan. "You blocked the Cara."

Teyr whipped his head up. Even I glanced at the dragon in surprise.

"How?" Teyr pinned Declan with a stare.

Declan set his mouth in a harsh line. "I'm sure Bash can explain how magics of the mind work. And I'd love to know exactly what I blocked."

"But…you don't have magic," Teyr said.

"Obviously." Declan's voice dripped sarcasm. "I was promised details, so let's hear them. I believe we're in some hurry to reach this Council."

Shade whined again and tucked his tail between his legs. Declan's hands tensed like he had to restrain himself.

Teyr stroked the dismal wolf's ears. "You do know you're the one upsetting him."

"That doesn't seem like my problem. I'm not here to be lied to and shit on." Declan's easygoing, curious manner had disappeared. He turned to Bash. "What you did to me yesterday was a complete violation."

I flinched. The color drained from my second's face.

The wood nymph who ran the inn walked to the table with a tray of porridge, fruits, nuts, and more coffee. We fell silent. She snapped her fingers, and Teyr's spilled coffee sank into the wood before she unloaded her fare. Declan avoided our gazes. The nymph seemed to sense the tension and fled. Declan dug in like he hadn't eaten in days.

My father used to tell me the best way to judge a man was by how he dealt with inconveniences. A kind man would always find a kind way. Shame washed over me.

Twice, Bash opened his mouth. Twice, he closed it again. He stood and walked out the front door without even a grunt. I *pulsed* support and understanding to the dragon, but I wouldn't follow him. He needed space.

I glanced around the common room. This early, we only shared the space with the nymph and the satyr, though, as I watched, another satyr joined him at a table well within hearing distance. I didn't know they were that plentiful in this part of the wilds, but most satyrs were too obsessed with their own sexual conquests to worry about us.

"How much do you know about Anam Caras?" I reached for a bowl of porridge. I had to find a kind way to explain.

Declan swallowed and scooped up another spoonful. "Nothing."

"An Anam Cara's basically a magical fighting unit," Teyr said before I could continue. "Five fae, all male, called by a soul bond—the Anam Cara. They train at the Academy until they achieve balance, usually years, then take a vow to formally combine their magics. If one dies"—the ember studied his coffee—"the entire group loses effectiveness until the magic finds another good fit."

Teyr refused to meet my gaze. He didn't like the lie any more than I did.

"When this fae is found"—he ran his thumb along the rim of his mug—"the Cara returns to the Academy for assessment and retraining."

Declan nodded as he ate. A bit of the tension loosened in his shoulders.

Teyr took a deep breath. "The magic you're feeling is our magic. The Cara wants to bond with you, but that shouldn't be possible. Nothing against you. Humans aren't selected for Anam Caras."

"We're bringing you to the Lower Council to correct this," I said. It wasn't any kinder to keep lying, regardless of how bad the truth sounded. "Caras can only be as strong as their weakest link. Your addition was a mistake."

Declan swallowed and wrinkled his nose. "How close does this Anam Cara make the group?"

I met his gaze. "Very."

Declan held my gaze for a long moment, then looked back down at his food. "You're all, um, physically active? Together, I mean?"

I raised a brow. Teyr laughed, lightening the mood for the first time that morning. A faint blush covered Declan's cheeks, and I smiled.

"What we share goes deeper than physical pleasure," I said. "We're mentally connected, literally unable to get away from each other. My mates are closer than family."

Declan glanced at me before stabbing some eggs with his fork.

"Sex—" Teyr said.

"You'll not be part of an Anam Cara for long enough to need that information." I gave my mate a quick, quelling look. "The more you know, the more we talk, the more solid our bond will become. That will make it harder for the Council to remove you."

Declan pursed his lips but nodded.

"You suck all the joy out of a Cara, Zel." Teyr refilled his mug from the carafe of coffee the wood nymph had left on the table.

"So, it's you two, Bash, and Shade?" Declan speared a red berry with his fork.

"Why can wolves be part of a Cara but not humans?"

I sighed. Teyr flinched. We had to put all our cards on the table.

"Shade isn't a regular dire wolf," I said. "He's a fae, a divar, who's taken on this shape."

A long moment of quiet passed.

"He took the death of your fifth hard then?" Declan watched the wolf with such care and concern I had to swallow against a lump in my throat.

Hard was an understatement. Shade blamed himself for his brother's death. After six years, I didn't know if he was remaining a wolf to hide from his grief or from the fact that other people might think the same. I'd spent most of that time convincing Teyr not to even mention anything around that guilt.

"How did you know?" Teyr asked quietly.

The man looked up at our solemn faces. "It's not a hard leap."

"Our fifth was Shade's twin, Light." I bowed my head. Unbidden, I realized Light would've loved Declan.

"I'm sorry." He turned to Shade and patted him on the head.

Shade wagged his tail once at the human's touch, but his low whine wrenched my Cara into a knot.

"And I get it." Declan's voice became as smooth and emotionless as iron. "I'm the imposter. The connection I feel to you is magical, not real. I'm sure someone worthy of your Cara is out there. I won't cause you trouble. I just want to go back to my old life a little bit richer."

Teyr recoiled. I ran my hand through my hair. Declan looked so polished and professional, I almost believed him. That pleased me. It had to. If he kept his distance, following the Council's orders would be all the more painless. So, I bit back the confession I'd offered Bash before the others had woken and sipped my coffee.

"Buy me a horse." The man turned back to his breakfast. "I'm not riding double anymore—we can't solidify the bond, right? And I don't have the...energy to run the rest of the way."

I kept my expression blank as I stood and gestured for Teyr to do the same.

He nodded and knocked back his cup of coffee. "Have another cup waiting for me when we get back."

"Will do." Declan didn't look at either of us.

Shade scooted closer to the human and rolled over. Teyr and I turned for the door before we could watch that conflict play out. Everything had worked out for the better.

15

TEYR

I tugged on my horse's reins, intending to drop back next to Declan. The human still followed the orders Zelimir had given at the Waltzing Willow a few days ago. He always rode the spotted gelding we'd purchased for him a bit apart from the group, and his Cara remained muted. Hardly anybody spoke anymore. Even the sun seemed dampened by our mood, hiding behind a rare blanket of clouds.

Zelimir steered his horse into my path, cutting off the route to Declan. I huffed.

"Don't get attached. Don't let the Cara grow," he said.

"You're on repeat, Zelly." I rolled my eyes. "Anyway, Declan's ingenuity did a better job than we could have."

I couldn't figure out how he blocked the Cara. Runes required magic to power them, and a rune caster to write them. Ooproot tea required no magic, but I didn't know where he would've gotten any, much less how he would've known the leaves blocked magic.

Bash rode up on my other side.

"Talking to the dragon is like talking to a wall." I scowled at Zel. "And you're too busy brooding to be good company. I want to play with our new toy."

The dragon growled. "He's not a toy."

"We're letting other fae play with it when we stop at inns." I wiggled my eyebrows at the moody dragon.

"It's not playing, it's conversation." Zelimir sighed. "Humans are... intensely social. His interactions at the pubs exhaust that, so he doesn't bond with us."

I rolled my eyes. "Just because you broke it doesn't mean I can't have a turn."

Bash's already stony expression darkened. A large rock floated telekinetically up over his shoulder. I dove sideways off my horse as the rock shot forward, and I hit the ground as it clipped my saddle.

I rolled onto my back and ignited my frustration into a large fireball in my palm. "If you hurt my horse...."

"Enough!" Zelimir bellowed. "Bash, go scout ahead. Teyr, just...think before you act. We can't fix this if you mess it up."

I flashed Zelimir a grin, extinguished the fire, then jumped to my feet. I remounted. "Don't worry, I've been thinking about it."

The dragon disappeared into the trees.

Declan trotted up beside me. He narrowed his eyes as I guided my Andalusian next to his shorter, spotted mount. The two horses put their ears back. Mine nipped his, and they settled. I grinned and patted my horse's neck before looking down at the human blessed to ride in my company. We had a little over a week until we reached the Academy. I'd have my fun while I could.

Declan raised an eyebrow. "Do you need something?"

I shook my head. "Conversation was a bit dull at the front."

He snorted. "I thought Zelimir had a 'no talking to the human' rule."

I winked. "Rules were made to be broken."

"Is that what you said to Bash before he tried to take you out with a rock?" Declan smiled.

"No." I puffed out my chest. "But did you see me make that fireball?" I'd never met anyone who couldn't be impressed by fire magic. It looked good and worked well.

Declan bit his lower lip. "I saw your hand glow. The balls of lights that float around the taverns are bigger."

I deflated. "My fireball was bigger than a fif."

"Fif. Finally, I have something to call those lights," Declan said. "I kept forgetting to ask. There's just so much stuff. I met a brownie last night, Teyr. A real brownie. I can't believe they're made of the same stuff as treants. He was only a foot tall and had spotted skin like my horse and the most adorable little spear."

I pouted. "Adorable *poison* spear. Why are you more impressed by that than my fire?"

Declan scrunched up his face. "Why do you care?"

I scowled. "Because I'm an ember—one of the most powerful embers to ever live. Everyone's impressed by me."

"Sorry," Declan said. "I didn't know glowing hands were impressive."

I narrowed my eyes. Declan bit his lip, but the corners of his mouth tugged up. I wished I knew him well enough to know what that meant. He looked tired. Deep bags sagged under his eyes, and he slouched in his saddle.

My Cara reached for the man. I swallowed. Every evening, we let him wander the common room of whatever inn we stayed at, and he talked to anyone interested. Yes, it kept him away from us, but it meant he learned about the wilds from strangers who could be telling him anything.

And they didn't tell him about us. The human didn't know me. He didn't know the shaved side of my head, even the straight hair brushing my chin, made a statement against my people's traditions. He'd never heard any stories or watched me fight to victory in the Emberhold Arena.

My horse twitched and rotated his ears. The quiet clop of hoofbeats on dirt filled the air, but with none of the usual birdsong. My skin prickled. In front of us, Bash's horse came into view, abandoned, but his Cara stopped in the forest ahead.

I pushed my mount closer to the human's and kindled my worry into fire. Reds and oranges danced over my palm. Zel *pulsed* an order to remain at Declan's side before he vaulted off his horse and charged into the forest. Where he vanished, a single tree, bleached of all its color, stood amongst the bright reds and purples.

Declan tried to urge his horse toward the tree, but I cut him off. The man obviously lacked proper horse training. After a few attempts, he gave up with a huff.

"What is that? Part of Earth?" His voice broke on the final word.

My Cara spiked with adrenaline. My mates had disappeared, but I'd guess they'd found an open rift. I itched to help them. But Declan seemed fragile. And, of course, I valued following orders. At the Academy, I'd heard rumors Earth was white like the pieces of Thrae that Tech had siphoned off, but how would Declan know that?

I turned my attention back to him. "It's not Earth," I said slowly. "It's what happens when a rift isn't closed. Tech dig cables into the ground and siphon out the magic of Thrae. The very essence of life. I saw them siphon from a fae once." I shuddered. "The troll didn't live long."

"You promised me no rifts." Declan wrapped his arms around himself and gripped his own biceps so hard his fingers went white.

Guilt swirled, but I ignored it. I'd done nothing wrong, and warm currents of Zelimir and Bash's magic sealed the rift. No harm done.

"This isn't a rift." *Anymore.* "And it wasn't a promise. More...an assessment of the current situation. There were no rifts open that we knew of when I made that promise."

Declan looked up at me with hurt in his blue eyes.

"We'll do our best to stay away from rifts. But closing them and fighting EarthTech is why Caras exist. Shit's gonna come up." I flashed the man my most charming smile. "Relax, we won't involve you."

Declan grunted in frustration and grabbed his waterskin. I glanced in the direction of the rift, and the sun glinted off something silver. What? Bash and Zel had closed the rift. There shouldn't be any silver left, and certainly not over here. I was about to dismount and check it out when my mates emerged from the tree line. Oil covered Bash's cherrystone axe head, but he and Zelimir looked untouched.

"Just one cable," Zelimir said as they remounted.

Bash took off immediately to scout once more.

"Nothing we couldn't handle. Less than six inches across, but the cable had lodged deep in the ground. A few blasters defended it from

Earth's side." Zelimir sighed. "I don't know who's patrolling this area. It must have been open for at least two days."

"Is that unusual?" Declan asked.

Zelimir narrowed his eyes and kicked his horse into motion. "Yes."

Declan paled. I looked back at where I'd seen the glint. Maybe it was the remnants of the cable, or a blaster that had fallen through and needed to be destroyed. But as we passed the spot, nothing caught the light.

I looked between Zel's tense riding stance and Declan's unsteady grip on his reins. I deserved some entertainment for keeping out of the fight.

My prissy horse pranced unhappily as I settled next to Declan's once again. The bushes next to us rustled, and a gray-and-purple possum skittered across the road with her babies dangling from her stomach. Declan reined his horse back, and the possum hissed up at us, displaying mismatched eyes, before running along.

"What the hell was that?" Declan demanded.

"Possum." I steered my horse over to him again. "Thought you'd recognize it, since it's one of the animals that came over with humans. The coloration gives it away."

He shook his head. "It looked like a big rat with a dozen other rats attached."

"Rat?" I asked.

"Never mind."

I studied him for a moment, then decided we needed to talk about something more interesting. Me. "Embers used to be a type of elf—tinggi elves, or tall elves, if that's easier."

Declan eyed my mates ahead of us. "Won't Zelimir get mad at you for giving away your secrets?"

"He can be as mad as he wants." I winked.

Declan flushed, and I grinned. The man put up a strong front, but I'd spend the time to see it crack. Finally, he relaxed into his horse's gait.

"Elves are short and squat, with wide heads and long ears. Tinggi elves"—I patted my chest—"are perfectly proportioned. A gift to faekind, really, and only improved by becoming elementals."

Declan snorted, and I took it as a compliment.

"Some of my shorter ancestors are okay. You'll meet Councilor Odhrán, of the Lower Council." I scrunched my nose. "I guess one of the greatest conjurers of all time can be short."

Declan bit his lower lip. "You sound personally offended by that."

"I am. They're the first version, and we're the improvement." I pressed my hand to my heart and held my breath, waiting for him to ask. I swear the man bit back a smile.

"So, what's the story?"

Ah, attention at last. I draped my reins over my thigh, trusting my mount to plod along so I could use both my hands to accentuate my words. "Long before humans came to Thrae, the whole world was alive. Elements themselves walked these forests, devastating and blessing in equal measure. A group of tinggi elves, at war with a much greater enemy, impressed Fire with their determination and passion." I grinned. "Thus, Fire made embers, elemental fae blessed with powerful fire magic. Since there were so few, priests devoted to Fire instituted a system of arena duels and bloodlines to create strong lineages that could lead us into the future."

Declan cocked his head. "Like dog breeding?"

I wilted. I didn't know what a dog was, but it sounded bad. "You really don't know anything."

Picking up on my mood swing, Declan nodded. "Zelimir mentioned that titans were decedents of old fae. Were they elements, or gods, or what?"

I wiggled my fingers. "Ooh, theology. My favorite topic because every conversation goes on endlessly."

Declan snorted again.

"I don't know what humans believe." I splayed my hands out in front of me. "But fae know the magic of Thrae started everything. There were the elements, there were ancient fae, but nobody really knows what changed. Some fae think they became our magic, others they're still out there meddling in our lives...." I barked a laugh. "Some fae even believe they *are* gods."

"Oh, Teyr, I'm sorry to burst your bubble, but...." Declan trailed off with a sly smile.

Old memories flooded through my head, and my heart squeezed. "I know I look like a god, but I'm as far from one as you can get."

Declan narrowed his eyes. "I've never heard you say something bad about yourself before."

I glanced at Zel's back, my broken Cara bleeding. "That was an...old joke of mine. Before I got called to the Cara, I was a duelist with very few losses to my name in that arena I mentioned. The Anam Cara only amplified my power." I released a harsh breath. "But then Light died."

"And Light was Shade's twin?" Declan glanced around, no doubt for the absent wolf.

I nodded. "Divar, to circle back to your theology question."

Declan raised an eyebrow.

"A very rare clan of fae infused with raw magic from Thrae itself. They're the only true mages, don't even need runes to talk to the world." I swallowed.

"Runes being those letters," Declan said. "If they talk to Thrae, why didn't I see them in human territory?"

"You need magic in the land and the user." I shrugged. "Runes used to work over there, but without fae, the magic just isn't able to cycle like it needs to."

Declan shook his head. "That seems stupid."

"I don't make the rules, I just tell the stories." I gestured broadly. "Which I believe you were enjoying?"

Declan laughed and rested his chin on his fist in a mockingly attentive pose.

I smiled as my chest warmed. "Light was amazing. I've never heard of a fae his equal. He had power like you wouldn't believe, but the most impressive thing was his heart. He might have been the only genuinely good fae I've ever met." I clenched my fist. "I didn't do well in our Anam Cara at first. On our first day at the Academy, I told Zelimir to shove his orders up his ass, then set part of an obstacle course on fire."

Declan laughed, and I joined in. The look on Zel's face had been priceless.

"While Zel threw a hissy fit, Light took my hand." I rubbed my palms together, still feeling that first touch. "He took me away from all of it, and we drank until I admitted—"

Declan's wide, blue eyes never left mine, all hope and curiosity. I wanted to tell him everything. He would be gone in a little over a week.

I picked up my reins and pushed down the tears brimming in my eyes. "Well, Light never broke my confidence."

A wolf's howl rose to my left, and I pictured Light's face, covered in dark blue veins when we found him. I sent a wave of comfort, of promise that I didn't blame him, to Shade. Even if his animal brain didn't understand, it seemed like the right thing to do.

Declan leaned forward to brush his horse's short mane. "Loss is never easy. I understand wanting to keep pieces for yourself."

Silence fell over us. The human breathed slowly and evenly, like he focused all his attention on the effort. Something in my heart tugged. I wanted to know who he lost. Zel *pulsed* a rebuke, sharp and insistent.

I nudged my horse toward Declan and bumped our knees together. "Enough sadness. We're staying at the Partying Poppy tonight. Pari, a fairy who looks like a tulip, runs the place."

Declan turned to me, his somber moment already replaced by curiosity. "How can someone look like a tulip?"

I smiled.

16

BASH

Days passed uneventfully on the road. Zelimir let me spend most of the ride scouting ahead. I couldn't stand to be within arms' reach of the human. I had ridden past Punaky's Pub to get a sense of the path ahead while the others halted for the night, but sunset finally forced me to head back. Guilt churned my stomach near constantly, and Declan's accusation played over and over. The human had been kind in his phrasing.

I shouldered open the door of our stop for the night and stepped inside. The roiling clamor of fae laughing and talking in every corner of the long common room of Punaky's Pub washed over me. I should have expected the crowd. The pub squatted at the intersection of three main roads. More than one crimson-wearing Anam Secca dotted the tables.

Two elven bards played on a large stage in the far corner, but they seemed more interested in each other than the audience. The stone and wood walls had only a couple windows along their length, too small for my shoulders to fit through should I need to escape by that route. The only doors were the one I entered through, a small one behind the bar, and one in the back that looked like a kitchen entrance. A small army of gray goblins wearing rough, brown pants and matching shirts served drinks and food. They skittered around and used strange machines to rearrange furniture as groups came and went.

Declan sat at a table in the middle of the room with a petite tinggi elf, but I couldn't find Zelimir or Teyr. I snorted. Zelimir had no doubt already retired to the suite to page through history texts like he might find some reference to a human Cara mate every fae in the wilds has missed, and Teyr—well, with a pub this crowded, he had likely already found someone to slake his desires. Even Shade was absent. It was my turn to oversee Declan while he socialized tonight. My struggles with him might be clouding my thoughts, but I hadn't stopped feeling watched as we traveled. A bit of distance would tell me if the worry had any basis.

I selected a table far enough away that the man shouldn't believe I could hear him and with a superior eyeline to all three doors. Many fae looked at him, but no one reached for weapons, murmured spells, or even seemed to be taking notes. Despite the clamor, my ear fans allowed me to pick out his voice easily as he chatted with the tinggi elf, whom he called Norrila.

"Do all humans have gray bags under their eyes?" Norrila flipped a tendril of her high, golden hairdo over her shoulder.

"No." Declan smiled. "We're traveling fast, and I've been staying up later than I should, talking to all sorts of lovely fae like yourself."

He seemed to be eating up the elf's attention. My chest tightened. I couldn't imagine how anyone could have a pleasant time in this place.

"So much flattery." Norrila tittered. "I guess we fae are interesting to a human."

"My travel companions aren't the most talkative folk." Declan leaned closer to the elf. "They think if I spend every evening socializing, I'll be less likely to talk to them during the day."

I grunted. He'd seen through our transparent plan. But he hadn't been talking to us, which meant it worked.

"Oh, how very fae of them to manipulate you." Norrila giggled and trailed her fingers down Declan's forearm.

I growled. Presumptive little witch. I started to reprimand the man through our Cara, but the connection remained too thin for communication. I took a deep breath. Something about this human inspired intense reactions, but I was neither my Cara nor my instincts. I wanted nothing to do with him.

"Bash!"

I turned toward the sharp, nasal voice to find Councilor Xerxes walking toward me. I'd never seen a councilor outside the walls of the Academy except for General—Councilor Drax, and him, only during the civil war. Councilor Xerxes didn't even wear the rainbow robes of a councilor now, just a plain, dark hood.

I straightened. "What can I do for you?"

He perched on the chair in front of me. His dark, billowing robes blocked Declan from view. As spymaster of the Lower Council, everything about him, from his carefully clasped hands to his long, birdlike face, demanded my full attention.

"I'm here to meet with a contact," Councilor Xerxes said. "Though now that I've found you, I might as well get an update on your progress with the mistake."

Discomfort pinched my heart. For a moment, I wanted to defend Declan. I had already caused the human enough trouble. The councilor sounded completely casual, but the noise in the room rose to a dull nothingness. The spymaster could affect others' senses, and it seemed he'd chosen to protect us from eavesdropping.

I schooled my features. My inner conflict was mine alone. "We made contact in the *Cross Roads* and convinced the man to travel with us for a small sum. He has since been informed of the truth of the situation and is equally interested in being removed. We had a brush with a barghest and closed a small rift. The Cara has not solidified."

The councilor's piercing green eyes remained fixed on my face as I spoke. I understood why such a fae would be given the position of spymaster. Even I almost wanted to keep talking.

"I see more scales have appeared on your face," he said. "You're a dragon?"

"Part dragon." I leaned slightly to the left in an effort to see Declan past the fae, but he matched my movement. My skin prickled.

"I understand some dragons struggle with their possessive natures.

This is a very difficult situation, and you failed to mention anything personal regarding the human. How are you coping?" The Councilor steepled his fingers.

I fisted my hands under the table. "I didn't mention it because it's not an issue."

He gave me a hard look. "You have lived many years, Bashu, but you have less than a century as a Cara. I might be a better judge of what is or is not an issue. Understanding is of great value to all fae."

I steeled my expression and waited for him to leave.

He pursed his lips. "Did you stay at the Waltzing Willow?"

I nodded tersely. I would never forget what Declan said to me there. I turned my ear fans in his direction, but only the low white noise of the councilor's magic reached me.

"A rift opened not far from there about four days ago. Nobody found it until the day after." Councilor Xerxes cocked his head to one side.

I remained silent. Four days lined up with the morning we'd left, so I doubted the rift had anything to do with us.

He smiled. "I look forward to seeing you at the Academy. If I could give you all my wings to hasten the journey, I would."

"Thank you, Councilor."

"If you find you have more to tell me...." He stood.

The noise of the room doubled in volume as he walked away.

The chair where Declan sat was empty. I stood and scanned the room for him.

Nothing.

My heart slammed. Councilor Xerxes vanished into the crowd. I stood and ran my gaze over the pub once again, but still nothing. I closed my eyes and reached for our bond. Still uselessly faint. I cursed. I'd had one job. I wrenched my eyes open again.

Frenzied barking broke out at the back of the tavern, and a rush of Shade's fear flooded into me. I hadn't felt emotion from Shade in six years. I raced toward the wolf, shoving fae out of my way. I rounded the bar to find him scratching at the small, half-hidden door I'd noticed behind the counter. I should've known that door meant trouble.

I pushed the wolf to the side and wrenched the knob. Locked. I oozed telekinesis into the cracks around the door and tore the wood from its frame until the door burst open. Shade darted inside, and I followed on his heels. He disappeared around a long shelf of liquor and barked.

"Yeah, my doggy here doesn't think I should do that." Declan's voice emanated from the direction Shade had gone.

I rounded the shelf and found Shade stationed in front of the human, hackles raised. One goblin stood behind a low bar, while another stood halfway between Declan and the bar. Neither looked armed. A few kegs lined the walls, and a single low table strewn with empty glasses stood in the corner. That elf, Norrila, dangled off Declan's arm with a goblet in her free hand.

I stopped short. "Declan, what are you doing back here?"

"I was just about to give him a tour of the cellar." Norrila batted her eyelashes at me as if to distract from the intelligence in her slit-pupiled eyes. She extended the sloshing goblet toward Declan as she tugged him toward a large set of double doors behind her.

Declan's excited bounce made his curls bob. "Norrila said they have a special liquor made out of punaky. I don't know what that is, but they distill it using scraps from Earth—not Tech parts, just basic materials. I had to see."

I didn't need to hear more. I reached Declan in a single step, pulled the drink from Norrila's fingers, and shattered the blown glass against the stone floor. Her nostrils flared in agitation.

I smiled a hungry smile. "I'd love to see this as well. Maybe a paid pour, straight from the source, would be more to the human's liking."

"Of course." Norrila untangled herself from Declan's arm and motioned to the goblins.

The one behind the bar began to clean the broken glass while the other opened the double doors. Shade sniffed the patch of spilled liquor and whined.

I slipped between Norrila and the human. "Punaky," I murmured to him, "is a purple root vegetable grown primarily in the mountains around here."

Norrila observed me coolly as Declan grinned. He opened his mouth

—no doubt to ask another annoying question—but the goblins ushered us inside before he could. Fifs flooded the second room with light. I'd never seen this much manufactured steel in good condition. The large tanks that heated, cooled, reheated, and eventually distilled the punaky sprouted meters and pipes like branches. The goblin closed the door behind us, and I realized only one small, high window provided an alternate exit from the room.

Declan shifted uncomfortably. "I didn't think there would be quite this much Tech. How did all this get here?"

One of the goblins puffed out his chest. "We have a Jalan on the books."

Declan's eyes widened. "You're kidding, right? Jalan don't...there aren't any Jalan in Thrae."

"Ah." The goblin furrowed his brows. "No?"

"What?" Declan took a step backward and crashed into a cherrystone support holding one of the tanks.

The goblin hunched its shoulders and scampered away from him.

"Do they live in the wilds?" Declan demanded.

I'd never seen the human truly frightened. Even when I forced my memories upon him, he became angry and determined. But I recognized the animal terror in the set of his shoulders, the fear no amount of training or practice could ever really tamp down. I'd felt it in the Cross Roads.

The goblin glanced at his companion, then at me—or, more likely, the brown pants and cream-colored tunic of my Cara uniform. "We don't actually have a Jalan. We buy what they salvage from the great Anam Caras' battles. Jalan aren't welcome here."

I *pulsed* to Declan that I would explain later, but it fizzled.

"Liquor," I snapped.

Norrila watched Declan.

"Liquor, right. Yes, sir." One goblin rushed over to a shelf to get a few glasses identical to the one Norrila had been holding.

"Did you know they deal with Jalan?" Declan asked me softly.

I grunted and shook my head. He pursed his lips but dropped it.

The sound of liquid being poured into glasses bounced off the hard surfaces of the small space. I never took my attention off the elf, but she remained frozen as the goblin offered us each a glass. I motioned to Shade. The little fae's hands shook as the dire wolf sniffed the drinks. Shade snorted, adding some snot to our tasting, but wagged his tail. We accepted the samples from the goblin.

Declan cocked his head and swirled his purple liquor, studying it. His blue eyes glowed in the fif light when he looked up at me. I grunted and downed my drink. He flashed me a grin before following suit.

"Oh, wow. That's weird." He studied the last few purple drops in the glass. "It's sweet. Is everything sweet in fae?"

"You are such a charmer." Norrila laughed and batted her eyelids again. She crossed to Declan's other side and linked her arm with his.

Declan seemed oblivious, his attention on the liquor. "Do you sell this by the bottle?"

Norrila tittered and motioned toward the goblin.

"We do, sir," the goblin replied. "Two gold."

Declan bit his bottom lip. Shade sighed happily as Declan absently curled fingers into his fur.

My heart jumped. A foreign, floaty sensation filled my chest. "He gets to fill his own bottle, right here, right now." I pulled three gold out of my pouch.

The goblin's big eyes grew wide, and he darted forward to relieve me of my coin.

Declan beamed and clasped his hands in front of him. That feeling didn't fade. I snorted, nodded toward the metal stills, and gave him a little push.

Norrila's mouth fell slightly open as Declan pulled out of her clutches like he'd forgotten her completely. I shot her a triumphant smirk. The human poked the metal with a slightly trembling hand, but when it didn't move, his shoulders relaxed. As the goblin showed Declan how to work the spout, I gripped Norrila's arm and pulled her aside.

"Who are you working for?" I demanded. "Was Declan your target, or just a gullible bystander?"

The elf's already pale face went white. "I don't know what you mean."

I tightened my hold on her arm. "Don't play dumb with me."

In a flash of light, her body shrank, disappearing from my grip. A small, purple itzal sprang out of the pile of clothing that hit the floor. Declan and Shade whirled, and we all watched the rodent dart through a grate I'd missed below one of the stills.

I hated shifters. Hair that high could've hidden any ears, and itzals didn't have tails.

"What was that?" Declan demanded.

"Watch your pour!" The goblin jumped up and down.

Declan spun back just in time to keep his bottle from spilling over.

I toed the elf's dress, but she had disappeared. I cursed.

The human turned to me. His smile almost split his face as he held up his bottle like he'd distilled the liquor himself. My scales relaxed, and I couldn't keep from returning his grin. For the first time in days, the guilt in my stomach eased. If I could make Declan happy enough, maybe I could make up for forcing my memories on him.

I choked down a sudden urge to ruffle the man's hair. "We're going to have to add 'no wandering off' to your rules."

17

———

KINNIA

I TWIRLED MY KATANA IN MY HAND, STEPPED INTO A defensive position, and braced against an imaginary opponent. Despite the thick orange and purple tree cover, morning sun blazed down on my armored shoulders. I spun into the next position and swiped away a river of sweat from my temple. A scant twenty feet away, Bash grunted as he swung his bright-red, black-veined axe through his own morning routine.

For the past week, the dragon had gone out of his way to find a spot as far away from me as possible for his exercises. I'd thought my very existence somehow pissed him off, and after the incident where he forced his memories onto me, I'd appreciated the space.

Until last night. He bought me that bottle of alcohol and sat at the table with me for the rest of the night. He didn't talk much, but his silent presence had been steadying as other fae had flitted to and fro. A girl could get used to it, if the girl wasn't a *mistake* the guy in question was traveling miles to fix.

Bash gripped his axe in both hands and slashed the weapon in a wide circle, then dropped into a crouch and swept his invisible partner's feet. He'd smiled for the first time last night. It softened his scaly features and warmed a rusty place in my chest.

I swung into a low stab that would gut any fleshy enemy, not that I faced many of those these days. The Cara in my gut had shrunk to a quiet, fuzzy throb since I surrounded it with my *energy*. I'd liked it better when I could blame my attachment on magic.

Something in the bushes behind Bash reflected the early morning sunlight. Weird. Most things here glowed on their own, but that looked like a reflection. I rubbed my eyes and squinted. A few heartbeats later, the bushes rustled, and I glimpsed the light again. Bash swung into a crouch and gave no sign of having noticed.

The light shone again, and my stomach clenched with its familiarity. I knew the shine of sunlight on metal as well as I knew my own hands. Despite every fiber of my being telling me to run, I caught Bash's attention and mouthed "bathroom," then pushed into the orange and purple undergrowth.

My senses had been on high alert since last night. The distilling tanks chilled me to the bone. Their pipes looked like the cables that connected everything on Earth, and the buttons and gears were obviously ancestors of the Tech that haunted my nightmares. I'd struggled to fall asleep knowing there were Jalan on Thrae. I'd run across a few of them on Earth, humans who built Tech into their body, and the very thought of them turned my stomach. Bash had explained they were scavengers, allowed to stay in the wilds because they made some kind of deal with the Lower Council, but that hadn't kept me from tossing and turning. I didn't understand how anyone could look at Tech and see something good.

Movement caught my eye, and I crept toward in that direction. The undergrowth thinned as I approached the back of the pub. A few well-worn trails wound away from the back door and deeper into the forest. My fingers buzzed, like the moment before a storm. A chunk of sharp-edged, symmetrical metal lay on the most worn path. I knelt beside it. A thin, green board covered in tiny boxes of various sizes poked out of the leaf litter. Hadn't the goblins I'd seen running from the barghest been wearing pieces of this? I picked it up.

"I dropped that," someone said in a nasally, male voice.

I snapped my gaze up to find a goblin with long, greasy black hair pulled up in a bun two feet from me. Unlike the uniformed goblins I'd seen in the pub, this one went shirtless and wore a thick belt boasting an assortment of small weapons over his brown pants. Most threateningly, a long, thin blaster of pounded metal was strapped to his hip. I hadn't seen a blaster since Earth.

"What is it?" I pointed at the metal, ready to run if his hand so much as twitched. I had felt a blaster's burn too many times to discount the weapon.

The goblin rolled his eyes and stuck out his hand. "Circuit board."

I didn't recognize the term, but I couldn't mistake the gesture. He wanted his property. Pointy, crooked teeth peeked out from between the goblin's cracked lips. I wished he hadn't caught me kneeling.

"Where did you get the blaster?" I got to my feet, board in hand.

"My uncle built it." He looked me up and down. "I can get you one, for a price."

I narrowed my eyes. "Does it work?"

The goblin grinned, wide and confident. "It will."

My whole body broke out in goose bumps. I shoved the circuit board toward him. Anything to get away from that smile.

"Declan!" Bash shouted.

The goblin snatched the board and bolted back the way he'd come.

The dragon emerged from the brush behind me "What did we talk about last night?"

"Um," I said dumbly. "Norrila?"

"We talked about not wandering off." Bash huffed and placed a hand on my shoulder.

"I just—" I broke off, surprised by his warm hand on my shoulder. Concern pulled at his brow. I'd expected anger. I bit my lower lip and looked away.

"This is too far, even for a bathroom trip," he murmured. "It's not safe."

The back door of the pub swung open, and Teyr poked his sleep-rumpled head out. "Breakfast on the road again." He rolled his eyes, indicating his feelings on the pace Zelimir set.

Bash's gaze went distant for a moment in a way I'd realized meant the fae spoke to each other through some kind of magic, then he took off toward the horses. I trailed behind. I didn't like seeing Tech coming through rifts, but Tech laying around in the fae wilds disturbed me even more.

I caught up with Bash. "The goblins are making some weird stuff, huh? Are they all like that?" I hadn't gotten a close enough look at the metal-laden goblins fleeing the barghest that first day on the road.

He shrugged. "Goblins experiment. They're small, and their magic is weak. The distilling tanks aren't that strange."

I frowned. Bash hadn't seen the blaster or the way that goblin smiled, but maybe goblins were just like that. And, I reminded myself, I didn't care about the problems of the fae.

The farther away from the goblin we got, the less the air buzzed against my skin. I rubbed my arms. The feeling disappeared as we reached the clearing at the front of the pub. Neither Bash nor Teyr had mentioned the feeling, and I certainly wasn't about to be the first. I'd learned that lesson well enough. My second foster mother dumped me on the streets for saying too many "unnatural things."

I shuddered. Bash rubbed a calloused palm comfortingly along my arm, then snatched it back and continued toward the stable without a backward glance. He'd touched me twice now. The same warmth bloomed in my chest as when he'd smiled at me. I would keep the electricity to myself.

And try to forget the way that goblin smiled.

18

TEYR

Later that day, my knee brushed Declan's as my mount side-stepped a poisonous mushroom. The brief contact sent a thrill up my leg.

"So, the wilds has all kinds of different birds, but you still call them birds, generally?" he asked.

"I guess?" I shrugged. "I know stuff like zainacs and akuri are unique to the wilds, but you have bhelrians, right?"

The human laughed. "You just said a bunch of nonsense words. I've never even heard of a bhelrian."

"No way." I shook my head. "You've definitely seen a bhelrian. You can't miss them in the daytime."

"A bhelrian is larger raptor, a bit like one of your hawks, but completely gold," Zelimir called from in front of us.

Bash grunted. "Big talons. Decent meat."

Declan shook his head. "Never seen one."

"What do you even look at in human lands?"

He returned to his favorite pastime, ogling the same navy blue and mint green trees we'd been traveling through all day.

Zelimir *pulsed* to contain myself. I sighed. We'd been on the road a little over a week, and already my day flowed around Declan's mood.

Teasing him out, giving him space, answering his questions, coaxing that quick flash of smile. I kept almost forgetting how things used to be, the years of trying to talk to my brick-wall mates, and spent more time doing stupid things to draw Declan's constantly distracted eye.

The road ahead opened into a small, grassy clearing, shot through with morning sunlight. Maybe I could convince Zel to break, get in a little nap--

Three fae surged out of the forest on dark mounts, their hooded cloaks flapping open to reveal brown Cara pants. Bash *pulsed* that there were another two behind us, cutting off any retreat. A full Cara. I channeled my desire to impress Declan into brilliant fire on my fingertips and braced to fight our way out.

A fellow Cara used to be cause for celebration, not combat.

The tallest rider stopped in front of Zelimir and dismounted, then threw back the hood of his cloak. Dull gray skin stretched over his lumpy muscles, and double-layered ears widened his already broad face. His curly orange hair frizzed as if trying to escape.

Geminai grinned. "Zelimir."

I scowled. That had to be the rest of his Cara surrounding us. We'd been at the Academy together, racing to see which of us would graduate first. I knew their abilities well. Brettrus, his minotaur second, could harden his body to take hits and dole them out. I recognized him by the custom stirrups on his Shire horse, which accommodated his hoofed feet. Judging by the slim build of the third fae in front of us, he had to be Terris, Brettrus's air elemental. That meant Exilis and Gorar, his fairy healer and ophican poison wielder, pinned us in from behind.

"Geminai." Zelimir's voice sounded calm despite the suspicion he shared across the Cara. "What brings you this far out into the wilds?"

The Councilors usually kept their Cara close to the Academy, like a lot of their promising graduates.

Geminai grinned, exposing the jagged boulders of his teeth. "We were on patrol and wanted to check out your…special assignment."

I narrowed my eyes. Nobody should know about Declan. Zel had been right, there had to be a leak. Worse than that, the troll carried himself with a new confidence. The sort people only have when they know the establishment won't let them fail. I knew it well from Emberhold.

"So? Let's see it." Geminai crossed his arms like he had all the time in the world.

Zelimir *pulsed* a reminder that Geminai's complete Cara pulled rank over us and urged his horse to the side. I bit back a sigh and moved to the other side of the road, giving Declan a clear path to ride forward. Nothing happened. I glanced back to find Declan frozen on his horse with his brow furrowed in what looked like confusion and worry.

"Human, come," Zelimir barked.

Declan clenched his jaw, but he urged his spotted gelding forward. The beast trembled, unused to life without another horse's butt in front of its face. The animal retreated when Declan encouraged it to pass Zelimir.

Brettrus laughed long and loud, tossing his cloak back from his minotaur horns. "What a prize. It can't even control its horse." The golden ring in his nose caught the light as he threw back his head and laughed again.

Geminai's mates burst into laughter. The fire in my hand burned brighter as my desire turned to something darker. Part of me wanted to laugh with them, to step outside the target. I'd noticed Declan's weak riding. Another part wanted to ride in front of him, block him from view, and hurl fireballs until our old rivals cried mercy. Zelimir pushed calm across the Cara. I rolled out my shoulders in an effort to shake off the sting.

Brettrus leaned forward. "Why don't you get down off that thing and show us what a human's good for?"

Declan flinched. I glared at my impassive commander. The human didn't deserve this. Zelimir didn't look at me. I dropped my fireball and urged my horse forward to intervene. A low wail cut through the clearing, and everybody looked in the direction of the sound. At the tree line to the left, a low, reddish mist oozed along the ground toward us.

I froze. I'd heard rumors of this, the fog of war preceding spirits still fighting long-settled battles. Fire, what were they called? I'd stopped paying attention in class after Ambrocio admitted they hadn't been seen in fifty years.

"Wraiths!" Zelimir bellowed as a foggy hand clawed out of the cloud.

A half-solid, armored fae comprised of the same reddish mist followed the hand. Another followed that, and another. I dug my heels into my horse's ribs, and the animal leapt toward the tree line on the other side of the clearing. At the trees, I grabbed a branch, swung out of the saddle, and spun to face the clearing.

Bash and Zelimir leapt from their saddles and sent their horses for the trees as well, but Declan dangled from a branch over his horse, which bucked with its reins tangled in a different tree. Geminai's Cara remained still.

The smoky red fog roiled across the ground toward us. Dozens of fae-shaped wraiths formed from the mist and rose up. As a new wraith formed, it pulled a misty scythe from nothingness and swung at its nearest companion with a whispered war cry. Maybe they didn't want anything to do with us.

A wraith in the middle of the clearing hurled a bolt of mist at Bash. The mist hit him in the chest. He stumbled back with a cry and unsheathed his axe, bright red against the wraiths' dull color.

So, they did want us. I hated being wrong.

"Clear it out!" Geminai stomped the ground. A vinelike blade jutted up out of the dirt, and he uprooted it with a grunt.

Zelimir grabbed his massive two-hander and swung at the wraith attacking Bash, then cupped Bash's axe with a line of force. Declan dropped from his branch as his horse scrambled away, and a streak of black-and-navy fur barreled out of the forest at him.

I ignited the sting of humiliation into a handful of small fireballs and hurled them at the thickest clusters of wraiths. The fireballs exploded, destroying a few of the figures in bursts of fog.

Terris, Geminai's willowy blond air elemental, leapt off his horse and landed with a gust of air which only barely drove the fog away from his feet. It leaked back in quickly, and more wraiths sprang up.

Zel cleaved through an axe-wielding wraith. The wraith burst into fog and sank back down to join the ground cover. A wraith with an eerily similar axe crawled out of the ground next to me, wobbling for a moment before it caught its footing. I swore. They were already dead. We couldn't kill them again. I kindled irritation into a whip of fire and cracked it into the wraith that reached me. It burst apart, then reappeared elsewhere.

Declan hollered as he launched himself into the fray with the wolf at his side. The human's sword sank through the fog, and Shade leapt and bit, but they each had to hit a single wraith more often to destroy it.

I channeled my frustration into a line of fire that shot across the battlefield , cut through tens of wraiths, and whipped around Declan's sword. He cast me a quick glance across the clearing, nodded, and turned back to the horde. I only wished I could do something for Shade.

Zelimir bellowed in pain. I summoned that burst of fear into another handful of fireballs. A blade made of mist split the back of his tunic and sliced through his flesh. I drew back to launch. Brettrus whirled for a new target and came face-to-face with the one attacking my commander. He hesitated.

My breath caught in my throat. We'd fought battle after battle alongside other Caras, when a rift got too big or remained for too long. The vows of the Anam Cara dictated that you had to defend another Cara as you would Thrae itself. Regardless of the mocking laughter that still rang in my ears, Brettrus would protect Zel.

Right?

The minotaur glanced at his commander, then charged away from Zelimir. My stomach flipped. Neither Gorar nor Exilis entered the fight. Terris had begun blazing a path toward the edge of the clearing with Geminai and Brettrus in his wake.

Zelimir *pulsed* for assistance. I tore my attention back to my commander and found him surrounded by wraiths. Politics later. Ghosts now. I launched several fireballs, dulling their heat to keep from burning Zel, and raked through dim memories of Ambrocio's ridiculous lecture on wraiths. The old councilor droned in a way I found nearly impossible to pay attention to—

Wraiths pinned Zelimir down in the middle of the clearing, Shade remained a wolf, and Bash—where was Bash? I hadn't seen the dragon since he took the first hit. The wraiths crowded the clearing, but not so much that I couldn't see anyone else. I ignited worry into a bigger fireball.

My Cara pointed me to the tree line the wraiths still emerged from. Bash slashed at the foggy spirits as they appeared, but mostly, he stared through the trees at something in the distance. A wraith slammed a ghostly hammer into his side, and he lurched to the ground. He rocketed back up.

Fear leaked into the bigger fireball in my palm, turning it sickly green. Bash never fell out of a fight like this, even when injured. I *pulsed* to ask if he was okay. He met my gaze across the fray and jerked a thumb over his shoulder. A wraith launched itself at him, and I dodged the thing.

I spun, breathing heavily. Nobody had seen a wraith in fifty years, but the crotchety old Ambrocio believed in using the past to inform tactics. He'd said something....

"Wraiths are caught in a cycle." His voice warbled in my memory. *"But cycles can be broken."*

Ridiculous. I pelted across the clearing toward my mate.

Geminai, Terris, and Brettrus had ridden to the far edge of the clearing, just out of reach of the fray and a bit away from Bash. Geminai released his vine blade back into the dirt. Exilis beat his four green wings frantically, holding his tiny body over his pony a little deeper in the trees. Gorar coiled his serpentine lower half around his saddle.

They were fucking leaving. I *pulsed* the news to everyone.

Zelimir wheeled, ignoring the wraiths around him. "Cowards! Traitors!"

"Let the human save you, if it can." Geminai swung onto his horse, and they thundered away.

The fog lapped at my feet. Wraiths outnumbered my mates on a scale we could never overcome. The Battle of Light glowed in my mind. We had fought eddying waves of Tech with little hope of survival. We had to break the cycle.

Zel *pulsed* a warning. I dodged a wraith's claw and skidded to a stop in front of Bash. His purple skin darkened with bruises and a few gashes leaked gray blood down his left side. Still, he kept looking into the trees.

I blasted a handful of wraiths out of the way and glared at him. "What in Fire are you looking at?"

"Civil war ended over that ridge." He flinched as a wraith barreled through him and into the trees.

The civil war…the battle the wraiths were still fighting.

"Talk to them," I said. "You were there when it ended, right? Tell them about it."

Bash frowned as a misty wraith fist collided with his shoulder.

"We have to break the cycle!" I shouted.

Bash *pulsed* a worry that he couldn't convince the wraiths. Then something happened on his side of the Cara. I blinked and the vision of the battlefield surrounded by navy blue and mint green trees with an army at my back filled my vision. Councilor Drax, in a uniform I'd never seen before, held a blade to the throat of a tinggi elf I didn't recognize.

"As commander of this army," the elf hissed, "I, Kellam Enceran, hereby surrender on behalf of my men and agree to negotiate peace with General Drax on this ground, three days hence."

I blinked again and found myself back in the fog of war as a wraith swung at me. I dodged and raised an eyebrow at Bash. Since when could he project a memory into someone? He shook his head. Shade yipped painfully, and I wheeled back to the fight.

A dozen wraiths pressed in on Bash and me from all sides, sometimes peeling off to fight each other. I put my hands up in surrender and nudged Bash to do the same. He sheathed his axe reluctantly. Zelimir *pulsed* a furious request to know what the hell I was doing, but I had to see if this would work.

"Commander Kellam surrendered!" I bellowed. "General Drax has won the war. Put down your weapons."

The wraiths kept fighting. More oozed from the trees. I stared into the forest in frustration, as if seeing the place I'd stood in Bash's memory would help me. Another wraith clawed into being, then wobbled for a moment before lashing out.

I *pulsed* to Bash to grab a wraith as it formed. He unsheathed his axe and slashed through the spirit in front of him. It sank back into the mist and reformed nearby. In that moment of hesitation, Bash seized it with his telekinesis. The form quivered in the air.

I stepped up to the frozen wraith. "I don't think the news has reached the edges of the battlefield yet, but Commander Kellam surrendered." I put a hand on its smoky shoulder, hardened by Bash's hold. "General Drax won. We can lay our weapons down."

The wraith creaked its head to one side as if questioning me.

I forced a relieved grin. "It's over. We can stop fighting."

The battle around me went suddenly still. Zelimir looked at me. I held up a finger. *Wait.*

"We can go home," I said.

The wraiths burst into mist all at once, leaving a thin, red film in the air. I inhaled to cheer and coughed on the metallic taste. Bash thumped my back until I regained my breath.

Zelimir, Shade, and Declan joined us at the edge of the clearing. Shade had a pretty nasty gash across his face and a small limp. Zel looked cut up, but no worse than would heal in a day. Declan moved achingly as if bruised, but I couldn't see any blood.

"What happened?" Zelimir asked.

I grinned. "I broke the cycle."

Bash looked at Zelimir. "Geminai had two communications bowls on his mount—both within easy reach."

Zelimir nodded and I didn't need our Cara connection to know what he was thinking. The troll would only need two communication bowls if he answered to multiple masters.

I wondered which councilor never wanted us to reach the Academy.

19

———

KINNIA

A FEW LONG DAYS OF TRAVEL LATER, I SAT ALONE AT A TABLE in yet another tavern and cupped my hands around a red stone mug—cherrystone, Bash said—full of fruity ale. Only half a week of travel separated us from their Academy now, and Teyr had babysitting duty. He chatted with a tall, baby blue fae on the other side of the long, pink wood common room and glanced my way occasionally. Zelimir had turned in for the night and Bash hadn't come in from the stables yet. Shade snoozed at my feet. After Punaky's Pub, Zelimir no longer tried to lock up the dire wolf.

Untethered, permanent oval portals of bronze-colored wild magic floated through the otherwise monotone pink room. Inside the portals, I glimpsed other connected pubs. When we'd arrived, Teyr had explained this tavern collected wild magic, a side effect the material used to build it, and the owners channeled it into these portals. Drinks appeared out of thin air with no centralized bar or fire pit to draw the eye. Fae faded in and out, wandering the wilds in the blink of an eye, but most of them still took the time to stare at me, like seemingly everyone had along our last few stops.

My heart jumped to my throat as Teyr stroked his companion's glowing blue arm. I had lost control of my mount yesterday, and Teyr had seized the reins before the gelding could shoot off into the forest. His hand, smooth and long-fingered, had landed on top of mine. I could imagine exactly how his fae companion felt.

I drained my ale and squashed the thought. They believed me to be a mistake, not their friend. At least Teyr and Bash sometimes spoke to me as we rode. The conversation ate away at a little of the loneliness.

One of the oval portals floated close to my table. I caught sight of the side profile of a fae man wearing a high-necked black shirt. He had thick, blond hair and tawny skin and sat alone in his pub, nursing a thin-stemmed glass. He looked familiar. Where had I seen him?

Before I could get his attention or investigate further, an old bard, so small I doubted she reached my elbow, hopped onto a table near the middle of the room. I smiled. In the few taverns my little family snuck into before we went to Earth, I always had to shush everyone when the storyteller arrived. I could imagine David flipping me off but falling silent, and Alex swinging an arm over my shoulder as he settled in to listen.

With a deep breath, the bard began a new story. "When the rift that changed everything opened, the sky was clear and blue." Her light, musical voice seemed at odds with her wide, wizened features. "Humans had been appearing for some time, in funny suits with funny robots, and they poked and prodded and took, but this was different. When the rift that changed everything opened, the humans came through screaming. They came in hundreds and thousands, all of them running. And the monsters followed." The little bard's face grew solemn as she spread her hands in front of her.

"War overtook our land. We had fought before. We'd always been fighting. In truth, we fought ourselves, and the funny humans, and whatever Thrae saw fit to throw at us. But fighting and war are terribly different things. The sky became smoke-choked and bloody. We turned weapons against whatever was closest, people or fae or the Tech that ravaged our world."

She smiled slightly. "But amidst the darkness appeared a glimmer of hope. Varsina was a squadron commander, a glorious leader with an eye for the future. She believed things could change if fae could only unite."

The bard clasped her hands together. "So, she handpicked her squadron from disparate tribes and groups, from long-standing rivals and distant cousins alike. The first night the five of them fought together, when Thrae needed it most, something changed just as Varsina said it would. Their magic broke across the battlefield like a firework and the first Anam Cara formed."

An explosion of laughter blotted out her next sentence. I glanced around the tavern and realized not a single other person listened. The storyteller sighed, her shoulders falling as she looked around the room. Her startlingly wide, orange gaze with catlike pupils that reminded me of Teyr came to rest on me, and she smiled. With a graceful hop, she jumped off the table, grabbed her tankard, and strode toward me. She seemed spryer than her wrinkles and bent posture suggested.

She reached my table. "Mind if I join you? My stories don't seem to be drawing much interest tonight."

I smiled and gestured to the seat across from me. "Please. I can't wait to hear what comes next. My name's Declan."

"Rydel." The bard sat, though her eyes barely cleared the tabletop. A flower-shaped pin held back her graying hair, the fluorescent green of the petals melting into the gold outlining them. She held out her hand in a very human gesture.

I had to stand to reach across the table to clasp her hand. Her palm warmed in mine and immediately put me at ease. She winked before she released me and picked up her drink. A soft, orange glow lit her face as she took a swig.

I eyed the drink. "What are you drinking?"

Rydel gently set down the wooden cup that fit perfectly in her hands and smiled. "That's not the real question you have for me."

My heart leapt. Days of speculation and unanswered questions demanded my attention. I took a sip of my ale to keep from tripping over my own tongue. As I put my drink down, I met the bard's gaze.

"Varsina was a woman?" I flexed my shoulders. "Women can be in a Cara?"

Rydel chuckled. "They told you only men could be in a Cara?"

I almost asked how she knew who I traveled with, but Shade still slept at my feet. It couldn't be hard to figure out.

"They did."

She tsked. "It's very rare. Only three women have been called to the Cara, but all of them powerful." She tapped the table with one finger. "I shall finish my story now."

I flushed with excitement and nodded.

Rydel stood on her chair and climbed onto the tabletop. "Months and years of fighting passed. The Anam Cara led charge after charge. More and more clans united under their guidance. We lost many. The humans, perhaps more. It seemed the sky could do nothing but bleed. The Anam Cara figured out how to close rifts, but there remained only one Anam Cara. No one had managed to replicate the magic the five of them worked."

She smiled down at me. "A great battle was waged to close the rift that changed everything. Human and fae fought side-by-side, all in the desperate hope that something could be done. The Cara reached the rift. Bloody and bruised, they traced the runes to close it and strike a blow against the heart of the Tech invaders. At that moment, the Tech invaders struck a blow against our heart. As the rift closed, Varsina fell, and her lifeblood leaked into the soil of Thrae.

It is said that in her final moments, Varsina spoke to Thrae herself. Varsina drove her fingers into the dirt and poured all the magic in her body into the ground. For the first time in years, the sky became clear and blue. Across the wilds, magic awoke in groups of five as the Anam Cara spread across the land. We lost Varsina, our greatest hero, but with her sacrifice we won the war."

I wrinkled my nose. "Why don't humans and fae live together if Varsina united them?"

Rydel dropped her hands and scowled. "Unity and peace never truly last amongst fae." She jabbed a finger at me. "And humans were greedy. They feared us because they had no magic to counter our wildness with. We fought the humans for decades after Varsina's death. In the end, we agreed on splitting the world and keeping out of each other's hair." She scooped up her drink and took a big gulp. "Everybody just wanted the fighting to stop."

I raised a brow. "What happened to the rest of Varsina's Cara?"

Rydel set her drink down hard, wood thumping against wood. She climbed back down to her chair but didn't sit. I had a perfect view of her clenched jaw and pinched eyebrows.

"My storytelling's lost on the youth." She huffed. "They survived, unlike most Caras who lose a member, and founded the Academy as the Upper Council."

"When Caras lose a member, the rest of them die?" I glanced at Shade.

"Most of the time. The Anam Cara bond is like nothing else. It's the only magic with a purpose, and without all five, that purpose is thwarted." She peered at me. "It's not just raw power. The first Cara worked because they loved and trusted each other."

I scoffed. "What does love have to do with fighting units?"

"Why do you think Varsina fought?"

I ran a finger over the handle of my mug. I'd never really had time for whys. They belonged to people with more time, less loss. I fought because I needed money and because I'd gotten good at it on Earth. It suited my *energy*. I didn't have any other skills.

I looked toward Teyr. He stood at the side of the table beside the glowing blue fae. Horns of frothing water sprouted from her head. She blushed and laughed, making the tops of her breasts jiggle. Teyr wiggled his eyebrows.

Rydel snapped her fingers in front of my face.

I jumped and winced. "Sorry."

"No need for that, I have my answer." She grinned. "Now, do you have a story for me? It's only fair."

Shade shifted his head onto my feet, and I ran my fingers through his soft fur.

"He needs his rest," Rydel said as if reading my mind.

Her gaze burned into mine. I leaned back and grasped the handle of my mug of ale. She wouldn't let me leave without a story.

"I'm not as good a storyteller as you, but I can try," I said. "Let's see, I have a very human one about—"

Rydel put her hand on mine. "Actually, I'm looking for a specific story." Pale orange light sprang to life where our fingers touched.

I blinked and leaned forward. My skin warmed under her touch with a small tingle. Rydel flipped my palm to the ceiling, and her fingers brushed over the inside of my wrist. Shade made a noise in his throat that vibrated my feet, but he didn't move.

"Right." I tried to focus. What were the rules? No running away. No deals. No…something else. "I can't promise anything, but what story are you looking for?"

"Do you love life?" Rydel asked.

I blinked a few times. "I'm not sure what you mean."

"It's a simple question, girl." Rydel pressed her fingers into my skin. "Do you love being a part of the world? Living and being part of its workings?"

I raised a brow. "Girl?"

She sighed. "Give an old bard some credit."

I swallowed and tried to pull away from her. Her long fingers glowed. My anger and discomfort vanished. The fae knot bubbled happily in my gut.

"I've never wondered if I love life," I answered slowly. "I guess I do."

Rydel rubbed circles on my wrist with her thumb. "You guess?"

"I've fought to live." I gnawed on my lower lip. "I love parts of life. Seeing new things, meeting new people." My stomach knotted. "But there are so many awful things too. Sometimes, I think it would be easier if I hated everything."

"Love and hate are different sides of the same coin." She nodded. "Why do you pretend to be a man?"

I swallowed. "It's easier. Nobody looks twice at a tall, strong man." I closed my eyes. Alex's blood coated my hands. I opened my eyes. "And… Declan doesn't let people down. He protects them."

Rydel narrowed her eyes. "But not you. Are you not worth it?"

I shook my head. "I'm just one human, living in other's stories until mine's over."

"Clever." She rubbed my wrist again before flipping my hand over, but she didn't release me.

Shade stirred, and I wiggled my toes to reassure him.

"I want to make you a deal." Rydel brushed her fingers over the inside of my wrist.

"Zelimir said I'm not supposed to...."

A wave of calm and trust followed more of the bard's pale orange light.

She met my gaze, and her eyes looked so wise. "Your Anam Cara is traveling to toss you away like the trash they think you are." She frowned comfortingly. "Did you ever think some of those rules exist to keep you under their control?"

Tears stung my eyes. In the short time we'd been together, I already looked forward to Bash's silent company. To Teyr's teasing. To Shade's fur between my fingers. Zelimir moved with such confidence and acted with such surety. That confidence drew me to him like a moth to a flame. Just like that moth, I knew I would burn trying to follow him.

Rydel smiled softly. "Just hearing my offer won't hurt."

I brushed away the tears with my free hand. The bronze magic of this strange tavern swirled around me. Voices that had been low rose into a blur of sound. I picked Teyr's voice effortlessly out of the swell.

"Yup, that's my charge over there," he said. "He's kind of obsessed with stories. He listens to me talk all day, as he should."

A peal of feminine laughter rang out, but her response disappeared in another shift of magic that dampened everything once more.

Rydel tapped my wrist with her index finger. "You're destined for something greater than yourself. I want your final story." She leaned forward. "In exchange for that, I'll give you two summons that can be used for anything." She stopped stroking me. "A third summoning will happen automatically at the end, so I can witness your final moments and hear your story."

I swallowed. "I don't understand."

Rydel gave me a knowing look. "I can project myself to anywhere in the world, as long as I have someone to anchor myself to. I intend to leave a bit of myself in you, just a bit, to give me that."

Unease crept up my spine. "I'm not sure—"

"Only my spirit travels." Rydel's hands glowed. "I will merely be a visitor, a friend, a confidant. Two times, I will come when you call and answer anything you ask within my knowledge."

"And you won't be able to find me unless I call on you?" My thoughts moved like tar. "But what if you're wrong? What if I'm no one special, and I just end up discarded back in the human world?"

"Until the final time." Rydel met my gaze. "And I'm willing to hedge my bets—to use a human turn of phrase."

I couldn't look away. I couldn't even blink.

"Knowledge is power." I nodded to myself. "And it's not like anyone else cares about my story." I swallowed. "Answers have been the most difficult things to get."

Rydel nodded encouragingly. "I can't lie. It's part of my magic." She winked. "I no longer need to trick the world into giving me what I want."

I studied the bard for another heartbeat. Her catlike pupils had widened until they nearly blotted out the orange irises.

"Deal," I said.

Rydel dropped her head to my wrist and sank her teeth into my flesh. I hissed with pain, but no blood oozed from the wound. Instead, it felt like she pushed something under my skin. She straightened, and I yanked my hand to my chest. The sounds of the tavern dipped to nothing before returning to normal. The swirling bronze of the room's magic dulled, though I didn't remember it looking particularly bright.

No blood ran down her chin. She licked her lips and smiled. I frowned. The stinging pain had already dissipated. Where she bit me, three pale orange dots, their middles filled with an intricate latticework of runes, ran in a nearly invisible line along my skin.

Rydel picked up her glowing drink and smiled pleasantly. "I've taken up too much of your time tonight. But don't forget your Cara's advice entirely." She rose from her chair. "No more deals. I look forward to seeing you in the future."

I nodded, rubbing my thumb along my new marks. The odd sensation of comfort dwindled with every step Rydel took away from me.

20

____

ZELIMIR

AFTER TWELVE DAYS OF FORESTS AND VILLAGES, THE landscape abruptly changed. Stark mountain peaks separated the lush trees from miles of barren, cracked red land called the Mud Pits of Saltair. As darkness fell, we gave up the climb, found a safe enough ledge, and made ourselves a sparse camp with a small fire. The smell of bland stew wafted from Teyr's cookpot.

Shade had proven himself impossible to control, and I didn't have the energy to keep trying. The years of not allowing myself any hint of irritation with the wolf in case he interpreted my actions as accusation about Light's death had started to fray. Tonight, he inched toward Declan, but the human stared off at the mountains around us. He'd been rubbing his wrist for the past day. I took a breath to ask him why but swallowed the instinct. I shouldn't care.

I kept wanting to know. Not just what he thought about, but everything about him. He had a love of life and a mental fortitude I found exhilarating. I'd never been particularly drawn to men before, but something about even Declan's shape tugged at me.

Once again, I let my gaze wander over his form. He didn't have the curves that typically drew my eye. Still, his shoulders sloped softly down to the muscles of his arms. He smiled at Shade, and dimples bloomed on his angular face. He bent and stroked Shade's thick coat. I ran a hand through my hair. I'd always been an ass man.

I dropped onto my mat, gripped two of my twists, and yanked them apart. I didn't like men. Especially human men mistakenly attached to something they could never be a part of. I quelled my interest and forced my thoughts above my belt. Otherwise, I'd turn into Teyr.

As if called, the ember stepped to Declan's side with a bowl of stew. Excitement burst through my Cara from the human, though whatever block he'd put up muted the feeling. My blood rushed. He took a big bite of stew, and the bond turned to pleasure. I clenched my fists.

Teyr frowned, and asked Declan, "Is your Ooploroot running out?"

If I were half the leader I claimed to be, I would have bought a supply of the stuff before we'd left the *Cross Roads*. Feeling the man's emotions should be classified as torture.

Declan spooned up a bite of stew through a blast of worry. "Sure."

Teyr returned to the pot and dished himself a bowl. "We need to find you more."

Bash tensed. "No."

I couldn't help but notice my second had seated himself between Declan and myself. He'd spent much less time scouting lately. I released a frustrated breath and stood as Teyr sat next to the human. I didn't need a third mate to keep an eye on. I ladled out dinner for Bash and myself, then set the cookpot on the ground in front of Shade.

Teyr balanced his bowl on his knee and gestured with his spoon. "I think it's slowed down the Cara more than we possibly could have."

Bash crossed his arms. "It's not safe."

"It's Ooploroot!" Teyr waved his spoon so wildly he almost dumped his dinner on the ground. "We give it to babies."

My second grunted.

"Babies, Bash"—Teyr jabbed his spoon at the dragon—"you know what those are, right? Little fae with dangerous magic they can't control?"

Bash grunted again. Teyr sighed, then dug into his meal. Longing shot through our Cara, leaving unhappy ripples on my skin. The human focused on our fire as he inhaled the simple stew, but the hunch of his shoulders gave him away. He wanted to belong.

Shade whined, completely ignoring the pot I'd given him, and wiggled closer to Declan. Declan glanced at the wolf, and his defensive posture eased. He offered his empty bowl to Shade, who eagerly lapped at it.

Declan stood and pulled out a bag he'd picked up in the last town. The bag contained a few simple toiletries and a stone rune that produced water when touched to the dirt.

"I need a minute." He walked toward an outcropping of rocks until the night swallowed his form.

After days of crowded common rooms, the silence was deafening. We hadn't been able to stop at a tavern for the first time in our journey. The bright-eyed human, who was excited to see new things had disappeared and left behind a man struggling to stay away from us. I didn't like it.

"Not going to happen," Bash said.

My brain fumbled until I remembered we'd been talking about Oopleroot.

Teyr licked his lips, firelight dancing in his eyes. "That was four words. Give me one more, and I'll leave you alone for the rest of the evening."

"It was six syllables." I smiled.

Teyr groaned. My second ignored us both to stare at our mounts, or more likely, the rocky outcropping behind them which hid Declan from view. I focused on my food. Teyr barely knew how to cook, but long days of traveling meant we all knew how to eat. I missed the days when Shade ran our cookpot like a maestro conducting a symphony.

Soon enough, the human returned.

"You shouldn't go so far," Teyr said. "Anam Caras are close. There's no shame in the natural process of digestion."

Declan didn't look at him. "I'm not one of you."

"Well, regardless." Teyr stood and cleaned his bowl over the fire.

I finished my food, set the bowl down, and closed my eyes. The arrogant ember rarely became flustered, and I found it harder and harder to set a good example for my mates. Councilor Drax told me to stay strong and trust the Council. My mentor wouldn't lie to me. Magic, though, had always been tricky. This could be a test, or the natural result of the almost six centuries that had passed since Varsina's sacrifice.

The Council's orders had never gone against the magic before. Our magic had never gone against itself before. My gut twisted unhappily. When I opened my eyes, Declan sat with his back to the fire.

"I'm going to sleep," he said through a yawn.

He smoothed down his bedroll and kicked off his shoes. The man unloaded daggers I hadn't realized he carried into a little pile on one side, as well as his bow and arrows. He kept his sword close to his right arm.

"You're with us." Teyr stretched. "You don't need to keep those in reach. Just relax."

"Ha," Declan barked.

My heart skidded. He might not have been one of us, but I'd explained we'd get him to the Council safely. He should trust us.

Declan pulled off his leather gauntlets and greaves, then reached for his cuirass. He looked back at us. With a sigh, he left it on and tucked himself into his bedroll. Within minutes, his breathing slowed, and mixed with the sounds of the night. Sleep fogged his Cara. I'd never given him any reason to feel unsafe. I never would.

I whistled to pull my mates' attention away from the human's back. We weren't supposed to be looking. Teyr turned his attention to the fire. Bash didn't. I frowned.

"I'm glad he's getting some rest." Teyr tossed the last of our wood onto the blaze. "He'll need it for Saltair tomorrow."

Bash finally looked at us. "Rifts."

I nodded. "Saltair is known for them at the best of times. Now, with rift activity heightened, I can't imagine getting through without encountering at least one."

"Declan can hold his own." Teyr looked back at our human. The human.

My gaze drifted back to Declan as well. Shade had already curled around him. Teyr looked at me with an eyebrow raised. With real tiredness pulling at my eyes, I couldn't lie about being too exhausted to stop

Shade. I'd felt the wolf's fear when he couldn't get through the door at Punaky's Pub. No, not the wolf's, Shade's. Something was changing in him. Uneasiness churned my stomach. Giving them time to bond would only make everything harder in the end, but stopping Shade seemed increasingly cruel. To both of them. I didn't want to think about what would happen when Declan left.

"Just for tonight," I said softly.

Teyr put two fingers to his forehead and mockingly saluted me. "Whatever you say, boss."

I scowled, then stretched out on my bedroll. We didn't need a tent with the warmth of the Mud Pits. My mates followed my lead. I couldn't face them, couldn't see the looks on their faces as they wondered about Shade and Declan and me, so I turned on my side and let the fire heat my back. The coward's move.

From our higher vantage point, the Mud Pits looked like nothing more than dry dirt under the stars. Superstitiously, I reached out to whatever ancestors would still listen to me after I abdicated the throne. Sleep wound gentle fingers through my thoughts.

THE NEXT MORNING, I WOKE TO BASH AND DECLAN DOING their morning warm-ups. Not together, but on the same side of our little camp. The two occasionally eyed each other when the other wasn't looking.

It didn't take me long to stoke the coals of our fire into a blaze and prepare coffee and porridge. I poked Teyr awake and shoved a mug of coffee into his hands. We needed to get moving before the sun burned off our energy.

Declan finished his routine first and sat next to Teyr, then pushed his sweat-covered hair back from his face. The ember looked at him and narrowed his eyes. Declan smelled himself before standing to grab his own coffee. When he sat back down, he sat on the opposite side of the fire from Teyr.

Our morning continued, silent and awkward. Declan kicked dirt over the fire before I boiled our bowls clean, which meant the task fell to Teyr and his fire magic. He sighed dramatically, halfway through removing our horses' feedbags.

By the time we packed up and mounted, the sun's heat reached me through my boots. I scowled. "No scouting today. We stay together through the Mud Pits. Bash and I will trade off point. The human will ride in the back."

My mates *pulsed* their affirmatives, and our horses began picking their way along the uneven ground of the mountain.

The sun reached its zenith and started its descent to the other side. Heat rolled in rippling waves over the caked earth. Sweat poured down my skin, darkening patches of my horse's bay coat. I loosened my reins once more as my horse struggled to find footing that wouldn't give way to the bubbling mud under the thin layer of dirt.

I glanced behind me and narrowed my eyes. Declan walked alongside his mount. The spotted gelding, not as prepared for the heat as our trained horses, dripped with sweat. Shade's tongue lolled out of his mouth as he padded so closely alongside the human that his tail bumped the man's ass, another testament to the horse's exhaustion. The animal couldn't stand Shade.

A bhelrian screeched. The sun glinted off its golden feathers. I swiveled in my saddle to watch the bird. Shade summoned up the energy to yip at the bird hundreds of feet overhead. Declan's mount pranced and reared. I cursed. The human dropped his reins and dove to the side. The terrified horse fell backward onto his saddle. The air pressure dropped.

No. Not now.

A blinding silver light engulfed Declan, Shade, and the gelding. The human and I locked gazes in the instant before he and his horse toppled into the rift that sliced the air behind them. Before I could say anything, Shade leapt after him.

I froze in disbelief. Matching shock radiated from my mates. A wave of Declan's terror and adrenaline screamed over our surprise, followed by searing pain from Shade.

Flanked by Bash and Teyr, I sprinted toward the hole in our world and jumped.

21

BASH

I hit the chalky surface of Earth in a cloud of dust. Blood rushed in my ears and thrummed with the thrill of a fight. I shot to my feet, drawing my axe. In an instant, my commander sharpened the head with a line of force in readiness for me to slice through the thick metal of Tech. The pain radiating from Shade's Cara spiked before fading into a dull roar as our wolf lost consciousness. Movement to my left caught my eye.

Two DogTech lunged at Declan. The man jumped to his feet next to the body of his gelding. The arm-length, headless, spike-covered metal torsos of the DogTech soared through the air, their four legs ending in smooth balls braced to land.

The human yanked his sword up and blocked the first DogTech, but his blade tangled in the creature's legs. The second DogTech hit Declan in the chest, sending him flying with a cry of pain.

Shade's Cara dimmed. Tech surrounded the prone human. In my mind's eye, I saw Light's golden wings wilt in the instant before he fell. I hadn't been strong enough to save him.

I drove my nails into my palms. My commander dashed forward while Teyr landed at my back. Blood screamed in my veins. A SpiderTech advanced on Declan. I wouldn't lose another mate—temporary or not.

I wouldn't fail Declan.

I shook my head. I wouldn't fail my mates.

Zelimir *pulsed* for me to go to Shade. A spear of my commander's purple magic flew toward the Tech surrounding Declan. Teyr's fire raced alongside the weapon. I tried to turn toward Shade, but my feet wouldn't budge.

My desire—my need—to go to Declan yanked so hard I thought my insides might rip through my skin. But I couldn't go to Declan. I needed to obey my commander's order to go to Shade. I gritted my teeth, trying to remember how to walk. Teyr's fire engulfed a SpiderTech, and it scurried away from Declan's motionless body.

Fear pinched my heart. I desperately searched for our Cara. I couldn't feel anything from Declan. Zelimir *pulsed* again, reinforcing the order to attend Shade. Once again, I tried to move and couldn't. The compulsion to go to Declan nearly doubled me over.

A searing heat split my head. I dropped my axe and fell to my knees. White spots raced across my vision. I gripped my head as if to keep my skull from splitting. Sharp claws dug through my brain and made themselves at home in my thoughts. An animalistic growl ripped from my chest. A second, smaller consciousness awoke inside me and roared in defiance.

My dragon.

He demanded we save Declan. I bellowed, equaling my dragon's roar, and focused all my thoughts on Shade. The wolf bled onto chalky white earth barely ten feet to my left.

My mates protected the human. We had to trust Zelimir.

Sweat poured down my face as the dragon struggled for control of my body. The vibrant red of my cherrystone axe and Zelimir's purple magic on its edge stood out like a beacon against Earth's pallor. I grabbed my weapon, buried its head in the ground, and hauled myself up.

I'd always known I had dragon in me, probably more than I thought, but not enough that I'd ever thought twice about the strange way true dragonkin spoke about their dragons in the third person.

Zel launched a purple force spear and pinned a DogTech to the ground. Declan vaulted to his feet, sword in hand. The dragon stopped fighting me, and an intoxicating wave of joy washed through me. My commander slid to a stop at Declan's side, and that joy turned to raw jealousy.

In his distraction, I wrested control of my body back from my dragon and bolted to Shade, sheathing my axe. The dirt beneath the wolf had become a deep and troubling red. His guts leaked out of a gash in his stomach.

Shade would die soon.

I cursed. The newly awakened dragon in my head coiled and uncoiled, itching for something to do. An explosion came from Declan's direction, and I jerked my head up.

A few hundred yards away, a seething horde of Tech had spotted us. My dragon and I went still. If we didn't get out of here before the mass arrived, we didn't stand a chance. I took a deep breath and focused.

With thick bands of telekinesis, I pulled Shade's body back together. His shallow breathing evened out, but if I lost my hold, I would lose my mate. Declan let out a scream somewhere between terror and excitement. My dragon fought me for control once more.

"Stop!" I shouted. "We're a Cara." I swallowed. "All of us."

I extended a mental hand. The coiled consciousness in my brain let out a final, frustrated roar before rushing forward and sinking his teeth into me. The magic maintaining Shade transferred to my dragon. He would hold the wolf.

I opened my eyes, and my dragon's voice joined mine. Our battle cry echoed above the hissing hydraulics and the clash of metal-on-metal. I drew my axe, shoved to my feet, and spun toward my mates.

22

ZELIMIR

Declan swung up onto the torso of a SpiderTech with half its skin melted off and plunged his dagger into the monster's eyes. A second SpiderTech skittered around, firing beams of energy out of its arms. DogTechs jumped and circled, but they'd already done their damage. Declan's cuirass hung, shredded and red with blood, from his chest.

The emotional turmoil filling Bash's Cara evened out, and he *pulsed*, letting us know that Shade needed a healer but was stable for now. Bash bellowed and charged another cluster of DogTech.

I raced forward and cupped the shaft of another force spear. The magic responded a second late. A DogTech leapt up and sliced into Declan's calf. The man cursed and yanked his dagger out of the Spider-Tech. He couldn't defend himself and attack. The DogTech landed gracefully on the ground and spun to lunge again.

Search lights twinkled as the army of Tech raced toward us. We had to get out of here. I launched my spear. It rocketed through the DogTech and caught enough cables to pin the beast to the ground. Sparks flew. Oil dripped onto the dry earth as the monstrosity twitched.

The SpiderTech under Declan spun before freezing in place. A stream of smoke curled upward from the monster's head. It tilted. Declan leapt off as the tangle of metal crashed into a heap on the ground, and he sailed toward the second SpiderTech. It dodged Declan and a much faster DogTech pivoted to occupy the spot where he'd land. I cursed and threw a shield of force over the thing. Declan bounced off the purple shield and landed hard, but he hadn't gotten skewered.

"SISTER." The low, inflectionless voice of Tech rumbled through the air, but I couldn't pinpoint from where. "Parameters specify Zone One. Please proceed to Zone One."

The DogTech scurried away. I dropped my shield and palmed the hilt of my two-hander. The white world around me lit with a purple glow as I conjured a sword the width of my arm and almost five feet long. I swung into the second SpiderTech. Pure force of the sword's magic cut through flesh and metal alike, biting through its legs and up into its torso. The two halves of the SpiderTech collapsed.

Teyr *pulsed* a warning to look left. I spun and threw my weight to the side just as a DogTech leapt toward me. The spikes scraped along my arm and the flesh beneath the long sleeve of my tunic lit up with pain.

My two-hander would only slow me down against the smaller DogTech. I released my hold on the hilt and the magic. In its place, I jammed my left arm into the straps of a translucent purple shield the size of my torso and gripped the lighter, one-handed sword I so rarely used.

With a roar, I charged the DogTech in front of me and struck. The blade plunged past the creature's spikes and into its cabling. Sparks flew. Something impacted my shield. I turned just as a curl of fire wrapped around the second DogTech trying to breach my defenses.

The hiss of hydraulics grew louder. I *pulsed* to Bash and Teyr to buy us what time they could and realized I couldn't see Declan in the fray. I searched my Cara. He thrummed with focus and fear, but the block prevented me from sensing his location or the extent of his injuries. I slashed at the DogTech trapped in Teyr's fire whip and severed the cables connecting three of its legs to its body. It twitched once, then went still.

Bash skidded to a halt in front of Shade and closed his eyes. The muscles in his bare, lilac chest tensed. Bleach-white rocks and dirt rose into the air between the oncoming army and us. He lifted a curved wall of churning debris not quite high enough or long enough to protect us entirely, but he had to save part of his mind for Shade.

Teyr slapped his palms together, then thrust them forward. Bash's wall lit with swirling fire. The two of them stepped back toward the rift. I *pulsed* rapid-fire orders for them to find us any way out.

The last DogTech of the original group fell to the wall's fire, and I found Declan frozen behind it. He stared up at my mate's wall. Red blood seeped down his greaves.

I sprinted toward him. The heat of Teyr's inferno screamed against my skin. Declan didn't move until I skidded to a halt at his side and braced my arm as I extended the shield around me to cover us both.

Although his bright eyes glowed with flame, his face had paled. He sheathed his sword and drew his bow in one clean motion, then nocked an arrow. Tilting his head to look up at me, he raised an eyebrow.

I waited for him to *pulse* what he wanted, but he only poked my shield with the tip of his arrow. An arrow slit. I pulled out a hole in my shield for him to shoot through and began walking us backward to the rift. The horde would arrive soon. We couldn't look away.

Declan's eyes reflected my purple. "Can you anchor the shield to me?"

The first signs of magic exhaustion tugged at my muscles. "Not for long."

"Then you'd better find us a way out fast." He slotted his arrow into the slit.

Teyr yelled, "Zel, I need a boost!"

The oncoming swarm hit Teyr and Bash's wall of magic with a *boom*. The wall bulged. A DogTech raced around the edge of the wall on our left. Declan aimed and shot with a grunt of pain. His arrow sank into one of the Tech's legs. The limb stiffened, and the sprinting DogTech smashed into the ground in a cloud of white dust. I grinned. Maybe Declan had something to offer, after all.

"Don't just stand there!" Declan lowered his bow and glared at me. "Run!"

I sprinted as fast as I could backwards toward Bash and Teyr. Declan kept pace with me, firing arrow after arrow into the encroaching horde. I risked a glance behind us. Shade lay at Bash's feet, below the rift shimmering dozens of feet above their heads. The wolf remained unconscious, but his chest rose and fell with uneven breaths.

I whirled back as three more DogTech loped around the edge of the wall. I stopped. Declan's arms shook as he brought his bow up. He took a steadying breath, then released and pinned one of the DogTech in the side. The creature didn't slow. I couldn't fight and protect us. I had to trust the human.

"Cover us." I released my sword and anchored my shield around the soft skin of his bow arm before turning and sprinting the last few feet to the rift.

The ember pranced like his horse beneath the rift and *pulsed* for me to hurry. Time for an old Academy maneuver. Bash and I stood on each side of Teyr. He jumped up and landed in our hands. I nodded at Bash, and we squatted and drove upwards in unison, launching the smaller fae into the air. He disappeared through the rift, taking his fire magic with him. Only a naked wall of white dirt now held back the army.

"SISTER." The inflectionless voice boomed around us again. "Parameters specify Zone One. Please proceed to Zone One."

Sister? Zone one? Tech couldn't speak.

Bash's wall cracked. Bowed. Shattered. The horde burst through.

I pulled Declan close and *pulsed* to Bash. My second grabbed Shade and stepped to my other side. I spread a spherical force shield around us, but my muscles shook, and the sphere barely contained us. I shouldn't be exhausted this quickly. My magic shouldn't arrive late. It had to be something about being on Earth.

The dried-up husk of Earth looked purple through my translucent shield. The quiet hiss of hydraulics and thumping, inhuman steps seemed louder. A SpiderTech's blast dented my shield. I sucked in a breath and pulled every bit of power I had to thicken the purple sphere.

Bash looked at my hand, still around Declan's shoulders, and growled. Before I could process that, resignation washed through Declan's Cara.

He sighed. "One arrow left."

"We're getting out of here. Trust Teyr." I squeezed his shoulder. "And put your bow away."

Declan swallowed, distrust and fear replacing resignation, but did as I ordered. The swarm of silver reflected in his wide eyes. A DogTech threw itself against the shield, and its spikes punctured deep, scraping toward Declan. I crushed the human to my chest. It wouldn't end like this. I *pulsed* to Teyr that he had to act now or never.

As if the ember had been waiting for the order, a rope tumbled toward us out of the rift just within my reach. Bash *pulsed* that he had to maintain focus on Shade, or we'd lose him. I grabbed the line and wrapped force magic around its length before the edges of the rift could sever it.

A blast of energy hit our shield. I cursed and shook. I couldn't hold the shield and the rope. I dropped the shield and created a bowl of force large enough to hold us. I yanked Declan to my side, stepped into the bowl, and gripped the pole in the middle I'd created for us to steady ourselves with.

"Hold on to me," I whispered.

Declan wrapped his arms around my waist while Bash stepped closer and gripped the pole with his thighs, Shade pressed to his chest. A DogTech leapt at us, and Declan barely knocked it off course with his sword. I gripped the pole with one hand and the rope with the other. My skin tingled as Bash telekinetically bound us together.

I *pulsed* to Teyr as a blast of Tech energy scattered off Bash's shoulder. He bellowed in pain. A tall, tubular Tech I'd never seen before emerged from the center of the horde, shuddering forward on telescoping metal legs.

The rope jerked. Pain lanced through my arms. I grunted and hoped Bash had enough power to keep me attached to the rope as we careened upward. Declan whooped just as a sickening *pop* sent agony blazing across my shoulder and down my arm. My muscles strained. Without Bash holding us together, we would've fallen back to Earth.

We rocketed upward and out of the rift. I had just enough presence of mind to wrap my aching hand and arm in a shield of force before I slammed into the fragile dirt of the Mud Pits. I cracked right through, drenching myself in hot, red mud.

Declan pushed out of my grip and scrambled away from the mud. I rolled onto my stomach, breathing hard and fighting the urge to vomit. Bash's magic dissipated, and my hand dropped limply from the rope. A spike of worry shot through his Cara, colored with something I couldn't identify.

After a long moment, I scrambled up, surprised my second hadn't offered me a hand. Instead, he sat next to a muddy Declan with Shade in his frail, human arms.

"Zel." Teyr pulled me up. "We need to seal this."

I cradled my dislocated shoulder as I dashed for the edge of the rift opposite the ember and began drawing synchronized runes with my good hand. The hum of magic almost made me forget my injuries. With a faint pop, the rift vanished as if it never existed. That, too, came easier with Declan around.

"Back off, Bash," he said.

A foreign rush of anger and frustration sizzled out of Bash's Cara before he roared and sat down hard. He closed his eyes, shutting his Cara completely, and his shoulders shook.

My shoulder throbbed. With a grunt, I slammed a wall of purple force into the shoulder and popped it back into the socket. My natural healing didn't work nearly as fast as that of a completed Anam Cara, but our partial status granted us some ability. The muscle began to knit.

I took a deep breath. The heat of the Mud Pits washed over me, along with the buzz of insects and the screech of a bhelrian. Teyr looked bruised and battered. He'd taken a bad blaster shot to the chest. Bash rocked back and forth, mumbling to himself. I rolled out my shoulder. If Bash needed help, he'd reach out.

"Shade." Panic tinged Declan's voice.

The situation collapsed on me. I'd almost lost another mate. I'd almost lost everything.

I rushed to the human and wrapped my arms around him and the wolf. "Shade's stable," I murmured. "Bash is holding him together, but he needs a healer."

My nose filled with Declan's smell and the coppery tang of human blood. I flushed with shame. The human held himself together so well that I'd forgotten I couldn't feel his injuries through the Cara.

I released the man and scanned his body. Cuts covered his legs. The top of a slice in his cuirass peeked out of Shade's fur. Red blood and chalky white dirt coated his pants. If he'd been in the saddle with me, or even riding in the middle of our group.... But he hadn't been. I'd put him behind us to keep him away.

"Can you ride?" I asked.

Declan nodded and disentangled himself from Shade. I scanned him again, cursing the block. The cut on his chest looked bad.

He narrowed his eyes. "I'll live." He grabbed the neck of my tunic. "Save Shade."

I took a deep breath and put my trust in the human's words. Like I'd trusted him to cover us. I shoved down the thought and *pulsed* orders to my mates for us to ride. Bash opened his eyes, stood, and flattened his lips into a hard line before mounting. I lifted Shade and draped him over my second's lap. Shade barked painfully before slipping into unconsciousness again. My heart squeezed.

I turned to Declan. "You ride with me."

Teyr mounted. Bash growled low in his chest, making his horse dance, then grimaced and muttered something. He *pulsed* an assurance that he would be fine and would explain later.

I nodded and swung into my saddle, then held out my hand. Declan ignored the gesture and struggled much more than I'd like to mount behind me on his own. Once he settled, the sound of ripping cloth filled my ears. He was making bandages.

I frowned. "You said you were fine."

"Compared to Shade," Declan hissed. "Fucking ride."

23

———

TEYR

I SIGHED AS MY HORSE PLODDED ALONG BEHIND ZELIMIR'S. The oppressive heat of the Mud Pits burned away. Patches of tufted black grass grew out of red soil. A matching lizard I didn't recognize skittered past.

I glanced behind me at Bash. Scales flooded his face. He muttered something and tightened his hold on the wolf draped over his lap. The scales receded back down his neck as he took a deep breath. He'd tried to close his Cara, but spikes of conflicting emotions jabbed outward. I winced and sent him a wave of support.

Looking back just reminded me of Shade's body bleeding into the chalky earth anyway. My eyes burned with unshed tears. Memories of Light's splayed body plastered themselves across the inside of my skull. We couldn't lose another mate. I couldn't survive being broken again. Not when Declan made us whole.

I exhaled slowly, releasing tension I'd carried for the last week and a half. I'd said it finally, at least in my mind. My days improved when he seemed happy. I daydreamed about his eyes. Fire, I just wanted to spend my days explaining the wilds to him.

It would be easier to go back to Earth and fight that horde of Tech than ask my mates if they agreed. My cheek itched. I scratched another bit of chalky earth glued to my face with mud. The dirt covered all of me, but the stuff on my face bothered me most. I scrubbed a hand across my cheek for the hundredth time.

I needed a shower. Badly. Real fights got so dirty. I much preferred magical duels. Short, sweet, and often including cheering fans. There had been no crowds on Earth.

I'd never actually gone through a rift before. The dead world had shaken me to my core. There had been no magic on Earth. I had been able to reach through the rift to Thrae to fuel my fire, but it still felt like drinking from an empty cup. And Mud Pits rifts closed naturally. If it had closed while we were Earthside.... Who would I be without my fire?

I shivered and shook my head. Somebody needed to banish our somber mood, especially if it'd started infecting me. I dropped back to ride next to Bash. The dragon stared at Declan's back, and hunger juddered through his Cara.

"Did you see the size of my balls?" I asked.

As I'd hoped, Declan sniggered, though it quickly turned into a pain-filled wheeze.

Zelimir *pulsed* a warning. I returned the equivalent of an eye roll. The human would live through a laugh. Zelly needed to relax.

"Do you always stab the eyes first?" I asked Declan.

He didn't turn. "If it works." He snorted. "And are you really critiquing my methods? Zelimir saved us with a magical umbrella. I didn't even know those existed."

I laughed. Humor trickled in from Bash's Cara. The tension in the air started to melt away.

Zelimir stiffened. "An upside-down force shield with an extended handle."

Declan laughed himself into another wheeze. "As I'm still alive, I'll praise the mighty umbrella."

Bash grunted. "You held your own, human."

"I did a little more than that." Declan rested his cheek against Zelimir's back so he could look behind him without twisting his waist.

I obliged the man's fish for compliments. "You were an excellent distraction. Next, we'll teach you to run them to us, since we already know running's one of your strengths."

"Har-de-har." Declan smiled. "It helped that the Tech started farther away, though their sensors still picked us up." He sighed. "Fighting Tech would be so much easier if they weren't so damn attentive."

I pressed my lips together. A normal human wouldn't know about Tech sensors, much less understand them.

Zelimir grabbed one of Declan's arms and wrapped it around his waist for balance. Bash growled as his scales raced up his face. No, wait. They normally moved from his body up onto his face, but this looked different, like new scales actually sprouting from his skin instead of just shifting.

He clenched his fist and pounded his thigh. The scales started melting away. I raised an eyebrow at Bash. The dragon had always been a little rough around the edges, but he used to only growl when he got really worked up.

"What crawled up your ass?" I murmured. "Jealous Zelly gets to touch the human?"

Bash glared. His scales whirled on his face, collecting in larger and larger patches. Everything clicked.

"It's your dragon, isn't it?"

He nodded tersely.

True dragonkin were far too self-absorbed for me, but I'd heard rumors. Some fae said they not only took on the winged, scaled form, but a second personality to match.

I leaned toward him. "Can you change shape?"

"No." He scowled. "At least, I don't think so."

"And Declan?" I looked at the horse ahead of me.

The human flinched as Zel's horse stumbled.

Bash started to growl but thumped his chest and stopped. "Something's changing."

"I suppose I have to say it," Zelimir cut in. He twisted and looked back at the human riding on the saddle behind him. "You've been through rifts before."

Pain, emotional this time, shot through Declan's Cara. Bash and I exchanged a look before urging our horses forward on each side of our commander's mount. Declan studied Zelimir's back as if it held the key to life. A mixture of anger, regret, and sorrow leaked through the weakening block he'd placed around our bond.

"I have been through rifts," he said slowly.

Somehow, that still surprised me. "How? What happened?"

Declan continued to stare at Zel's back. I opened my mouth to press him, but Zelimir's quick *pulse* cut me off. The human plucked Zelimir's waterskin off his saddle and took a long drink. I busied myself braiding my horse's golden mane, so I didn't watch his throat move.

He replaced the waterskin on the saddle, then said, "I was so naïve."

I bit my lip to keep from interrupting.

"We all were." Declan sighed and rested his forehead against Zel's back. "None of us had any family, so we became each other's family." He brushed a hand across his face. "We weren't cute little orphans people felt bad for anymore. Just teenagers who had been on the wrong side of right too many times." Declan paused as if remembering something. "I miss those days."

He shook his head. "One day, we stumbled across this book. David read it to us. He was the only one who could read, though he taught me. We all looked at these pictures, a technological utopia where humans lived peacefully. Everything looked so…perfect." He laughed bitterly. "Alex got it into his head that if we went back to Earth, we could change something."

I raised a brow. "Change what?"

Declan glanced at me. "I'm not really sure. None of us had seen Earth, a rift, Tech, nothing. We had no idea." He snorted. "But we spent months stealing supplies, weapons, and gear. Alex became convinced Earth would be a better place for us."

Zelimir shifted like he didn't know what to do with the human's weight. "How did you get into the wilds? Rifts don't form outside of them."

"We snuck across the border one night." Declan poked at a slash hole in Zel's tunic. "I don't know if we were lucky or what, but a rift opened within the hour. Nothing came out, so we just waltzed in."

I started another braid. "That's not weird. Rifts are random, so sometimes they open without any Tech nearby. That's why we have to close them. Tech seem to patrol the whole Fire-damned world, so some of them always shows up eventually."

Zelimir ran a hand through his frizzing twists. "That a rift opened right where you were, especially on the edge of fae, is strange."

"I don't know what you tell you." Declan wiggled his finger into the waterskin spout. "I mean, one opened at the back of the caravan when I first arrived, so they can't be that rare."

I frowned. Until recently, maybe thirty rifts opened at the border of the wilds a year. That's why Drax assigned broken Caras like us to border patrol in the first place—even a partial Cara could handle a few piddly rifts.

Bash grunted. "What happened then?"

Declan grimaced and pulled his hand back. "Nothing good."

Without thinking, I sent a wave of love through my Cara to him. The man didn't respond, so he must not have felt it. Disappointment and relief mixed in my stomach.

"I was stuck there alone for almost five years," he murmured.

I swallowed and looked away. A human will always be the weakest link, Ambrocio said. But Declan had survived alone on Earth for years when our whole Cara had barely survived five minutes. Ambrocio couldn't have been more wrong.

Declan fell silent, and for once, I didn't want to pry.

I dropped back and let my horse return to his comfort position in Zel's horse's butt. My brave, well-trained mount preferred his place in our little herd to striking off on his own.

24

KINNIA

ANOTHER WAVE OF DIZZINESS MADE ME SWAY ON THE HEELS of bright pain. We arrived at a perfectly round tower, a Cara outpost, and were ushered into some wooden room with tables and an undyed canvas divider by a group of fae nobody bothered to introduce me to. It took all my attention just to remain standing. Now, only the healer remained, a greenish fae in a cream tunic and brown pants that matched the fae I'd been traveling with. I found a small, dark stain on the wood floor and focused on that to keep the vertigo at bay.

Earth. I'd been back on Earth.

But I'd escaped. No cables had burrowed under my skin. No one had died. The healer put Shade back together, and now he slept on a table beside the stain I stared at. Teyr said the wolf would sleep all night.

I rubbed my arms, banishing my fear. Not only had we escaped, but we'd done it together. I took a deep breath and allowed myself a small smile. Something compelled me to look up. Bash's gray gaze bore into me over the healer's shoulder as the healer worked on him. The dragon had barely looked away from me since he set Shade down.

The healer's gold magic sparkled through Bash, drawing my attention away from his eyes. Minor cuts disappeared like they never existed.

Larger ones knitted, leaving behind faint, weeks-old scabs. I wanted to run my fingers along his freshly healed skin.

The healer stepped back and cocked a finger at Teyr.

"I'm good." The ember pressed a hand to the middle of my back and pushed me forward.

Even that small movement pulled at the edge of the huge gash along my chest. Pain lanced through me, and I jerked away with a hiss. Teyr frowned and shoved his hands into his pockets. Bash growled like an animal and clenched his fists. I looked to Zelimir for guidance. He nodded.

I sighed and stepped forward. The wound running from the right side of my stomach to just below the center of my bound breasts radiated heat. Another wave of dizziness made me fight for balance. As the adrenaline from the battle had slowly faded, every injury had come screaming into focus. I'd landed on my back in the white dirt of Earth. I only stood in this weird, round room because Shade had thrown himself in front of the DogTech who pounced first. I'd thought he was dead.

I took another unsteady step forward. The healer would take away my pain like he had Shade's. Two more steps brought me to the edge of the cloth-draped table, and I held on to keep from collapsing.

"I don't touch humans." The healer skittered away from me, palms out in front of him.

I gritted my teeth.

"This one's part of an Anam Cara." Zelimir stepped closer to the healer.

The healer scowled. "That one's a parasite on its way to being removed."

A wave of exhaustion washed over me. This wasn't my world. Why had I ever thought a fae would heal a human?

"Just leave me your suturing supplies," I said through the pain. "I've patched myself up before."

I'd done this to myself. I knew the risk taking this job entailed. And now I had nothing. My horse had been slaughtered on Earth, and I hadn't had time to grab my pack. I'd lost the gold I'd been paid. My medical kit. The liquor Bash bought me. I hadn't even gotten to taste it. Anger unfurled in my gut like a molten butterfly.

The healer looked down his sharp nose at me.

I met his gaze with a glare. "Leave your shit and piss off."

The healer's jaw dropped.

Teyr stepped up to my side. "You heard him."

With a click, the healer snapped his mouth shut. He spun and marched away. I rolled my eyes, but my burst of anger left me as fast as it came. If I hadn't been holding onto the table, I would have collapsed.

"Is there a bottle of something strong in this shitty tower?" I asked.

Bash rushed away before anyone could answer. I didn't look at Zelimir or Teyr as I boosted myself painfully onto the cloth-covered table still stained with Shade's blood. My body ached too much to turn, but my wolf breathed steadily behind me.

Over the last week and a half, Shade stuck by me no matter what, defying friend and foe to keep me safe. I didn't care that he belonged to the group hellbent on getting rid of me. I needed him to be okay. A tear slid down my cheek. Everything hurt too much to scrub it away.

Teyr stepped toward me. "Declan—"

"Out," Zelimir barked. "I need a word in private."

Teyr wrinkled his nose and scowled before muttering curses as he shuffled out.

Zelimir grazed the side of my face with one knuckle, studying me as if I were a puzzle. "Bash will help you."

My insides fluttered. I wanted so badly for him to comfort me that even my wounds ached. He held my gaze, and for just a moment, I thought he would lean down and kiss me. My heart raced.

"Do you know anything about the voice in the rift?" he asked.

I blinked, my mind pulling back from my previous thoughts.

"Voice?"

He nodded and it took me a minute to focus through the haze of pain. He was talking about the Tech that had said "sister." I'd never heard Tech call for a sister. In fact, in my time on Earth, I'd never heard Tech speak. The memories splashed cold water over my desire. I was a mistake Zelimir needed to fix. I wasn't his lover.

"I didn't know Tech could speak."

I jammed my hands into my pockets to hide the tremble that was working its way up my arms. Something cold touched my fingers. Curving lines, metallic bite. That crappy golden rune charm the fae who promised to cure my Cara gave me in the *Cross Roads*. Of course, that would be the only new thing that survived the battle. I pulled it out and tied it to my belt for something to do with my hands.

Bash reappeared with a heavy, clear glass bottle, saving me from trying to understand why Zelimir had furrowed his brow. The titan gave me one last look before leaving me in the care of his second.

Alone. Like we hadn't been since he attacked me with his memories. I trembled as much from pain as from the recollection. Since that day, he'd either gone out of his way to avoid me or gone over the top to make me happy. Bash pulled the stopper out of the bottle with a *pop*. The sound was so normal that I giggled before groaning and clutching my chest against the pain. The dragon narrowed his eyes.

"Never mind." I brought the heavy bottle to my lips and drank. The clear liquor burned on the way down my throat, leaving an aftertaste of lavender and violet.

Bash stared at me as if I would burst into flames.

"What's your problem?" I set the bottle down and slid one of my daggers out of its sheath.

He growled. "You."

I jerked back from the animosity in his voice and winced when pain seared up my side. Bash stepped forward, his hand extended as if to comfort me but stopped. He muttered something, then grabbed the bottle of liquor and took a swig.

Another wave of exhaustion swept over me. I had no energy left to deal with fae mood swings when I still had to pull off my greaves.

"Look, I'm injured," I said. "Either help me or leave."

Bash froze. Scales poured onto his face, then back to his neck and shoulders. He set the bottle on the table. "What makes you so special?"

My jaw dropped. "I'm sorry?"

Bash leaned forward. "Are you trying to destroy my Anam Cara?"

I burst out laughing. Destroy them? With what, my unmagical

katana? My not-so-feminine wiles? Scalding pain rocketed through my ribs. I choked and curled in on myself. Whatever anger Bash had, vanished. He gripped my shoulder to steady me.

"Fuck off." I reached for the liquor as my humor turned black. "You tracked me down and bribed me to follow you to some unknown location." I waved the bottle. "I don't know what kind of fae crazy you're dealing with, and I don't really care. I'm just trying to survive."

I'd been fighting for that as long as I could remember. These shithead fae reminded me I could want something more, but I couldn't want them. Another tear slipped down my cheek, and I prayed the dragon didn't notice. I took a big swig of liquor and started tugging one greave off over my boot.

Bash leaned forward and wiped the tear away. "You're right. This isn't your problem."

I looked up, expecting to see more suspicion. Instead, Bash's shoulders drooped, and his gaze looked distant like it had when they had silent conversations around me, as if I wouldn't notice everyone going quiet. I held my breath.

"I will have more questions for you." He snapped back to attention. "But for now, you're my mate, and you're hurt."

I exhaled slowly as the greave came free.

He plucked the dagger from my hand. "Now, strip."

I spluttered. "No!"

Bash frowned. "Your legs are covered in cuts. At least take off your pants."

I scowled. "No."

The dragon rose to his full height, shorter than mine, and crossed his arms across his wide chest.

"Piss off." I gulped liquor until the pain started to fade out of my notice, then pulled off the other greave quickly.

He snarled and my heart crashed against my ribcage. He clamped his hand over my thighs, caging me in place. I closed my eyes and braced. This was it. He would expose my secret. And then what? Would this be the final nail in my coffin? Did he already know by some fae fuckery? I gasped for breath against my wounds and racing heart. I couldn't be Kinnia. I didn't want to be her.

Something tugged at the material around my upper thigh, running down toward my knee. I opened my eyes to find Bash delicately shredding my leggings into shorts. I sucked in a deep breath. He didn't know about me.

"I would do anything to take back what I did that day," he said. "I will not violate your wishes again."

My heart stuttered. In the last minute, we'd gone from accusations to apologies.

He finished cutting my leggings. The two sides fell to the table, exposing the bloody mess of cuts crisscrossing my skin. He set down the dagger and repositioned me so both my legs lay flat on the cloth-covered table.

"That fae crazy's doing a number on you, isn't it?" I grabbed a clean bandage from the healer's pile and dipped it in the water basin, then rubbed dried blood off a cut.

Bash plucked the cloth from my hands and took over with a snort. "It is. I don't understand why it's here." He paused. "Or what it wants with you."

I pressed my lips together, feeling the easy buzz of *energy* under my skin. "I think not understanding is the hardest part of living."

He met my gaze for the first time since I flinched and nodded with a small smile. My heart warmed, though that could easily be the liquor. A few of the cuts opened as he worked, but only a couple needed stitching.

I grabbed the liquor bottle to sterilize them, but Bash took that as well. His lilac fingers brushed across mine. Heat tingled up my arm before the searing pain of liquor hitting open wounds dashed it. The dragon took a swig before picking up the healer's threaded needle.

"Lie back. It will hurt less if you don't see it." He grasped one shoulder and pushed me until my head rested on Shade's soft back.

The pressure warmed me like the liquor. I locked gazes with the dragon who had done so much to me. His gray eyes softened in the dim light to something like kindness.

My gut churned. The fae knot of magic, my Cara, hummed. Instead of sitting back up to watch him, I closed my eyes and braced. If he really wanted to hurt me, he had his chance.

He grunted and started stitching the few cuts in gentle, tugging strokes. His rough, calloused fingers moved dexterously over my skin, and the tension drained out of my body. I couldn't remember the last time somebody else had patched me up.

Bash paused twice for both of us to take another pull of liquor. The air filled with the scent of violets, mixed with a smoky, mineral smell I slowly realized belonged to the dragon.

I opened my eyes. "Where did you learn to do this, if you have all these healers?"

Bash's needle hovered in the air at the edge of my vision. "I wasn't always part of an Anam Cara." He slid the needle into my skin.

I hissed and stared at the stone ceiling.

"Healers are not common outside of Caras." He grunted. "So, I learned to stitch myself up when I fought in the civil war."

I chewed on my lower lip. "Tough way to get good at something."

Bash picked up the liquor bottle and took another swig before handing it to me. I sat up and did the same. He took the bottle back and set it next to my legs on the cloth-covered table. My pale skin had become a collection of black stitches and red scratches.

He motioned to my chest. "It's time."

I sucked in a breath. "I can do this one alone."

"But you won't." He touched my shoulder.

My heart fluttered. If not for the pain, I would have thrown my arms around the dragon. I could let him help me without giving away my secret. I pulled at the sliced leather. It might be the only thing keeping my guts from spilling out. Or worse, the only thing holding my breasts in. An insane giggle bubbled out of my mouth. Bash's eyes narrowed, and I stopped. I shouldn't be more worried about my breasts than my guts.

With a final swig of liquor, I covered my chest with my arm again and began painfully unfastening my cuirass. The wad of cloth I'd stuffed in to stem the bleeding fell to the table, crimson-soaked, but the wound didn't open further, and my chest bindings stayed in place. I sighed in relief. Bash grunted.

The still-damp blood on my long, gray tunic pulled easily away from the wound. No point trying to keep it in place over my crotch after he'd stitched all the way up my thighs. A line of sticky blood seeped down my abs. As I suspected, the gash ran from the right side of my stomach to the center of my chest, close enough to just nick my bindings. I exhaled sharply. My secret remained safe, for now.

"This wound should have been treated on the battlefield." He shook his head. "I can't believe you haven't passed out yet."

I gritted my teeth. "I have a lot of experience with pain."

Bash's gaze hardened. The number of scales on his face doubled. My heart raced. He clenched and unclenched his fists, then took another massive gulp of the liquor.

His scales receded. "No one should have to say that."

I nodded agreement.

He took a deep breath, set down the bottle, and picked up the wet cloth. "Lie back and take off your tunic."

"No."

Bash scowled. "Your human modesty does you no good here."

"Stitch it as is or leave me." I dropped my tunic and gingerly crossed my arms over my chest. The edges of the wound pulled, and I choked back a scream. The Mud Pits had taken everything from me. They couldn't have this.

His eyes shifted from my face to my arms, and his brow furrowed. A few of his scales shifted. He leaned over me, gaze lifting to my face. I smacked my lips and grabbed the bottle for another sip. Bash sucked in a deep breath, and my tunic slid up my stomach without either of us touching it.

I gasped. My liquor-warmed stomach fluttered, making my core tingle. He devoured every inch of my exposed flesh with such intensity that my fear of discovery vanished under a need so sharp I ached. Lust tore through me, drowning out the world.

My tunic caught on a patch of dried blood, and the sting shocked me back to reality. The long shirt stopped its climb just below my breast line, exposing the base of the faded, dirty bindings.

"I meant what I said." Bash murmured. "I don't want you to fear me."

I studied the deep lines in his chiseled face. Swirling navy tattoos even replaced his eyebrows. I couldn't read a thing.

"We can never take back what we've done. Only move forward." I took his hand and squeezed it.

He smiled, softening his frown lines. I lay back against Shade, Bash's hand still in mine, and studied the dark stone ceiling once more.

"This is going to hurt." He picked up the liquor bottle, then brushed a heavy leather strap across my lips.

"More stitching, less bitching." I released his hand and took the leather between my teeth.

"On three," he said. "One."

Agony lit my body on fire as the liquor burned into the gash. The leather barely stifled my scream. I dug my nails into Bash's hand.

I yanked the leather from my mouth and demanded in a rasp, "'Three?'"

Bash grunted, already sewing. I lowered my head back against the still-sleeping Shade. Bash braced against the curve of my hip, then paused and traced it lightly. My heart raced. Fear and another stab of lust twisted my gut.

"Is your chest injured higher up?" he asked in a soft voice.

Heat filled my cheeks, and I hoped I wasn't blushing. "That would be a no."

"Why the bandages then?" His voice held an edge this time.

"Work around it." I wrapped my arm around my front just in case he decided to cut the bindings.

His gaze shifted to my chest, and he traced the edge of the bindings with one finger, where the fabric didn't quite meet the flat surface of my ribs. The warmth of his skin left a trail of fire where it touched me and—

"Bash," I said sharply.

He yanked his gaze onto my face.

"Let's finish this." I struggled to keep my voice as manly as possible and my body from responding to his touch.

His gaze bore into me for three heartbeats. Then, he grunted and returned to his stitching.

When he finished and put down the needle, his gaze lingered on my stomach. My heart thumped. He had to know. Had he already told Zelimir through their Cara?

"One more dash of liquor to burn away anything introduced by the stitching?" I asked.

He nodded.

I narrowed my eyes. "Everything okay?"

He jolted from staring at my belly. "Yes."

Gently cupping my hip to keep me still, he dashed his work with the remainder of the liquor. I hissed as I burned. He released my bloody tunic from his magic, and it tumbled back down over my lap. I pushed myself upright, wincing, and Bash held out his hand to help me up. I rolled my eyes and ignored him.

Another hiss escaped my lips as I slid off the table. I found my feet, wobbled, and had to lean on the table for support. The cloth-draped wood dug into my hamstrings. Tiny shorts that used to be leggings exposed miles of my legs and disappeared under my long tunic. Bash chuckled.

I stared at him. "Are you laughing at me?"

A full, genuine smile softened his features. Warmth filled my chest as I smiled back.

The warmth spread. The Cara pushed against the barrier I'd built around it. My stomach fluttered. The knot swelled, filling my gut like I'd eaten too much, then compressed. A luminous new string connected me directly to Bash. I gasped, clutching my stomach as guilt, joy, and bliss fought like a thousand bees inside me. Bash threw his arms up and tilted his face to the ceiling with his eyes closed. Euphoria, not my own, flooded me.

"Isn't this what you were trying to stop?" I pressed my fist into my gut despite the pain.

He opened his eyes. His smile made him look years younger. "Yes."

I furrowed my brow. "It feels like the connection I have to Shade, but...lighter."

"Yes." His smile dissolved into his usual frown.

I leaned forward, hoping for more information. Bash looked away.

"Does everyone in the Anam Cara feel it when, um, this happens?" I wrapped my arms around my middle.

He shook his head. "No."

"Right." I took a deep breath and chewed my bottom lip. "So, my bonds with each of you are individual?"

He adjusted his belt and nodded. I waited for more, but his gaze went distant, like one of those silent conversations. Great. Whatever trust I'd just built with the dragon, I'd destroyed.

"Are you telling Zelimir?" I demanded.

He licked his lips and looked at me for a long moment. "Not yet."

Something bright filled my chest. Maybe he just needed time to process. "Do you think I can get new pants?"

He smiled at me, a smaller and more reserved smile than his grin moments ago. "You can use mine."

25

———

KINNIA

Bash ran his hand along the bottom of my bindings. Pain spiked from somewhere in my belly, but I ignored it and leaned toward him. His face blurred as he shoved the rest of my tunic out of the way and unfastened my bindings with a snap of his lilac fingers. I should have fought him. Instead, I closed my eyes and moaned as his mouth covered one of my exposed breasts. A sense of floating surrounded me. He dragged his rough hands over my bare chest, and warmth sparked between my thighs. I shifted.

A spike of pain snapped my eyes open to an unfamiliar dark, stone ceiling. Every muscle in my body screamed, and my heart raced. Where was I? How had I gotten here? The end of my evening had blurred into the scent of violets and the heat of strong arms. I closed my eyes. Two people breathed evenly somewhere in the room. My heartbeat slowed. I hadn't realized how much I missed the sounds of others.

I ran my hand down my body to find myself dressed in Bash's over-sized pants and tunic. Someone had taken off my shoes and left my katana within easy reach. My greaves and gauntlets lay nearby. A warm, tight feeling overtook the pain in my chest. I opened my eyes and eased myself up as quietly as possible.

Early morning light streamed through the round window and onto my utilitarian cot. Zelimir's bulk dangled off a matching cot far too small for him. Teyr lay tangled in a green blanket, a sleeping smile on his face. No sign of Bash, but as I stood and threw my hands out for balance, I brushed something in the air.

Silent comfort rippled through me, a warm presence at my shoulder and a smile in a room full of glittering metal. I tried to grab the phantom, but it slipped through my grasp like water, leaving a lingering impression of a thin, strong thread—and Bash.

Bash. The knot in my gut rippled with recognition of him, below me and to the west. I swept my hand through the air around that invisible string until I found impulsive exuberance, a heart so full it didn't think twice about how sharing his emotions might look. Shade, downstairs.

Dim, blurry emotions floated across his thread, like someone had turned the intensity down. We'd spent a long time trying to keep the Cara from fusing, but now that we'd failed, its presence comforted me. I liked being able to find the dragon and the wolf.

I picked up my shoes and weapons belt before hobbling to the only door. Bash's cream-colored tunic swished silkily over my skin, and warmth filled my chest. He hadn't hurt me. Maybe I'd even made a friend.

Somehow, no one woke as I slipped out and found the washroom. I ran some water through my hair and over my face, but the bandages prevented me from doing more washing than that. Fastening my weapons belt made me ache, and I barely managed to get my shoes on without bursting stitches. I needed to stretch out to keep from getting stiff.

That stupid charm tinkled and caught the morning sun. I started to pull it off the belt, but a little of the gold paint had flaked away during its time in my pocket. It glinted dully silver in places, the mundane shine of iron or steel. Something so human steadied me in the midst of this fae nightmare. I left the charm in place. It didn't have any magic anyway.

I sighed and limped through the hall, past one of those purple rodents Bash called itzals. It squeaked and scampered away. After a few wrong turns, I found stairs leading down into the healer's room, the last place I remembered before my evening grew fuzzy.

The string connecting me to Shade hummed with his closeness. I rushed to his side behind the canvas and ran my fingers through his fur, trying to find the wound he'd taken for me. I could just barely make out where the healer stitched him back together. The injury looked weeks old already. The memory of glittering gold magic left a bitter taste in my mouth.

I patted Shade on the head and took a deep breath. I'd gone twenty-some-odd years without fae healing. I could withstand another twenty or more. I scowled and left through the first exterior door I could find.

I stepped out onto stairs leading down to the courtyard. Morning sun streamed down onto my face. A few fae in the same creams and browns milling about stared at me. I limped down the few stairs leading to the courtyard proper and between two sheds. Out of sight, and out of mocking commentary about the fact they refused to heal me. I hoped.

Working out would be tricky. Every core movement pulled at my stitches, and my legs sparked painfully with each step. I lay flat on my back and pulled my knees to my chest one at a time. My Cara hummed happily. I pulled one leg in too fast and winced as a shadow fell across my face.

I set my leg down and peered up at Bash, who raised one tattooed eyebrow. The magical string between us hummed. I strummed my hand through the air, attempting to play it like an instrument, but nothing reacted. None of this made any sense.

Bash crouched next to me. "Your block's still up."

Hazy memories of Zelimir demanding I remove the block floated to the top of my addled brain. "Huh?"

The dragon pushed up one of my pant legs to check the bandages. "My commander said removing the block would be safer. I agree."

I didn't know what safety I'd gain by letting them in, but my *energy* didn't hold much back anymore. It just didn't play well with magic. *I* didn't play well with magic. I closed my eyes.

"Show me what you were doing," Bash said.

"Not going to comment on my smell or warn me to stay away?" I cracked an eye open and peered at him.

Scales collected around Bash's gray eyes. He dropped to his knees and braced a hand on each side of my head. Fear fluttered into my stomach and away, leaving behind an aching need. If I told him to leave, he'd ask how far. I barely knew anything about this man. I only knew he'd been hurt and gotten back up. He'd seen horrors and greeted the next dawn. He'd taken no for an answer.

I only knew I wanted him in my life.

"You can trust me." He brushed hair off my forehead. "I intend to show you that."

He hadn't told Zelimir that I was a woman. That was a good start.

My heart raced. I bit my lip. "Is this because of the Cara?"

Bash's stoic face twitched. "It's not that simple."

A shiver ran down my spine.

Bash growled, shrugging one shoulder as if trying to get something off his back before he straightened. "I'm going to stretch your legs for you." He picked up my ankle and bent my knee, rotating my hip.

I winced, but the uninjured inside of my thighs relaxed. After repeating the stretch a few times, he paused. "This is a bad one."

I set my hand on my chest and swallowed. If the wound didn't heal right, I'd never lift a sword again. I didn't want to think about that. He lifted me into his arms and stood. I let out a very unmanly squeak of surprise, then tried to cover it with a cough.

He smiled. "You're done for the morning."

I gripped his shoulder for balance. "But I want to stay in the sun."

He grunted and carried me to the stairs by the door, then settled me against the wall in the warm light. He set his waterskin by my side, peeled off his shirt, and began his morning routine.

I'd watched parts of his warm-up before. He moved smoothly, wielding his bright-red axe with a violent grace that matched his scales. His attacks gained speed as he combined them with jumps and rolls. Sweat glistened on his muscles, making his collection of scales and tattoos glimmer purple, white, and navy in the sun.

As his workout ended, I clapped my hands once and clasped them so he wouldn't know I'd almost applauded. He smiled, and heat rose to my face. Where had this Bash come from? Showing off and grinning. Had the Cara changed him? Unease prickled the back of my neck. I rubbed my neck, hissing against the pain of the movement.

This time, when the dragon offered me a hand up, I waved him off and stood on my own. Declan didn't need anyone's help. He kept his head in the game no matter how much someone made his—or Kinnia's—heart flutter.

Bash regained his usual neutral expression and ascended the stairs. I trailed after him. He led me into what I thought was the healer's room, now occupied by a handful of fae eating breakfast at the various tables and chatting. The fabric still sectioned off one part of the room, but the string didn't lead me to Shade there. Instead, it directed me toward the middle of the room.

Zelimir perched on a too-small bench near where the string stopped, and Bash headed that way. I followed. Whispers rippled through the room. I'd barely lowered myself into the seat across from Zelimir before Teyr stumbled down the stairs and slumped in the chair next to the titan. The ember snagged the coffee out of his commander's hands and chugged it.

Shade barked softly from under the table, and I grinned. He rolled over to lean heavily against my legs. Pain lanced through my muscles, but I didn't care. Just having him here soothed something in me. I wanted to bend down and kiss his head, but that would have popped every stitch, so I settled for rubbing both sides of his head and cooing at him.

A massive bowl of raw meat glittered into existence next to him, and he whined, clearly torn between breakfast and me. I released him with a laugh. He dove into the bowl, his tail wagging madly. The sound of crunching bones made me wince, and I looked away before I remembered just how dangerous the dire wolf could be.

Teyr shuddered. "That's a grown adult fae consuming an entire raw padena."

"What?" I asked.

He sighed. "Forest prey. Bright blue coat, at least around here. Big horns that look like roots. Now, no more questions until I've had at least three coffees, please."

"You're just grumpy in the mornings." I grinned. "Do you want me to rub the sides of your head too?"

Teyr scowled at his empty mug. "It's too early to flirt. Ask me again later." He rested his forehead on the table. "I'm sure I can come up with something for you to rub."

Heat rushed to my cheeks. I peeked at the titan, waiting for him to stop us. He only looked at Bash, who exhaled and sat decisively on my other side. Zelimir picked up his bowl and shoveled porridge into his mouth, his gaze unfocused. Bash went similarly distant. Could I talk to Bash silently now?

The dragon growled, stood, and left the room through a door I hadn't used yet. Zelimir turned to me and pursed his lips. I tapped my chin and stared back at him. Only Bash's return ended our little staring contest. The dragon dropped a bowl in front of me and sat with his own. Warm, sweet spices wafted from the sticky porridge. I lifted a spoonful to my mouth.

"The outpost quartermaster has informed me a rift appeared outside the Waltzing Willow," Zelimir said.

I froze, my spoonful of porridge in the air in front of me.

"One is a coincidence." He crossed his arms. "Three rifts in your area is something else entirely."

I dropped my spoon. It splashed a bit of porridge over the sides of the bowl. Bash put a hand on my shoulder. Teyr blinked and sucked down another mouthful of coffee.

"You're not a regular human. The more we know, the better we can prepare." Zelimir glanced around the mostly empty hall and leaned in. "I think—"

Two fae in cream and brown outfits that had to be Cara uniforms descended the stairs, talking loudly. They reached the eating hall and slowed to stare at me. Bash cracked his back. My new bond with him shifted as if irritable, and I prodded my stomach.

"The human smells terrible," a deep male voice behind me said.

I stared at my bowl. I did smell.

Someone else snorted. "I feel so bad for Zelimir. Imagine going from prince to top-ranked Anam Cara to laughingstock."

The first person chuckled. "Maybe they can use him for something."

"Ew." The second inhaled sharply. "Would you let your dog touch your cock?"

I took a bite of my porridge. The flavors turned to ash in my mouth. Just a pet, and unwanted pet at that. The Cara drew these four fae to me, and me to them. Zelimir had been right. We should've kept it from forming.

A short, froglike fae walked up to our table. "I heard you got your ass handed to you and limped here from the Mud Pits."

Teyr took a sip of coffee. "We had to jump into a rift after Declan and fight on Earth." He smirked. "You ever done that?"

The froggy fae chuckled wetly. "Did the human trip?"

Several fae gathered around us and laughed as I reached down to pet Shade and winced when pain seared along my side. I'd have a much easier time not feeling pathetic if I could use my arms.

The healer stepped into my line of sight. "Take your meal outside." He sneered. "Your smell is too offensive."

Bash slammed his fist on the table, making every plate and cup rattle. The crowd of fae fell silent.

"Maybe if you'd healed him"—the dragon shoved to his feet—"he could've bathed like the rest of us."

My jaw dropped. Bash stood up for me—and was maintaining my alias as Declan. Or did he really not know?

The healer narrowed his eyes. "He seems well enough, for a human."

Bash growled. "I had to sew every one of my mate's injuries closed."

Shade's matching growl rumbled against my leg. Bash loomed toward the willowy healer, making up in presence what he lacked in height. Magic wafted off the dragon in tingling waves that made my hair stand on end. If I didn't stop this, there would be a brawl. I stood, scraping the bench against the floor. Pain shot though my legs. Everyone looked at me.

"I was done anyway." I turned and took a step toward the door.

Despite the atmosphere, a smile tugged at the corners of my mouth. *My mate.*

Magic leached out of the air.

Zelimir spoke loud enough that everyone could hear him. "Saddle our horses. We're leaving within the hour."

I frowned. We'd been planning on resting here for the day, or I'd dreamt a conversation.

"I've decided to stop at Stoneheim before we greet the Council," Zelimir said. "We shouldn't present Declan to the Council in the shape he's currently in."

If my grin got any bigger, my cheeks would split. Zelimir used my name.

"We're going? Now?" Teyr asked.

I turned to face the room.

"Gather your things." Zelimir looked at me, his hard gaze unreadable. "Declan, you ride with me."

Teyr groaned. Bash smacked the table again, and the fae gathered around us scattered. The froglike fae oozed back to wherever he came from. I didn't know what alternate reality I'd woken up in, but I intended to enjoy it.

26

ZELIMIR

ALTHOUGH DECLAN STARTED OUR RIDE IN GOOD SPIRITS, after three hours, he radiated pain and anxiety even through his blocked Cara. He sat in the saddle in front of me, clutching his stomach. I didn't like it.

Bash and Teyr thundered behind me as we raced up the wide trail, Shade draped over Bash's thighs. It had been my second, not me, who stood up for Declan. I burned with shame. Caras existed to protect those who couldn't protect themselves. I'd spent all my time doing the opposite. Every fight. Every conversation. Every time the man did something exceptional, I came up with an excuse.

Pain thrummed through Declan's Cara. "How much farther?"

My insides twisted. "Hours. A half day still." I slowed to a trot, and anger simmered amidst my guilt. "May I?" Before Declan could answer, I wound my hand around his narrow waist and pulled him against my chest. Moving in rhythm with me would minimize the impact of the horse's gait.

For once, Declan didn't fight me. He relaxed against me, and the pain radiating through the Cara eased. Red, human blood coated my hand. I swore. His stitches had burst, and I couldn't do anything but pray the ride wouldn't kill him. He'd be seen to properly when we reached Stoneheim. Hopefully. I hadn't been home since the Cara united me to my mates.

Despite the warmth of the day, Declan shivered and burrowed into me. Despite the fact he hadn't bathed, his scent of leather and honey filled my nose as his hair brushed my chin. My blood surged with the same tingling excitement Declan's hands had given me ten days ago. I didn't want to admit it, but I'd dreamed about those hands. I'd banned myself from touching them to keep from spurring the thoughts on.

"What are you?" I murmured.

"Human." Declan's chuckle vibrated against my chest.

His answer echoed mine from our very first ride together. He dropped one of his hands onto my knee, and the motion of the horse made his fingers brush across it over and over. I suddenly understood why Shade never wanted to leave the man's side.

Just like my initial answer, *human* didn't seem to cover it.

I tried to focus on the path. "What does that mean?"

Declan yanked his hand off my knee as if burned. "Right, now that you have questions, we're changing the rules."

"No." I scrabbled for the right words. My ancestral home lay at the end of the day's path. I'd planned to talk to Declan there, but for the first time in a long time, my mouth ran ahead of me. "What if I gave you a gold back for every question I asked?"

He laughed darkly. "Fair's fair, I guess."

"So?" I adjusted my grip on the reins so that my arms rested against his waist. "What does it mean to be human?"

Declan didn't answer. Emotion clawed at my chest.

Finally, he spoke. "Humans don't have the same hard roles that fae do. People with red hair aren't fated blacksmiths or whatever." He leaned into the crook of my arm and shifted his head to smile up at me.

My chest melted into soft warmth.

"I guess...that's what it means." He shrugged and looked back at the road ahead. "The choosing. The getting to choose."

I nodded like I understood, but I'd never come across a concept more foreign in all my life. Everything important in my life had been chosen for me, even the Cara.

"Why did you choose this? Uh, mercenary work, I mean." I wished I could see his expression.

"It's simple." He straightened, and I wished I'd kept silent so that he would have remained relaxed in my arms. He stared at the trees ahead of us. "I like the freedom of the road. I like meeting people. Things are always easier when they're new."

He talked so casually about a life I couldn't envision. I'd always lived in a complex web of who gave orders and who took them. That hierarchy gave shape and reason to my days. I'd listened to my father until the Anam Cara called me. That day, I'd decided the magic of Thrae itself superseded any of the smaller hierarchies we'd made up. But that hadn't stopped me from choosing orders over magic when the magic led me to him. I wanted Declan to look up at me again. I wanted to stare into his wide, blue eyes and discover all the secrets hidden within.

"What would you say if I said I couldn't ignore my feelings anymore?" I murmured.

If he didn't hear me, Thrae chose my fate once more.

"What? Feelings for me?" he murmured.

I winced. "Well, yes."

Declan went quiet. My heart thudded in my throat.

"I like you too, Zelimir," he said. "I've honestly never been as physically attracted to anyone in my life."

I exhaled slowly. Teyr sent a curious *pulse* through the Cara, but I could only think of the man in my arms.

"I should have been the one who stood up for you first." As the words left my lips, my Cara tingled, and my body flushed. Magic fought through the dull static of Declan's block, and our Cara connected. Euphoria made me lightheaded. For one, halcyon moment, we were alone in our joy.

His pain returned tenfold. The heat of the gash burned, the further injury of our ride seared, but excitement bubbled underneath it all. Declan buzzed with hope and a desire to belong. His emotions remained dimmed by the block, but even feeling this much exhilarated me.

When Bash told me he'd connected with Declan last night, sharp feeling had cut through me like a knife. I'd tried to justify my reaction as frustration with the dragon for giving into the magic. Now, I recognized the feeling. Envy.

Decland shifted again to look up at me. It took all my self-control not to drop a kiss on his full lips. Commanding my Cara kept me busy enough that I barely looked at women anymore. I'd never had feelings like this for a man, much less a human.

Declan bit his bottom lip. "This is the opposite of what you wanted."

I looked away from his mouth and ran a hand through frizzy twists I'd be able to fix properly at the castle. "Things change."

The magic chose him. I'd seen Bash smile more in the last two days than in the last six years. Maybe longer. Teyr talked to us, rather than around or over. I could feel Shade. Declan didn't fit the mold, but maybe that was what we needed.

"I'm going to fix you," I whispered. "The healers in Stoneheim won't turn you away."

He squeezed my arm. "Thank you."

His touch was worth the price of facing my father.

WE THUNDERED THROUGH THE LARGE VILLAGE AROUND Stoneheim Castle. Hot pink and neon green trees blurred by. Brilliant red smoke floated up from the twisting towers of the gold stone castle I once called home.

We reached the courtyard in front of the massive, intricately carved, dark wood doors I had slammed behind me the last time I left. My heraldic colors, purple for the force magic than ran in the veins of our sons and gold for the rich stone of our castle, danced over its surface.

Declan laid a hand on my forearm. "Breathe, Zel."

I inhaled. I'd not realized I'd stopped.

Two titan guards in Stoneheim purple and gold with medals decorating their chests, stood on each side of the door. They saluted me while a third in front of the door placed his hand against a rune-covered stone, then stepped aside. The doors groaned open, and my horse shifted beneath us as my older sister, in a gown of purple velvet, stepped out onto the landing. A foot shorter than me but equally muscled and broad, Cordelia suited our ancestral home. Her hundreds of copper microbraids swooped up in a complex, structural bun, and gold sparkled around her neck and wrists.

She inclined her head regally. "Welcome home, brother."

My sister's voice had become smooth as butter in my near century of absence.

"Cordelia." I nodded in turn and tightened my hold on Declan. "Is Drek still in our employ?"

She looked me over. "He is. Are you hurt?"

I shook my head. "One of my mates is."

"Of course." Her gaze shifted to Declan. "That would be why you came home."

She clapped her hands, and attendants swarmed out of the stables to our left. One took control of my mount while another gripped my stirrup to ease my dismount. I tried to get him to help Declan first, but the human swung his leg over the pommel and slid down the opposite side. Although he didn't land hard, his features crumpled, and he gripped my leg to keep from falling over. I cursed and leapt down from my saddle.

Shade practically shredded Bash's pants trying to leap off his lap. The massive, thrashing dire wolf frightened my second's mount, and it reared, dumping wolf and dragon onto the glittering golden stone. A laugh bubbled out of Declan. Shade recovered first and bolted to our human's side, slamming into him as if they'd been apart for years. Declan's laugh cut off with a cry of pain.

"Shade!" I took a step forward.

He put his hackles up and snarled. I took a calming breath. Shade's attachment had become a problem. I'd been so busy trying to keep Declan at arm's length, I hadn't thought about who had gotten closer.

"The stories about the human are true, I see." Cordelia walked down the few steps to stand in front of us.

Before I could say anything, Declan steadied himself on Shade and gave Cordelia a stilted half-bow. "Declan, at your service, your ladyship."

She smiled. "A human with manners?"

"But still reeking of the road and bleeding, I'm afraid." He grimaced. "Save your tender sensibilities, milady, and stay back."

My sister's eyes twinkled as she inclined her head, obviously charmed. I clenched my fist, unsure whether I wanted to be angrier at Declan for flirting like a knight in a human storybook or Cordelia for enjoying it.

"Belinda," Cordelia called, "please take Declan and Shade to Drek."

A water nymph clad in the soft purple my sister preferred for her personal attendants drifted out of the door and offered her arm to Declan.

Cordelia smiled at me. "Zelimir, our father awaits."

I ran my hand through my hair and *pulsed* to Teyr and Bash to follow Declan. Duty called.

27

TEYR

I crouched down in the narrow stone hallway leading to the mineral pool behind Zel's castle so I could look into Shade's glowing eyes. "I'll keep the human company. Go bother Bash."

Shade barked and bared his sharp teeth.

"What? No one else is obeying Zel's stupid orders." I scowled. "I'd bet money you've already let the Cara bond. And based on Bash's handsy new ways, he has too." I poked Shade's cool, wet nose. "I'm not going to be last."

Shade snorted and gave me a flat look, the glow in his eyes simmering with warning. I had no idea if he understood me, but he turned and bolted back down the stone hall. I grinned and straightened.

Declan had disappeared for the baths as soon as Zel's healer finished with him, and I couldn't deny a bath sounded like a good idea. And I could picture him completely naked and relaxed in the steaming mineral water pool. I hadn't been the first of my mates to complete our bond, but I could be the first to make him moan my name. My cock stiffened in my pants, and my pulse raced.

Stomping my feet loudly to warn Declan, I approached the privacy screen separating the hall from the hot pool beyond. I didn't want to frighten the already nervous man. Steam curled around me.

"Declan?" I called. "Can I join you?"

The soft splash of a body slipping into water interrupted the quiet.

"Yeah." He sounded unsure. "I guess it's fine."

I grinned and stepped into the steamy night air. Fifs floated around the single, deep pool in the jagged rock. They illuminated a towel rack and danced in the drooping, soft pink branches of the trees that hid the pool from the sprawling grounds beyond

Declan sat, his back to me against the wall of the pool, staring out at the sweeping branches. A few drops of milky blue mineral water ran down the back of his neck, and he wiped them away without turning.

"Mood lighting's always nice." I smirked. With a flick of my wrists, I lowered the fifs' brightness. The space turned soft and warm-toned. "Don't you agree?"

"Ah, yeah." He sank deeper into the water.

I strutted to the far side of the pool, shedding my boots as I walked. The man hadn't technically indicated any sexual interests yet, but I'd be damned if all his little blushes didn't mean something. As I reached where the roots of the trees encroached on stone, I pulled off my tunic and stared Declan down. The man tried to look everywhere else, color rising to his face.

"Nice view, isn't it?" I slowly unlaced my pants.

Declan giggled nervously, then coughed. "You're so—"

"This tree looks to be over two hundred years old." I turned my back to the man and gestured to the behemoth branches. "Magnificent, huh?"

"It really is," he said.

I dropped my pants and patted my bare ass. "Don't I know it."

"Teyr!" he squealed.

I wanted—needed—to hear more. Stepping out of my pants, I turned and found Declan's face bright red. He quickly averted his gaze from my cock. I didn't know how far I could push him before he ran. Though maybe that would get him out of the water.

My cock twitched. Win-win.

I stared at him and slid into the pool. The opaque water lapped at my hips, just covering the curls of my reddish pubic hair.

He swallowed. "So, Zel's a prince and a Cara commander?"

I tried not to roll my eyes. "He is, but do you really want to be talking about our commander right now?"

If Declan's face got any redder, he'd boil the pool. "How many, ah, factions or kingdoms or whatever you call them, are in the fae wilds?"

I stalked toward him. I'd distract him from his endless quest for knowledge if it killed me. "Do you do anything other than ask questions?"

He scowled. "I do a lot more than that."

"Prove it." I flashed white teeth.

"I'll prove it if you answer my question." He rose slightly, exposing the tops of his curved shoulders.

I raised an eyebrow and slowed. Was that a playful note in his voice? Did I care about that more than his chest, hidden under the rippling blue water? He smiled, and I knew I'd play whatever game he wanted.

"Five big ones." I placed my splayed fingers on my chest, drawing the man's attention to my perfect flesh, and folded my thumb into my palm. "Four ruling families. Titans, dragonkin, short elves, and embers." I started toward him again. "The Council is a faction of their own." I slid my hand down my chest until it kissed the water at my hips and kindled my desire into a burgundy fireball that sizzled against the surface. "Between them, a thousand completely ungoverned patches of the wilds with a hundred other fae clans."

"That's hard to imagine." Declan watched the fireball just above my erection with wide eyes.

Good. I finally had his attention where I wanted it. I grinned and released my fire, leaving Declan gaping. "So hard."

In two large steps, I got close enough to touch. He reached for me. I closed my eyes. His foot connected with my leg, and I fell sideways, splashing into the water. That worked for me. I let the heat engulf me before pushing up to begin my slow walk in whatever direction he'd moved. As I swiped the water out of my eyes, though, I found him still in the same seat, grinning. What a pleasant surprise.

"I like the view here." He gestured at the trees. "So, do all the fae get along?"

I laughed. "Not even a little bit."

"But they all send people to train for the Anam Cara?" His brow furrowed.

I let out a dramatic groan. "Nope. I'm done. We had a deal." I pointed at him. "Prove to me you're not just a question machine."

Declan pulled his legs up to his chest. The tops of his knees popped out above the water, and he rested his chin on them. "Why don't you get closer so I can show you?"

I knew he liked what he saw. He studied me like I was a piece of art. I ran my hand through my hair and edged closer, drinking in his gaze. My heart raced. I needed to get my hands all over the frustratingly fascinating creature before me. He didn't move as I slid into his personal space, leaning my hip against his silky, bent legs. I trailed two fingers up his shoulder. I burned hotter than the mineral pool.

Declan's gaze twinkled. "Lean in, Teyr."

I braced my free hand against the pool's edge and leaned forward, my pulse racing toward my cock. I closed my eyes again.

He cupped my cheek. "I also kick ass."

I wrenched my eyes open. The man threw himself forward, knocking me off balance, before grabbing my right wrist and twisting it behind my back. The water around us surged as he stood to keep me firmly in front of him. I grunted and stepped back, but he stepped back as well. His body remained frustratingly far from mine. Two could play this game.

I twisted toward my free side with all the fae speed I could muster and managed to grasp his bare hip. His skin slid across my fingers like Fire. I took a smaller step back and tangled my right ankle with his, taking control of our balance.

Everything froze. The world around us fell silent except for the water dripping off our naked bodies and a cool breeze stirring the branches of the trees. Declan's breaths came almost as fast as my own. I ached to press our chests together, to gasp in unison. Could he drop back under the water before I turned? It would be a race.

"You might kick ass," I said. "But I'm still fae."

"And you're my friend." Declan released my arm.

Hot emotions flooded my stomach. Friends? Just friends? A splash echoed behind me, and I realized I'd missed my window. Water lapped against my hips, caressing my erection.

"Dammit it." I spun to find him back in his spot, looking at the tree with a carefully neutral face. The human might be brighter than we'd given him credit for.

My hand pulsed where I'd cupped his hip. He grinned and shoved his hair out of his face. In the flickering fifs, his slightly pointed ears jutted out of his dark curls. My jaw dropped. I rushed forward and cupped Declan's face, then traced the shape.

"Teyr, what are you doing?" He pulled out of my grip and balled himself up once more.

I *pulsed* to my mates to get there immediately. I had just begun pulling on my pants when Bash skidded around the privacy screen, Shade's scruff gripped in one hand.

"Really? Right now?" Bash's gaze caught on Declan.

I scowled. "Yes, right now."

Shade yanked free of the dragon and leapt into the pool with a splash.

"Shade!" Declan shouted.

"The human's busy with Shade." I nudged Bash toward the door, filling our Cara with urgency and excitement. "And we have something to discuss."

28

ZELIMIR

The first time I'd been allowed into my father's study on my sixteenth birthday, I'd marveled at the walls of lacquered purple and gray wood, broken only by rich, green-gold tapestries. Now, the dark walls seemed to close in on me as I sat stiffly in a high-backed chair with my hands folded in my lap and my sister seated to my left.

King Zephyr, one of the few fae in the wilds to hold true, united power over his territory, stood behind his purple desk. The only fae I knew who could still make me feel like a kid with his hand in the cookie jar.

"Both of my children, together at last." Our father beamed down at us.

He always stood when others sat. *"If you can command the eyeline, you can command the situation,"* he always said. It helped that he rivaled me in height and breadth, though his shaved copper hair had started to silver and his muscles to atrophy with age.

"It's good to have you back, brother." Cordelia smiled.

I spared her a glance, just long enough to note her gaze looked too intent to match her smile. So, this was to be the negotiation. The price for our stay.

"My Anam Cara thanks Stoneheim for its generosity in our time of need." I inclined my head. No promises had been made upon our arrival. If I guarded my speech carefully, perhaps I could get out of this without a formal deal.

"Of course." My father spread his thick-fingered hands before him. "What kind of a father would I be if I didn't help my son?" He glanced at Cordelia. "And what kind of son wouldn't help his father in return?"

To move the conversation this quickly, and to include Cordelia, his need must be big.

"Anam Cara members, much less commanders, are forbidden by oaths taken in front of the Lower Council to involve themselves in the politics of individual fae," I said slowly. "My life belongs to Thrae, and EarthTech is my only enemy."

My sister chuckled. "Still so serious, brother."

"Come now, I would never ask you to break your Cara vows." My father sauntered over to his drink cart and poured a finger of softly glowing yellow duskpepper liquor into three glass tumblers, then passed one each to me and Cordelia. He took a sip and smacked his lips in satisfaction. "I simply feel one good turn deserves another. Tell me, what have you learned of this human?"

I recoiled with unexpected vehemence. The thought of my father leering over Declan, steering him to political aims, turned my stomach.

"Nothing that would be of any value to you."

"That seems for us to decide." Cordelia frowned a practiced frown. "The truth is, rift activity has increased at an alarming rate these last few months, and we have seen no sign of increased vigilance on the part of the Councils to deal with them." She took a delicate sip of her drink. "Three rifts opened outside the wilds. Rifts stay open for hours, days because there aren't enough Anam Caras to close them. It's all very concerning."

"The Lower Council is at its weakest." My father grinned, and the hunger in his purple eyes, so much like my own, reminded me he had once been a legendary warrior. "They need new leadership. All the wilds does. We have too long been scattered. Think of how capable we were united against Tech, when we pushed back and regained control of our realm."

I stood so quickly my chair toppled onto the carpet. "Hundreds of thousands died. We lost half the world!"

"Only because we stopped working together." He crossed back to his desk and faced me with a hard look. "Because the Councils and their Caras put themselves above even magical law."

I thumped my drink down on the desk. "The Councils and the Caras form their own system. Not above the law, just alongside it. Why would a king be any better?"

My father sipped his drink and studied me with cool, purple eyes. My rage suddenly seemed immature and childish. A spike of pain, then relief shot through Declan's Cara, and I struggled to keep the wince off my face. If my father meant to destroy the Councils, I couldn't let him know I had defied a direct order and connected the Cara. He would use that regardless of my intentions.

Cordelia stood and offered me my drink once more. "Father is simply excited. You're right, a king would be no better. But the Councils aren't handling the rift problem effectively anymore. It's not safe. We need a new system, one that diverts power from the most powerful and gives it to those who want to better all faekind. To do that, we need to make radical changes."

I accepted the glass. When I'd left, she'd been working her way through the highest levels of schooling, which I had refused to do, and she had a knack for getting into and out of trouble. I barely recognized the polished princess standing in front of me as the firebrand I had known. I accepted the glass and took a deep gulp. The bittersweet liquor tingled over my tastebuds.

A wave of nostalgia washed over me. Once, Cordelia and I snuck out of lessons to the candy shop in Stoneheim Village and ate enough sweets to make ourselves sick for the next two days. Father had been furious, but Cordelia took the blame, and so received the brunt of the punishment. I set the glass back down and looked at my sister. She smiled warmly. I'd forgotten duskpepper induced pleasant memories. My father would never have picked this drink.

"I can neither support nor be involved in this...rebellion." I crossed my arms. "Even if it wouldn't shatter my Cara vows, more rifts mean more Tech, more cooperation, not an opportunity to sow further division."

"You've always been shortsighted, Zelimir." My father sighed and dropped into the violet leather chair behind his desk. "Change, fighting, this is the nature of the fae. Someone will seize the opportunity this unrest presents. You're fooling yourself if you think identical meetings aren't happening across the wilds right now."

Cordelia sat as well. "Wouldn't it be best if the power went to us, people who want to truly lead faekind to a better life?"

I flushed and remained standing out of stubbornness. "I'm more than a pawn to be used. I am a Cara commander."

Cordelia chuckled. "If you were being used, we wouldn't have had a meeting to request your help."

My father held my gaze. "I understand your vows, Zelimir, perhaps better even than you do. All I ask in return for my hospitality is that you do what you were already planning. Take the human to the Academy. Kick up whatever fuss you will. The busier the Lower Council is, the better."

I'd waltzed right into their trap. I looked at my sister. "What is your role in all this, Cordelia?"

Her gaze twinkled. "I'm an obedient daughter and loving sister."

I started to cup the hilt of my two-hander, then let my hand drop back to my side. Anger only made me look unreasonable. A cooler head would always prevail. My father taught me that.

I shifted my attention to my father. "The Councils need your support. Know that what I do, I do without desire to help your cause. Declan, too, is more than your political pawn."

My father smiled, showing all his glittering teeth. "You're quite fond of the human, hm, Zelimir?"

That hand-in-the-cookie-jar feeling I could never quite escape swallowed me. I turned, and Cordelia smirked as I strode from the room.

29

——————

KINNIA

My bare feet sank into the plush rug outside the door to Zelimir's suite. I hadn't seen the apparent prince since we arrived at his castle. Shade beat his damp tail against the loose purple pants and long tunic the healer, Drek, had scrounged up for me. My weapons belt dangled over my arm. I leaned closer to the door in an effort to distinguish what Zel, Teyr, and Bash were saying.

The voices stopped. I rolled my eyes. They were talking about me, of course, and my pointed ears. They weren't really that pointed. Maybe more than the average human, but not nearly enough to be fae.

I turned the handle, and Shade pushed past me to nose the door fully open. I got a nose full of the scent of wet dog in the instant before Bash came into view. He sat in a big armchair, his tunic discarded to reveal his lilac skin and navy tattoos, while Zelimir and Teyr lounged on opposite sides of a massive leather couch in front of a fireplace in clean Cara uniforms. Their gazes bore into me.

This morning, I'd been awash with peace and belonging. Three luminous strings connected me to the fae in this room. They hummed and tingled, waiting for me to join the group. I took a deep breath. With my next lungful of air, I stepped across the threshold.

Purple and gold surrounded me. Even thicker carpet than that in the hallway cradled my feet, and five circular beds with sprawling canopies dotted the walls between rich embroidered tapestries and well-oiled leather hangings. Bright fifs floated aimlessly through the space.

Shade yipped twice and bumped my legs. Zelimir motioned for me to sit next to him and poured a glass of something deep purple from the decorative glass container on the low table in front of the couch. He extended the glass toward me. I noticed the curtain folded up and over the canopy of each bed and a relaxed a sliver with the knowledge that I would have some privacy while sleeping. I tossed my weapons belt onto the only bed without saddlebags at its foot and sat. The couch probably cost more than I'd seen in my life. My Cara thumped oddly in my gut. Somehow, I knew it came from Zelimir. He huffed as whatever he did bounced off my *energy*.

I sighed. It might be wise to remove the block. The fae would be happier, anyway. But every time I thought about doing so, my skin broke out in goose bumps. I didn't want to give them unfettered access to whatever they got off the Cara, especially when I didn't seem to be getting anything.

He held the glass out again, and I accepted it. Everyone watched as I swirled the cup and sniffed like some of my richer clients over the years did, but I only smelled alcohol.

I took a sip just as Zelimir reached forward and ran his fingers along the side of my face, pushing my damp hair back from my ear. The contact sent a rush of tingles down my neck and straight to my core, mingling with the bitter fruit of the drink. I squeezed my thighs together. Our conversation earlier today whispered through my mind. Zelimir liked me back, though he seemed to hate admitting it.

He traced my earlobe. I pulled away as a spike of fear cleared my head. I couldn't do anything with Zelimir. Not if I wanted to keep my secrets. I leaned forward and set my glass down on the low table.

Zelimir topped it off. "I want the block on our Cara gone tonight."

Teyr nodded. "Pointed ears are a sign of fae ancestry. We just assumed you were human."

I frowned. "I am human."

Bash winked. "Sure thing."

The dragon had been paying enough attention to my words to copy me? I wanted to throttle and kiss him at the same time. I wanted to add *energy* to my hand, shatter the glass into a fine powder, show them who they'd really been traveling with.

"You have no scars." Bash's gaze could have set me on fire with its intensity.

I glared. "None that you've seen."

Teyr bounced up and down. "Is that a challenge?"

"It sure as shit is not." I grimaced. "You're right. No scars."

Teyr smirked. "See, being a prude isn't always helpful. You could've held onto that for a lot longer if we hadn't known your weakness."

I wrinkled my nose. "Har-de-har."

"You could've been stolen at birth." The ember scratched his head. "Or switched at birth. The changelings still do that, right?"

I picked up my glass and didn't crush it. "I'm not fae." I took another deep sniff of the liquor and realized the smell reminded me of Zelimir. My heart ached. "Do they make this here in the castle?"

Teyr scoffed. "That's not what we're talking about."

I looked at Zelimir. "I'm easily distracted."

"That's a fae quality." Teyr clapped.

"It's also a young human trait." The titan smirked. "And we call it aspage. It's a distillation of the fruits that grow on the aspagarium trees around here."

I frowned. "Did you just call me a child?"

Bash barked out one of his rare laughs.

The door burst open. I leapt to my feet. Zelimir grabbed my wrist before I could dump my glass in favor of my sword. I'd gotten too comfortable, stopped paying attention to my surroundings. My stomach twisted uneasily. What were these guys doing to me?

Cordelia, silhouetted in the doorway, struck an elegant pose. "You look cozy."

Zelimir sighed and released my wrist. He motioned to the empty armchair across from Bash. "Sit. I'm sure you won't leave even if I ask you to."

She smiled and glided to the chair. Shade shifted on my lap, his gaze following her until she sat and centered her attention on Bash.

"I didn't know you could laugh," she said.

Bash grunted. Teyr crossed his arms, something I'd never seen him do before. The gesture made him look petulant. I sipped my drink and tried to read the room. A new tension hung in the air.

"Have you talked to your mates about our discussion with Father?" Cordelia pulled a few loose copper braids over her shoulder to hang down over her breasts.

"No." Zelimir downed the rest of his glass and stood. "I'm sure you're here to rectify that."

"I'm actually not." She stroked a ruby pendant at the base of her throat. "I just wanted you to know the goblins are stirring up trouble again. They're gathering in larger groups than normal and traveling to the heart of the wilds."

I glanced at Bash. I hadn't mentioned the buzzing I'd sensed around that pub. The way the goblin's smile crawled down my spine seemed silly now. I didn't want to be the scared, foolish human.

"Father didn't mention goblins." Zelimir's brow furrowed.

She smiled. "He doesn't concern himself with less powerful clans."

I frowned. "Why wouldn't he want to know about everything?"

Cordelia looked at me like I'd asked the stupidest question in the world, then laughed. Teyr chuckled as well, but he stopped when I glared at him.

"*Everything* is a lot in fae," she said smoothly. "There's no reason for a fae king to deal with the squabbles of the less magical."

I took a sip to hide my blush. Her slick dismissal hit like a slap in the face. Of course, I had no idea about fae politics. Of course, I should keep my mouth shut.

Cordelia looked up at Zelimir. "There's never been a better time for the changes Father is talking about."

My heart raced. Changes? Did this have anything to do with me? I looked around, but Bash seemed as unmoved as ever, and Teyr just stared at his glass.

Zel scowled. "What are you proposing?"

"You always think the worst of Father." Cordelia laughed. "The wilds are on the edge of something new. You are a commander and a prince. Someone fae can look to. This is the time to act, not settle down in domestic bliss with some leech."

I blinked. Had she just called me a bug?

"That's an interesting word," Zelimir said in a soft voice.

"Isn't it?" Cordelia folded her hands primly. "I've always found Councilor Ambrocio unexpectedly poetic."

"*You* leaked the report." Zelimir clenched his jaw. "That's why everyone knows."

"We needed the eyes of the wilds on you, brother." Cordelia looked at me, no softness in her lighter purple eyes. "The human is a mistake, but his failure is now the Councils' failure."

Bash leaned forward. "Dee's not a mistake."

Butterflies filled my stomach. Dee? Had he nicknamed me?

The dragon faced me. Scales slithered around his eyes. I swallowed. The bond between us unfurled, and his strength and resolve infused my insecurity.

"Dee? You've given the thing a pet name?" Cordelia shook her head. "You're not thinking. We are not the only players in this game. He could just as easily be poison given to you by another. Can your Cara truly withstand another loss?"

The confidence Bash offered wilted and died. I didn't want to be a pawn, and I certainly didn't want to be a weapon.

"The decision will not be made tonight." Zelimir frowned darkly at his sister and sat back at my side.

"Think on our words." Cordelia's soft voice sent a shiver down my spine. "We merely need you to water the seeds we've planted."

She had to be referring to me. Was she asking her brother to side with the Council against me? My heart sank.

He sighed. "We're spending another day here to rest. Please, let's not spend it arguing."

Everybody looked at Zelimir.

Cordelia raised an elegant eyebrow. "You are?"

"We've already delayed a day. Another will make little difference. I'll not spend the entire time speaking of politics, but I'm open to more information." He clapped my shoulder and Shade snuffled. "After Declan's settled with new clothes, basic supplies, and a horse."

"Damn right." My heart raced at his touch, and I searched wildly for clues about his change of heart. His face remained carefully neutral. "It's your fault all my gear is gone."

Teyr spread his hands and summoned birds of flame. "I'm blaming the bhelrian."

I gasped, then clapped a hand over my mouth. He laughed, and three more birds fluttered into being and circled the room.

"Put those out," Cordelia ordered.

Teyr pouted and flew them in a circle around her head before they vanished. She pushed to her feet and stalked from the room. The door clicked shut behind her and Teyr visibly relaxed. Shade clambered into my lap, dampening my pants and shirt.

I bit my lip and looked at Bash. "I'm keeping your tunic. I bled all over it, so it's mine now."

His pleasure drifted across our bond. I smiled.

Zelimir frowned. "The urgency of our travel was…ill-calculated on my part. We'll not play into that fear any further."

Teyr folded his hands behind his head. "You think the Council rushed us? For what, just a power play?"

I wrinkled my nose. "Why?"

Zel sighed. "You would've arrived dirty, tired, and incapable of representing anything other than the worst human stereotype. And, if we'd been better at following orders"—he swallowed—"you'd also be isolated, maybe even hurt. The Lower Council intends your removal. Add to that the rifts that have been opening up around you, and there's not a fae in the wilds who would disagree with their decision."

I snorted. "You make it sound like I'm opening rifts. I have no magic."

Teyr cocked his head to the side. "But if a human gained access to magic, and rifts started opening around them…."

"Rifts are random." Zelimir's voice became iron. "Tech take advantage and enter Thrae through them, but neither fae nor humans open them since humans fled Earth."

A shiver ran down my spine. I didn't like the way he looked at me when he spoke, like he was weighing the possibility that I *could* open rifts.

Teyr clicked his tongue. "Could be a coincidence."

"I don't believe in coincidences," I blurted, then winced.

When we fought the Tech on Earth, from the depths of that battle, someone had called out to "sister." What did that mean? I'd been too busy trying to stay alive to wonder at the time. Tech wouldn't refer to itself out loud, much less as *sister*. Who—

My blood went cold. I had been the only woman present in that battle. But why call me *sister*? What else had it said? *"Return to...zone one."* I shook my head. None of it made sense.

I should never have returned to the wilds. My stomach churned around the liquor I'd drank. I stood, and Shade spilled off my lap with a thump. The room quieted.

"What's wrong?" Teyr demanded.

I tried to smile. "Tired."

Not technically a lie.

Zelimir reached for my wrist but stopped just shy of touching me. "Get some sleep. Your body needs rest."

I crossed to the bed where I'd thrown my belt, their gazes heavy on my back. I pulled down the thick curtain from the canopy and climbed on top of the mattress. Blessed privacy.

I loosened my chest bindings, sucked in a deep breath, and rubbed my sore breasts. I'd had to fight the healer just like I fought Bash for my privacy, and when Drek wasn't looking, I'd tightened the bindings even more. I didn't know if Bash had discovered my secret, but I wanted whoever owned this castle to learn the truth even less than I wanted Bash to learn it. At least the dull ache of the bindings and shallow breathing was easier to ignore than the screaming pain of the gash. I slipped between sheets so soft they had to be enchanted. Eventually, the conversation began again. I caught a few muffled words.

Tech. Rifts. Declan.

I would do almost anything to never see Earth again.

My curtains cracked open, allowing a line of light in, and Shade climbed onto the mattress and pressed his furry body against my side. I rolled and wrapped my arms around my dire wolf, damp dog smell and all. He hadn't transformed in six years, so I didn't have to hide my secrets from him. I should flee these fae and their complicated world. The only problem was, I didn't want to.

30

———

ZELIMIR

The next afternoon, I leaned against the banister of the balcony in the game room my father built for me as a child. He wanted to instill in me what he deemed a vital competitive streak, and he wanted to be able to watch. I'd mastered every game he threw at me over the years, from human billiards to the League board Bash and Teyr leaned over now, but victory held little thrill. I spent my childhood forever fleeing this place for the library or the training grounds, where I could learn something real.

The League board played a bright tune, and small fireworks erupted from Teyr's end of the three-dimensional map. Bash leaned back with an unhappy grunt. I expected Teyr to demand another game—he tended to grow obsessive on a winning streak—but instead, he looked toward the ceiling, through which Declan slept.

"I don't like leaving him alone." Teyr pursed his lips. "Especially with your family around, Zel."

I followed his eyeline. "If we stayed in the room, we would have woken him up." I glared at Bash. "He shouldn't have worked out this morning. Even magical healing is exhausting with an injury of that magnitude."

The dragon shrugged.

Teyr rolled his eyes. "Your sister's been circling like a vulture. You really trust her enough to take your eyes off Declan?"

"Shade's with him." I ran a hand through my twists and snagged on a mat in the back. Of course, I knew the risks. I hadn't left the human's side, even to fix my hair, since we arrived. But my father's final comment rang in my ears. Over attention would damn us. "And I don't think Cordelia would approach him by herself. He's too much of an unknown."

I wanted to be more confident about that, but my sister had transformed into a woman I hardly knew. We'd received the same lessons. She'd clearly taken them and run.

"Oh, right, Shade." Teyr rolled his eyes. "He's definitely sane and trustworthy."

I whipped a quelling *pulse* at Teyr. We couldn't think like that. I couldn't think like that.

Teyr shoved his chair back from the League board and stalked over to the billiards table. "Fine. Sure. When are we leaving?"

I leaned heavily on the banister and studied my youngest mate. His shoulders twitched as he grabbed a cue, and tension oozed out of his every pore. He didn't need to open his Cara for me to know he had something on his mind.

"What do you really want to ask me, Teyr?" I said.

The ember whirled, eyes blazing. "I guess I want to know how you sleep at night when you're such a hypocrite, Zelly?"

I steadied myself against the real anger in his voice. Even Bash blinked. Teyr wanted a reaction, and I didn't intend to give it to him.

"Can you specify?"

"You rode our Fire-damned asses about not talking, not bonding, not anything all the way here." He gestured wildly with the cue. "And now suddenly we're ignoring direct Council orders and leaving our own rooms to make sure Declan gets his beauty sleep."

I nodded slowly and gripped the banister so tightly the wood splintered under my fingers. Getting angry wouldn't help anything.

"Bash, do you feel the same?"

The dragon remained in the chair in front of the League board, his defeat still laid out in front of him. He studied the board for a long moment, then looked at me with scales thick around his eyes. He'd explained his dragon to me last night, but I couldn't imagine what called the beast to the surface now.

"I have noticed a shift," he said.

Eloquent defenses sprang to my lips. We couldn't drag Declan through the wilds in this shape. The Council wouldn't know how we were delayed. I needed to see my father. Under the weight of my mates' gazes, all my arguments died. I'd called the man a mistake while marveling over his reactions to us and the wilds. I'd policed my mates' engagement while explaining the wilds to him. I'd nagged them about Council orders while allowing our Cara to connect.

I spread my hands on the banister. "Perhaps there has been some change in these last few days, but the Lower Council ordered—"

"Fire, Zel, we haven't been following orders since Punaky's Pub." Teyr slammed the butt of the cue against the floor. "And I'm not here to follow their orders. I'm here for us." He swallowed. "What are we doing?"

The raw edge to Teyr's voice caught me off guard. Under all his anger lurked a well of pain. He'd taken Light's death particularly hard. A good commander would go to him, but as I looked out over the room my father crafted to turn me into the son he wanted, I couldn't. I never valued winning for winning's sake, but that didn't mean I liked admitting my losses.

"We'll rest here for another day, two if he isn't healed enough, then we will ride for the Academy."

Bash grunted. "The Academy or the Council?"

I clenched my jaw. My second so rarely questioned me. "They are in the same place."

"Fine, I'll say it." Teyr set the cue down on the billiards table and threw his arms out wide. "I don't want to lose Declan. And I don't think the rest of you do either."

I rocked back on my heels.

"I...do not," Bash whispered.

The delicate line in the sand I'd drawn between us and total insubordination dissolved. My mates wanted to defy the Council. And they looked expectantly up at me to support them.

I ran my hand through my hair. "The magic is making you say that."

Teyr laughed, thick and wet. "What difference does it make? The magic drew me to you, and Bash, and—" He swallowed, and tears glistened in his eyes. "You taught me the only thing that can tear us apart is a lack of communication, so I'm communicating. Fire, Bash is communicating. What are you doing?"

"I'm trying to follow orders. I'm trying to lead. What would you have us do?"

"I would fight." Teyr opened his Cara, full of determination and love, and stared up at me.

The distance between us seemed to stretch. The ember defaulted to fighting. He'd scraped his way to the top of Emberhold, battled for his place in this Cara, wrestled with where he stood in the world. I preferred looking over my options from a distance, seeing the whole field.

Bash still sat at the League board, tension in every line of his body. The dragon guarded his words almost as closely as I did, but his lack of rebuttal rang loud in the quiet room. I stood alone. I dug my nail into the banister and searched for a way out. My stomach roiled with the realization I must look just like my father from Teyr's perspective. I vaulted the banister and landed in front of him. He sucked in a ragged breath as I wrapped him in my arms.

"He makes me feel whole for the first time since Light died," he mumbled against my chest.

Bash didn't approach, but telekinetic pressure hugged us both.

"I miss Light too." He had been our peacekeeper, our equalizer. Sometimes I still found myself turning to the empty space where he used to stand when Bash and Teyr got out of hand. "And I know this journey has taken a toll on our communication, but I promise we'll work on that."

I emphasized my words with a *pulse* of apology. Teyr squeezed me in return. My Cara tingled with the knowledge Declan had just woken, and we released each other. Teyr looked back up, as if he could see the room where the human lay, and swiped at the tears on his cheeks. Bash stood. Even I found myself drawn to Declan. Somehow, my Cara had begun to revolve around this human.

And so, when Teyr looked at me with a question in his eyes, I simply said, "Two days. Then, we ride for the Council."

31

———

KINNIA

AFTER A FULL DAY OF REST STUDDED WITH DISTRACTINGLY sexy dreams about the three fae who barely left my side, I exercised carefully in a dewy clearing at the edge of the landscaped forest outside Zelimir's castle. Morning sunlight set the white leaves of a thin trunked tree aglow, their pink and blue veins pulsing with life above red-gold bark. I connected with the trunk and jarred a cascade of water into rainbow showers.

I spun again and kicked high before dropping to sweep out my imaginary opponent's legs. One of the seemingly endless servants in the castle had given me a pair of self-armoring pants that hardened to my legs without changing appearance, though I'd refused a tunic that would do the same. My injury tugged, but like tight skin over an old scar, and my right arm moved just as well as it used to.

The knot in my gut, my Cara, hummed. I ignored it. Cordelia's pronouncement two nights ago still rang in my ears, and I wanted to keep my distance from the fae attached to me until their Council could sever the connection. If the magic made us feel this way, gave me these dreams, then we'd know, and I could leave without hurting anyone.

If the magic wasn't inducing these feelings….

I shoved up from the ground, tossed my sword in the air, caught it underhanded, and spun. My heart crashed against my ribs with something other than exertion. Bash kept touching me. It made my heart flip-flop, and my core heat. Shit, I'd hidden myself in the forest because I didn't know what to do with his intense looks, the movement of his scales, the way he pulled back and leaned closer with equal suddenness. I didn't even know which direction I wanted him to move anymore.

I lunged forward into a low kick. And now Zel. He kept checking on me as I dozed the day away yesterday, delivering all my meals personally despite the army of staff in his castle. I flipped backward and landed in a squat. Someone cleared their throat behind me, and I whirled, bringing my sword up into a defensive position.

Zelimir chuckled and put his hands in the air, palms out. His shoulders shook, the half-done lacing at the throat of his tunic exposing the dusting of copper hair on his muscular chest.

"Don't sneak up on me like that." I sheathed my sword and forced my gaze away from his body to his face.

His purple eyes sparkled. "When you take down your block, that will be much harder."

I frowned. "I can't."

"Can't or won't?"

"Won't." I tugged on the golden charm on my weapons belt. "It's too risky."

"You don't understand the risks." He took a step forward.

The clearing suddenly felt small.

I scowled. "All the more reason for me to maintain the block."

I wiped away a bead of sweat that rolled down my face. Warm morning air kissed my stomach. I dropped the garment with a wince.

My breath caught in my throat when Zelimir prowled forward. A dazed voice in the back of my brain urged me to run. I had to keep my distance until we reached the Academy. But the heat in my core and fluttering in my stomach pinned me in place.

He stopped mere inches from me, his body heat engulfing my own. His rich, sweet liquor and vanilla scent filled my nose. If I just leaned forward, I could lave my tongue across those perfect chest muscles. I looked up into his eyes.

"I intend to keep you." His low voice surged down to my neglected sex.

I swallowed. "Don't you mean we?"

He smiled wolfishly. "I mean what I said." He cupped my face and brushed the hair away from my ears with his thumb.

My skin tingled, and my nipples hardened against chest bindings I'd taken to wearing tight everywhere in his father's castle. He handled me so easily. I had never felt small with a man before. A low sound rumbled through his chest. He grabbed my waist and pulled me to him. His fingers grazed the top of my ass. I leaned in. My Cara hummed as if dancing for joy in my gut, and my thoughts soured. The magic had to be making him do this. Making me do this.

I placed my hand on his chest and didn't think about the muscle beneath my fingertips as I pushed. "I can't do this to you."

"Then let me." Zelimir slowly leaned in, giving me every opportunity to pull away.

My heart ached. I wanted nothing more than to lean up, meet his lips, make a mess of his nice tunic and learn how his skin tasted. My resolve grew weaker and weaker as the distance between us disappeared. Maybe the magic wouldn't be able to maintain this electric chemistry when we kissed. I took a deep breath and prepared to be disappointed.

His mouth enveloped mine. Every thought I had melted away beneath the storm of pent-up need raging in my core. I wound my arms around his neck and pressed myself against his massive frame, suddenly glad for the armored pants that would hide the fact I had no bulge he would expect to detect between my legs. Zelimir slid his hands down my ass and effortlessly hoisted me up. I wrapped my legs around his waist, pressing my own damp undergarments into my core. He pressed his tongue against the seam of my lips, demanding entrance.

My rational mind surged forward. Zelimir obviously liked Declan, but if I wanted to keep being Declan, I couldn't let this go any further. Still, I could give him something else he wanted. I released the *energy* shield I'd constructed around the Cara. It dropped more easily than expected and slipped back into the stream of power under my skin. A blindingly brilliant knot of power exploded into my awareness. Four strings dangled out of the magic. One thick and stable, two clinging to fragile existence, and one still disconnected.

Zelimir broke the kiss and dropped me, blinking like I'd turned into the sun. I caught myself, but catching my breath proved harder. The need raging ramming through me refused to relinquish control while I could see skin through his tunic lacings.

I kicked the small trunk of the nearest tree, sending a cool wave of morning dew over both of us. The chilly droplets quelled the ache between my legs. Zel adjusted his pants. I refused to let my gaze follow his hand.

"What now?" I licked my lips, tasting him.

He took a few deep breaths. "Now, we go to the Academy."

My heart raced. I'd overheard enough to know the Lower Council and the Academy were in the same place, but I didn't know what that meant for my future with the Cara. Right now, I didn't want to know. I just breathed in the morning air, the beauty of the trees, the titan looking at me like the only woman in the world. One of us had to leave first.

I gave Zelimir a final once-over and slipped into the foliage behind me.

32

———

BASH

Teyr and I sparred on the manicured lawn behind the castle, only a few hundred feet from where I could feel Dee through the trees surrounding the castle as she, too, worked out. When Zelimir joined her and their conversation turned from talking to touching, Dee's lust filled my Cara as heavy and thick as syrup. My cock sprang to life, and I stumbled, twisting so I buried my cherrystone axe head in the ground instead of taking a chunk out of Teyr. The ember froze, but Shade pelted toward the manicured tree line where Dee had disappeared. I slammed him to the ground with my telekinesis and tried pointlessly to shove her emotions away.

My dragon clamored for me to launch myself after her. He had been voracious since I cupped her hip and stared at the swell of her breasts while healing her at that Cara outpost. He fed me images, glimpses I'd gotten while healing her, visions of what she might look like bent over various surfaces.

I clung to a wisp of control. Across from me in the basic sparring arena we'd set up at the back of the castle, Teyr wavered as he fought his own thirst to go after her. My dragon growled and reminded me Zelimir made her feel desire. I should've been the one to light this fire in her veins first, to make her scream. My dragon and I should destroy the commander. I took one automatic step forward before I caught myself.

After a moment, Dee's lust simmered down. My own raged on. Shade whined. If he wanted her that badly, he could drop his wolf form. Shade the necromancer wouldn't be pinned by simple telekinesis. I sent him a wave of who he used to be, strode to the steps leading to the nearest door, and sat.

I shouldn't have bonded with Dee before Zelimir. If I had been stronger, I would have held off long enough to at least bring Zelimir into the moment. My dragon purred his approval. I crossed my legs, rested a hand on each knee, and closed my eyes to center my mind.

From the first moment my commander laid eyes on Dee, he'd wanted her. I knew that before he did. But Caras needed order. Balance. They thrived on trust and teamwork. I was, now and ever, Zelimir's second, and that meant waiting for his call.

Dee's mixed-up emotions radiated through the Cara, as they would until she learned control. A useful tool in a fight, and a nuisance the rest of the time.

"Fire, our Caras aren't even connected yet," Teyr muttered.

I opened my eyes to find him standing in front of me. I'd been so focused on my dragon I hadn't heard him approach. He shot me a look that said he knew everything I hadn't told him.

The commander had been torturing himself over keeping his connection to Dee from Teyr, but I didn't have a flicker of guilt. The ember would push and push her. She needed someone who listened to her boundaries. She needed me. I gritted my teeth, reminding myself and my dragon that I belonged to a Cara. There could be no *me*.

The ember plopped down at the foot of the stairs, and I growled. Like always, he ignored me and adjusted the erection tenting his pants. We both stared at the little forest as our commander's and Dee's Caras drifted away from each other.

Teyr sucked in a breath. "Wow, that's all Declan. Zelimir's not giving us a single emotion. I mean, I get it. You've looked at Declan's ass, right? His body curves just right, and—"

My dragon roared. Before I could stop him, he swung my fist into

Teyr's face. The ember's head hit the ground with a satisfying *thump*. I reeled back and sucked down air, wrestling my dragon for control.

"Well, that's not how I expected to start the morning." Teyr sat up, rubbing his jaw before he scooted out of range.

My dragon watched him with narrowed eyes while I reminded him over and over that Teyr was my mate, my friend. We didn't hit our friends, no matter how annoying they might be.

Once I'd scraped back an ounce of control, I opened my Cara, letting Teyr feel my dragon's frustration and my regret. The ember nodded, and I closed it again. Hotheads were always quick to forgive.

He leaned back on his forearms. "I mean, I know we're not really connected yet, but this doesn't feel anything like Light."

I glanced at the forest and away. "It doesn't."

Teyr eyed me. "Care to elaborate?"

I shook my head. I believed none of my other mates had any idea about Dee's gender. The more I talked, the more I risked.

He sighed. "Talking to you is like talking to a wall."

I grunted and held back a smile. The ember had a hair-trigger lately.

"Declan feels more intense than Light ever did." He leaned in conspiratorially and glanced at the wolf, still pinned to the grass. "Even more than Shade during one of his episodes. So many more emotions at once, than—well, any of us."

Dee's secret danced behind my lips. The ember raised his eyebrows. I flinched back. Teyr and his golden tongue. But her secrets weren't mine to tell.

"Agreed." I looked away.

"Fine, don't share with your mate." Teyr stretched his legs out in front of him. "It's not like we've spent the last seventy-five years together or anything."

I grunted. The accusation hit closer to home than I liked. I didn't speak about my past because it held no relevance, so I'd never truly kept anything from my mates before.

I'd wrestled with the problem all that first night, but when I saw her in the courtyard, wearing my clothes and clinging to routine, something deep and warm and certain had bloomed in my chest. I wanted her to look at me like she had when she realized I wouldn't force her to remove her clothes, that dawning trust and belief. She almost seemed surprised. I would keep this from Zelimir, from all of them, until she told me otherwise, no matter how the lie gnawed at me.

Teyr huffed. "Fine. I'll just describe what I'm feeling." He scratched his smooth chin. "It's really…physical? Like, the emotions are fleeting, but they're so intense that it's sometimes less like sensing Declan's feelings and more like feeling it myself. Like he's all emotions." He shrugged. "A human thing, I guess."

I closed my eyes and focused on my bond with Dee. Her frustration and determination swirled into me, on the heels of embarrassment, a shred of lust, and more determination. My chest tightened with the emotions, and I exhaled slowly.

"Do you remember when the twins started enjoying the company of —what was her name? Abby, Able, Alissa?" Teyr sat up.

I grunted. Anissa, a succubus who hung around the little town outside the Academy, took an intense liking to our divar the week after they arrived.

"We all walked around horny as hell for a solid month." Teyr grinned like those had been the best days of his life. "No Anam Cara in the history of Caras ever learned to control their emotions as fast as we did."

Movement at the edge of the forest drew my attention. Dee emerged from the trees alone, and I sighed. I didn't know if I could have held my dragon back if she'd been in my commander's arms. She hesitated when she spotted us on the steps. I released Shade, and he bolted to her side.

Teyr winked at her. "Morning wood's a bitch to get out."

Confusion filled her Cara before it flooded with embarrassment. Dee turned bright red. Teyr howled with laughter.

"We were young once," I said. "You'll learn control."

Shade reached her and slammed into her hip.

Dee rested her hands on her weapons belt and bit her lower lip. "You're able to control what goes across the bond?"

Teyr wiped away a tear of laughter and caught his breath. "After about a month of oversharing."

Dee wrinkled her nose, her Cara tingling with doubt. I wanted to ask about that, but Teyr wouldn't have picked up on such a small shift in her emotions without the connection. My dragon grumbled at my inaction, and I reminded him we were the only ones who knew Dee's secret. Pride flooded my system, and he demanded we claim her. I cracked my neck. The moment I did something so brash, her secret would be out. Everyone would know. My dragon hesitated, as if that had never occurred to him. He curled into a ball and glared.

Dee released her belt. "I'm going to go dump cold water on my head. How do I get a coffee in this place?"

33

———

SHADE

The walls of Zelimir's castle caged me. Kept me away from my heart's desire. She shopped with Teyr and Bash in the village. I sat and howled my displeasure, but my pack leader didn't understand. He just reached down from where he sat in the chair beside me in the dusty book room and scratched my ears. I leaned into his touch and drank in his love and confidence that sank into me.

When he pulled his fingers away to focus on his reading, I huffed and collapsed onto the stone floor. My wolf had been my respite, a world where complex emotions and thoughts couldn't touch me. I ate when hungry, slept when tired. If I wanted attention, I'd lean against my mates until they reached down to oblige.

But my simple refuge diminished with each moment I spent in my Kitty's presence. I pictured her adorable face, curious and quick to smile, as delight coursed through her Cara. She had become ours. Our fifth. My world.

Her arousal from this morning set my mating instincts on fire. I'd wanted her from the first sniff. Powerful, strong, and smart, she could be everything our Cara needed and more. She would never replace my brother. No one could. But she could be more.

We could be more.

Bash had trapped me in his magic to remind me of my self-appointed cage. When I tried to go into town with my Kitty, my pack leader had pulled me to his side. With my fae mind awakening, I had no doubt I could have slipped his grasp. But I hadn't. Something smarter than my wolf kept me with him.

Zelimir's sister stepped into the room, and I growled. She rolled her eyes. The siblings exchanged a few words. Zelimir stood, and I did too. We followed Cordelia into a wide hall.

My Kitty's Cara tumbled through emotion after emotion. My head spun. Her uncertainty raised its ugly head and transitioned into sorrow that morphed into determination. In the market, one of my mates would point out something that sparked her mind. A wave of curiosity or humor would replace her unease. My Kitty's Cara rang with laughter. I joined her joy, chasing my tail. Zelimir cursed as I tripped him. I barked happily. Zelimir walked into a room with his father and two large fae I didn't recognize. I took up my spot at his feet and experienced life through my Kitty.

The afternoon sped by. When she finally returned, I tackled her and rubbed my scent all over her. Mine. Maybe the Cara's, but mine most importantly.

She didn't quail under the scrutiny of Zelimir's family as they picked at fancy food and didn't give me any. My muscles danced with pent-up energy as I watched them eat. I needed to run. I'd been cooped up all day.

Finally, Zelimir stood. The moment he opened the door, I bolted, only to skid to a halt and lope back when my Kitty's warm, sweet scent faded. I needed her more than I needed to run.

We returned to Zelimir's suite, and I pranced. I needed too many things at once. My mates talked and laughed. My Kitty kept up as best she could, but as time marched on, she grew restless. My mates wanted to go to the baths. She declined. Teyr had almost discovered her secret last time.

I didn't like waiting. I leapt on my mates, tried to chase them out. They threw a few things in my direction before they finally left my Kitty to her own devices. She laid out her new things on her bed one by one. I jumped up onto the mattress and sniffed them. None of them smelled like her.

Her shoulders fell, and whatever had been bothering her all day wrapped her in a dark blanket. I jumped into the middle of the pile and grabbed something to entice her into a game. She needed to be happy. I needed to cheer her up.

She snatched the bag away from me. "Don't chew on that."

Her hand shook as she placed it back on the bed. Fear, anger, and guilt fed her dark mood, turning our Cara to ash. My fae mind blazed to life and memory rose of my brother dying. I watched through eyes that weren't my own as his body twitched with my magic. *I love you.*

Grief lapped at me like dark water, threatening to drown me again. My Kitty sat heavily on the bed, her back to me. The reluctant determination in her Cara told me she thought about leaving us. I'd hidden when my brother left us.

I could no longer hide.

The song of Thrae, a wild, rhythmic melody only my divar ears—wolf or fae—could discern, wound through the air. Magic I barely remembered rippled along my fur. Hot, dark air surrounded me as I began to shift from wolf to fae, and my fur receded. The music swelled as I burst through the itchiness and fully transformed. The song dropped to a quiet hum, and my fae body lay across the objects my Kitty had spread across the bed. The bag dug uncomfortably into my hip. Sweet rot tickled my nose. Complex emotions and memories tried to crowd their way into my consciousness.

I had to focus. Only she mattered.

"My Kitty." I flinched at my dry voice.

She froze. The blackness of her Cara melted into equal parts fear and curiosity. I reached my long, pale fingers, still glowing with the blue-black of my magic, forward and brushed her shoulder. She didn't turn. She didn't run either. I rubbed her shoulders and the back of her neck, just like she did for my wolf. My thumbs didn't work quite like I remembered. She took even breaths and braced her hands on her knees.

My other mates *pulsed* curiously. They knew I'd shifted. My emotions spilled out of my control. I didn't know how long I'd been a wolf, but I knew I had been unreachable for that time. One by one, they opened their bonds, filling me with unwavering strength and support. Despite everything, my pack loved me. We needed to be whole. We deserved to be whole.

We could be with my Kitty.

I scooted closer and slid my legs on each side of her hips. The smell of dusty rot filled my nostrils as the tattered brown fabric of my pants shifted with my movement. No disgust tainted her Cara. As I grew accustomed to my fingers again, I pressed into her back muscles harder. She moaned softly, and her shoulders began to relax.

I placed my hands on each side of her spine and gently ran them downward. Her fear melted away. She didn't turn to look at me, just allowed me to comfort her like she'd comforted my wolf. When I tried to drag my hands back up, her long, baggy tunic wrinkled under my hands. I growled and pulled the tunic upward. She automatically lifted her arms, and I pulled the fabric over her head, then dropped the shirt on the mattress. Panic filled her Cara for a heartbeat, but when I returned to the massage, she calmed. Her chest bindings still obstructed me, but I didn't want her to run, so I loosened them to ease the pain in her ribs and worked around them.

I enjoyed having thumbs, I decided.

My Kitty let her head loll forward. "I'm lying to everyone. I want so badly to be a part of something that I'm forcing myself in where I don't belong."

"The magic called you." I kissed her bare shoulder through layers of facial hair I didn't remember having. "You belong. You could belong nowhere else."

"I make everything more complicated," she mumbled.

I kissed her other shoulder. "So do I."

"Zelimir kissed me." She sighed.

I nodded. "I can smell him on you."

She groaned. "He thinks I'm a man."

I laughed a raspy laugh. She didn't smell human or fae, but she smelled female. "Perhaps you can fool them forever."

My Kitty laughed, but her shoulders tensed. I placed my lips at the junction where her neck and shoulder met and ran my tongue along it before nipping the spot. A small dot of red blood welled up, and I licked it clean. Her taste exploded in my mouth. My cock hardened until it hurt. I searched our bond for something similar from her but found only a hint of passion lurking in her curiosity. The tail I didn't have sagged. She thought of me as more wolf than man.

I squeezed my eyes closed. "Don't leave us."

My fae mind couldn't face her response. The song wove through the air. Hot, dark magic swallowed me, reshaping my form. My world of simple needs and simple emotions engulfed me, and I opened my eyes. Except I knew it to be simple now. My wolf could never be simple again. My fur sprang up, and I leapt off the bed, rubbing my wolf body across Zelimir's fancy carpet.

I jumped up, wagging my tail, and put my face in my Kitty's lap in an invitation to scratch me. When she just blinked at me, I snapped up her tunic and bounded across the room.

"Hey!" She shot to her feet. "Give that back!"

I made her chase me until her laugher bounced around the suite, but in the end, I let her win. I would always let her win.

34

____

TEYR

I peered up at Declan and Zelimir, standing atop a steep hill of rock and dirt. Although the warm afternoon had dried most of the morning's rain, patches of mud still clung to the slope, so I waited with Shade and the horses at the bottom to protect my clean hands.

Zel claimed to have designed this outing to teach Declan how to handle his mount, but I recognized it for what it was: yet another excuse to avoid the Council. A few days' rest for Declan had turned into nearly a week at Stoneheim Castle.

I wanted to be angry with Zel for breaking rules he put in place, but excitement sparked into fire on my fingertips. If my stubborn commander stopped lying to himself, we could be whole.

He slid an arm around Declan's waist and leaned down to whisper something in his ear. My fire drained away. Just as he fixed us, the human broke us anew. My mates had started keeping secrets.

In seventy-five years, my commander had never once shown interest in a man. Bash could be more open if I caught him in the right mood. The dragon joined Declan and Zel at the top of the hill and took the human's hand in his.

Declan blushed. His unconnected Cara bloomed with lust and uncertainty. Being between them turned him on. Jealousy and joy rocketed through my veins. No, not jealousy. Disappointment. I'd been the only one excited to travel with the human, but somehow, I ended up last at everything. I hadn't been the first to connect our Caras, the first to kiss him, nothing. My so-called mates hadn't even admitted to their connected Caras yet, though everybody in the castle could tell.

Shade whined at my feet and thumped his tail against my leg.

"If you shifted again, you could climb up there and join them." I scratched his head. "The view should be incredible. You could see Stoneheim, the plains beyond, the volcanos, almost the Academy."

Shade pressed himself into my legs. I ran my fingers through his fur again and wished I could talk to him properly. Declan had even seen his first shift since Light. Fire, I was done being left out.

"All right," I shouted. "Shade and I are bored, time to go back to training."

Bash dropped Declan's hand. Zel released the man's waist without complaint.

Declan looked down at me and crooked a finger. "You come up first."

I looked at the mud on the slope. "I don't think so."

Bash lowered himself down using his telekinesis while Zelimir jumped down. A little purple parachute bloomed above him, so he landed softly. I glared at them both. Show-offs.

"Come on." Declan bounced. "I'm sure you can tell me something the other two didn't. The view is incredible."

I smirked. "The view from down here is pretty good too."

He turned red and wrapped his arm around his middle, embarrassment filling his bond. Under the embarrassment, I found a hint of pleasure. I sighed, looked at my nice, clean hands once last time, and began to claw my way up the hill. Dirt ground under my fingernails, and a patch of still-wet grass stained my tunic vibrantly pink. Finally, I hoisted myself up over the top and attempted to clean my hands on the back of my pants. The human, it seemed, didn't plan to give me that long. He launched himself at me.

"What in Fire!" I tumbled to the dirt.

Before I could defend myself, he landed on top of me. We rolled. Mud squished under my shoulder, and a patch of bright red moss stained the arm of my tunic another new color. I cursed. Declan laughed. Our legs tangled together, and he pressed himself against me. His humor not only rang in my ears but danced on his side of our bond, radiating toward me, and warming my world.

We rolled to a stop against the shrubs lining the hill's edge. Declan lay on top of me. The frustration and anger I'd held onto for the last few days eased, and I grinned up at him.

"See, you can be dirty and smile at the same time." He sat up, straddling my hips to keep me pinned to the ground.

My cock strained. I placed a filthy hand on each of his hips to keep him in place and barely restrained myself from grinding up into him. If only he hadn't gotten his hands on a pair of Fire-damned, self-armoring Cara pants that kept me from feeling if he responded to our closeness as I did.

"I'd get twice as dirty if it meant having you straddling me."

Declan groaned and tried to disengage my hands. "I just wanted to see you laugh."

My heart thudded, but I let him clamber off my lap. I wanted him to want to touch me, touch all of us. I wanted to know what his face looked like in the throes of pleasure. But when he settled back down in the mud next to me, my heartbeat calmed. A breeze tousled his dirty hair, outlined against the brilliant blue sky, and I set a hand on his knee for no reason other than to feel him. He closed his eyes and turned his face to the sun. My heart ached for something I couldn't identify.

"My parents didn't have much." The words spilled from my lips, a story I hadn't told in nearly a century. "They taught me that if you present yourself as who you want to be, the world will believe it."

He looked at me curiously. "And you want the world to know you're clean?"

I sat up and smiled ruefully. Sometimes I forgot just how little he knew. "Classism is the blood in Emberhold's veins." I rubbed the shaved side of my hair, my biggest insult to my home. "I was born in the lowest class, the coals, but my parents wanted more for me. They spent every penny on making me look like I belonged in the upper class and a special school to develop my magic."

I looked out over the horizon. If we could have seen far enough, I knew where Emberhold would be. I always knew. "They…died because we couldn't afford the final tuition payment." I swallowed. A day this beautiful shouldn't be sullied with the truth, that they'd been murdered in their home by vicious debt collectors as I graduated.

Sorrow filled Declan's Cara, and he placed his hand on top of mine. Even through the mud, his callouses scraped over my skin.

"I owe them everything. And now, I can be the son they wanted me to be. Staying clean is an easy part of that." I smirked and ran my hand up Declan's thigh a few inches. "Almost no one wants to bed a dirty fae."

He chuckled, but his gaze lingered on the horizon line as well. After a moment, he turned to me. "Well, I think you look just as much like the charming Cara mate I met in line that first day."

I grinned, and my Cara reached out to tangle with his. Pure, almost innocent joy burst through me, making my limbs buzz and the world spin. I reached out and pulled him against me. His chest met mine, and heat washed through my body. My heart danced. Instead of hiding it like my mates, I opened my Cara to share the moment with everyone.

Declan's blue eyes grew wide with the same dizzy glee, and I cupped his face to kiss him. He started to lean in, but Bash gripped the two of us with his telekinesis and lifted us down.

As our feet hit the ground, Bash and Zelimir opened their Caras. I could almost have sworn I felt something from Shade. We gathered around Declan, and I very nearly didn't resent the dragon for ruining my moment.

"I think this is cause for a celebratory orgy. Who's with me?" I smirked.

Shade began jumping around and barking, but Declan turned bright red, and panic shot through our Cara.

I patted his arm. "Don't worry. I'll guide you through it."

Declan's blush deepened. "Uh, that's not really the problem."

Bash stepped back a pace and bent forward in a full belly laugh, and Shade took the opportunity to race into the middle and chase his tail. I didn't know what made the dragon so happy, but I wouldn't change it for the world.

35

———

BASH

I FROWNED AT MY COMMANDER AS WE MOUNTED OUR horses. He wore his Cara uniform for the first time in days. He'd woken us early and hurried us through packing our things. The Lower Council had sent a message through the communication bowl last night, and they were not pleased.

One of the stable boys held Dee's new horse, a sturdy Arabian roan just a bit smaller than my Friesian, as she mounted stiffly. The relaxed and playful Dee we'd coaxed out over the last few days had vanished. In her place sat Declan, the hardened, take-no-shit mercenary we'd met in the human town. She wore fitted leggings, now paired with a long-sleeved green tunic that clung to her chest as close as she dared but still draped well over her leggings. She'd replaced her cuirass in Stoneheim Village, and the orange fae leather shone against the brown of her other armor.

I grunted and mounted my own horse. I couldn't begrudge her the transformation. Everyone felt the shift. Zelimir set his mouth in a hard line. Teyr frowned around his yawn. Even Shade stood motionless as we prepared.

At a single *pulse*, we moved. Zelimir took the lead with Teyr behind him. I jerked my head to Dee, and she maneuvered her mount between the ember's and mine. Shade would range, as always. My dragon purred. She belonged amongst us, not lagging behind.

We followed a small dirt track through the decorative forest, skirting to the backside of the castle, from which we could reach the main road. I watched the trees, trusting my mount to follow. In a few hours, we would stand before the Lower Council. What did my commander intend to say?

"Brother!" Cordelia called.

I jerked my head up. Zelimir's sister stood, flanked by guards, in the middle of the five-pointed intersection that would lead us off castle grounds. Beyond her, the first hints of the red and orange conifers of the volcanic range that ringed the Academy peeked out of the brighter trees.

"Cordelia," Zelimir said warily.

She crossed her arms. "Sneaking out without a goodbye?"

"It's early. I didn't want to wake you." He held his reins with an ease he wasn't feeling.

I eyed her crimson dress, golden makeup, and braided updo. She would've had to have woken long before us to prepare herself to such perfection.

"Oh, you know me better than that." Cordelia's eyes twinkled. "And I know you better than to believe you."

"I was trying to spare us another argument. My answer is unchanged," Zelimir replied.

"What answer, Commander Zelimir?" Another voice rumbled out of the trees behind Cordelia.

Geminai's Cara trotted into view, mounted and smiling. I drew my magic to the forefront of my mind and gripped the handle of my axe. They'd abandoned us to the wraiths, last we saw them.

They stopped abruptly before the center of the dirt intersection, farther away from Cordelia and her guards than was polite. That had to be the boundary line of Stoneheim Castle. My heart raced. They didn't want to start an incident. Which meant they intended to fight once we rode off castle grounds. King Zephyr only staffed titans, so those that bore his colors were tall, broad, and well-trained, but they were nothing compared to the might of a full-fledged Cara.

Something in the brush to the left rustled. I trained my ear fans in that direction, my gaze on the combatants in front of us.

Cordelia clicked her tongue and smiled. "I seem to have found myself right in the middle of Cara business."

Geminai attempted a diplomatic grin and prodded his horse forward a step. "It's always lovely to see you, your highness, but unfortunately, you are. Please step aside."

Cordelia studied Geminai's Cara, and I thought she might refuse. If she wanted to destabilize the Council, starting a war would be an effective first step. I didn't want to live through another civil war. She gestured, and her guards split to line each side of the dirt road. She stepped back to join them and placed a hand on her hip. My stomach sank. The princess intended to watch. Something rustled to the left again, this time farther back from us. It was leaving. Or getting out of range.

"Zelimir," Geminai bellowed. "Disgrace suits you."

"It's been too long, Geminai." Teyr urged his horse next to Zelimir's and put Dee firmly behind them both.

My commander let purple magic shimmer across his palm. "We have business beyond you."

"We're your escorts." Geminai spit on the ground. "You're to surrender your weapons and come under guard."

The rest of his Cara snickered.

Teyr scoffed. "We're being treated like criminals?"

"You disobeyed." Geminai grinned, almost vibrating with excitement. "You're not even a full Anam Cara. Some human doesn't change that."

I pressed my horse toward Dee. Cordelia raised an eyebrow and whispered to one of her guards. I hated politics.

Teyr's horse pranced. "You're living in a fantasy if you think we're surrendering our weapons."

"Last chance. We've been empowered to use force." Geminai flicked his gaze toward Cordelia.

She bowed her head. I growled. She would ask her brother to risk everything for her cause but wouldn't break the law in private to come to his aid.

"There are five of us." Geminai's grin turned ghoulish and triumphant. "And three of you."

I unsheathed my axe and dangled the weapon at my side, making my mount dance toward Dee. The cherrystone glimmered dully. A bhelrian screamed above us. The air pressure dropped.

A rift sliced through the air between Geminai's Cara and us. A single metal leg emerged from the opening and hit the ground, accompanied by the whir of hydraulics and soft hiss of well-oiled metal against metal. A SpiderTech crawled out with several DogTech scattering around its spindly legs.

I yanked my axe up and pinned Brettrus, Geminai's minotaur second-in-command, with a stare. He narrowed his eyes but nodded. *Truce.*

Their Cara spread out as a Tech I had never seen before climbed out of the rift. Like a SpiderTech, this Tech walked on telescoping metal legs but, instead of a torso, it had a clear, human-sized tube. A thousand tiny pieces of metal, constantly moving and shifting, formed terrifying arms. Silence froze the battlefield for two horrific heartbeats.

Cordelia's shout to her guards broke the spell. A DogTech leaped for Teyr, but one of Dee's arrows buried itself in the thing's body. Sparks flew. Dee's horse pranced and reared in fear, but Dee dropped gracefully backward onto her feet and spared me a nod before leaping for the nearest tree. I bared my teeth in a growl.

The Tech's lasers would chew my horse up. I vaulted off his back and sent him racing after Dee's fleeing mount. Battle shouts and the clash of steel filled the air. My blood raced, and I roared. Zelimir *pulsed* to close the rift.

I caught Teyr's eye and *pulsed* my need to the ember. Wicked blue flames flew from his fingers and burst across my axe head. I charged into the fray, reaching out with telekinesis to slow the Tech around me so my superheated axe could cut through their metal bodies like a hot knife through butter.

Zelimir *pulsed* a warning to my right. I spotted the DogTech leaping at my side just as it went limp, two arrows jutting out of its side. My dragon roared in approval. Another DogTech in front of me fell under my heavy blow. Two SpiderTech climbed out of the rift. I wrapped my telekinesis around a nearby tree, tore it out by its roots, and slammed it into them. They crashed to the ground in a pile of metal shards and oil.

I charged another SpiderTech only to pull up short as Zelimir *pulsed*. A fireball burned across my path and crashed into a DogTech mid-leap toward my commander. The SpiderTech reached for me. I grabbed it with my telekinesis, but something slammed into my ribs with a *crunch*. Pain bloomed. I tumbled to the ground with a grunt. My hold on my axe and the Tech dropped.

A second SpiderTech swung at me. I spotted my axe in the dirt and rolled toward it, only to immediately roll back as the first SpiderTech almost crushed me with a step. I flung my telekinesis around every moving thing within a five-foot radius. None of my mates were in range, and Geminai's Cara deserved any trouble my magic caused them. Together, my dragon and I lifted our catch.

I clapped my hands and sent everything crashing together over my head. Metal grated on metal. Sparks flew. A stream of slick, dirty oil and debris dripped out of the compressed hunk of technology and plummeted toward me. I hurled the mass into the forest and leapt to my feet toward my axe.

Teyr, side-by-side with Terris, held off three SpiderTech. Zelimir's raw, purple power radiated from the thick of the battle, but I couldn't spot my commander through the swarm of titan guards wielding runed swords. A boulder covered in glowing purple runes flew through the air and crashed into a pair of DogTech. Dee and Shade raced through the trees together in a cacophony of howling and rustling. I grinned. Nothing like battle to get the blood pumping.

With a roar, I charged for Teyr and stole a page from Dee's book. I grabbed one of the SpiderTech's legs to swing up, but my fingers slipped on the oil-slick metal. I snarled and leapt atop its abdomen instead.

The thing swiveled its head back and forth in an effort to get a line of sight on me. I'd never been this close to a SpiderTech's brain. Wrinkly, gray-pink flesh sat in a plastic dome with tiny cables running through the brain tissue. The brain glowed and flashed intermittently. Something cracked in its neck, and I met its all-too-human gaze. I expected madness or fury, but found only cold, clear calm.

I slipped and crashed to the ground. It slammed a leg down toward me. I flung myself to the side, and another leg crashed into the ground next to my head. I dodged again and again, but the SpiderTech corrected for my every movement, keeping itself overhead. I couldn't marshal my thoughts enough to use magic. Lines of gray blood welled along my shoulders where its jagged legs nicked me.

A gust of wind blew the SpiderTech back just enough for me to jump to my feet. I wound my magic around the thing's head and crushed the sides inward. The metal and plastic cut into the soft tissue of its brain until it erupted into a mass of blood, oil, and flesh. It shuddered and froze.

Nothing swung at me for a heartbeat. Adrenaline, fear, and excitement danced in Dee's Cara. My girl came to life in battle as much as me. I spotted her leaping from tree to tree with a small contingent of Earth-Tech in pursuit. I automatically *pulsed* the location and number of her pursuers to her. When she didn't react, I cursed. She didn't understand.

"Close that rift," Geminai bellowed.

Tech still poured through the split. I'd never seen this many arrive so quickly. It was as if they'd been ready. My dragon snarled a command to help Dee, and I snarled back. She couldn't be my priority right now. None of us would survive if we didn't close off Earth and its minions.

I rushed toward the rift.

36

———

KINNIA

My heart thudded as the HoldTech barreled after me. The clear-topped monstrosity seemed to have locked onto my location before it even entered Thrae. I channeled *energy* into my legs and flung myself to the next tree branch. My breath raced against bindings I'd tightened to their full extent again for the ride to the Academy. The ground shook, and I risked a glance back. In the trees a few hundred feet away, a fae I didn't recognize stood motionless.

The HoldTech's fragmented swirling arms spun like a massive saw through the tree beneath me. I leapt, but I landed hard on a thick branch lower than I'd hoped. Fuck figuring out what was going on with that fae I didn't recognize. Tech got you when you stopped moving. I picked my next target and crouched. My palms seared with heat like fire. I shot up, flexing my fingers, and the feeling vanished as I landed on the upper branch.

A DogTech jumped, and one of its spikes bit into my ankle. Pain burned up my leg. I pitched forward into the trunk and barely managed not to topple out of the tree. Blood pooled in my boot. Three DogTech charged the trunk, and my branch shuddered. I began to climb higher.

My ankle shrieked in pain. The bark slipped under my boots. I fell. I slammed into the ground on my back, and my breath exploded out of my chest. DogTechs surrounded me. Terror seized my heart. I'd stopped. I'd lost. I couldn't even get my breath back with the damned bindings I had to wear to fit into this world.

As if hearing my thoughts, the headless DogTech went impossibly still. My own gasping breaths filled my ears. To my left, trees splintered and cracked. An image—a memory, I realized—flashed of the cold plastic of the HoldTech's tub stuck to my skin. What the hell?

The final tree fell to the HoldTech's saw and my breath caught. As it drew close, I forced myself to my feet. I would die standing.

Two DogTech leapt toward me and sank their spikes into my legs. The pain forced me to my knees. I cursed and pounded the ground with my fist. They wouldn't even leave me my dignity.

Hydraulics hissed. A shadow fell across me as the HoldTech scuttled to my side. A round door whirred open, and the monster lowered its tub down over me. My scream died on my lips as my view of the world became distorted by thick plastic. The roar of battle dimmed as the HoldTech closed the door and raised me, along with an inch of dirt, back up to its full height. In a motion too smooth to be natural, the HoldTech began a lumbering run. *Toward* the rift, I realized in horror. I pounded on the plastic with my bare fists. I couldn't go back. I *wouldn't* go back.

My Cara thudded with the warm solidness of Bash, another silent message I didn't understand. My Cara thudded again, and I didn't need to understand. The Cara flared to life in my gut, burning with all my mates' hope and strength and resolve. I grabbed onto the feeling.

"You have people now." I forced a deep breath into my lungs with the admission. "People you can't just give up."

This thing hadn't reached Earth yet. And I hadn't fought this long to lose.

DogTech and SpiderTech encircled the HoldTech as if to guard its prize. *Me.* I drew two daggers and braced against the hard, rhythmic rocking of the HoldTech's pace as I beat the daggers' hilts against the plastic. I shifted on my knees and pain lanced through my injured ankle. My vision blurred, and I willed myself not to pass out. The dirt of the intersection where the rift gaped came into view beyond Tech carcasses and battling titan guards. One of Teyr's massive fireballs shook the ground to my right.

A blur of black caught my attention. I lifted higher on my knees and pounded against the plastic. "Shade!"

I focused on our Cara and forced whatever emotion I could grab into the bond. The wolf yelped loud enough for me to hear him through the plastic and spun. He stopped dead in his tracks.

I was thrown to the left, against the plastic, and pain lit my ankle like it was on fire. "Help me!"

His white-and-black eyes glowed, bathing one side of his face in light and covering the other in shadow. Blue-black power covered his body. It dissipated an instant later, and a thin, wild-haired fae in a rotting Cara uniform stood in the wolf's place. Every shadow reached for him. The nearest trees turned brown. Even through my plastic prison, his magic raised goose bumps on my skin. I turned slightly to keep Shade in my view as the HoldTech passed him.

He balled his fists, and power crackled over them as he growled, "You can't have my Kitty."

Piles of Tech shook. SpiderTech I'd have sworn were mutilated beyond repair lurched up on spindly legs. The metal groaned. What remained of their eyes filled with the same blue-black energy that swirled around Shade.

"Attend me, my pets." Shade's voice, rough from disuse, echoed over the battlefield and penetrated even the plastic around me.

Reanimated SpiderTech swarmed and began attacking their "living" brethren. I'd never seen Tech fight each other before. Laser blasts shorted out DogTech, making them crumple into twitching balls. Spider-Tech clashed in flurries of tangling limbs. I itched to be in the middle of the fray, until I turned more to see Shade behind us now.

Through the hair, I could only describe his expression as hungry.

The last "living" SpiderTech fell to the ground, then rose once more to join the necromancer's ranks. A shiver ran up my spine. Who—or what—had I been cuddling every night?

The sea of mangled Tech filled with Shade's magic went unnaturally still, poised to blow the HoldTech to bits. I forced myself to breathe.

They wouldn't hurt me. Despite this strange magic, I still trusted my wolf.

We drew closer to the rift. My heart thundered in my ears. Golden sunshine flooded the battlefield once more as the rift winked out. Titans in purple and gold stared at the place it used to be. The HoldTech halted so quickly, I crashed against the side of the tube. Pain stabbed the wound in my ankle, and I cried out. I didn't care. I was free. But the plastic tube remained high above the ground and its arms swirled wildly. I'd probably be trapped here for a few more hours, but with the rift closed, the battery would die. Even a HoldTech couldn't keep a charge forever. Zelimir sent me those weird, wiggly vibrations.

Geminai's musclebound minotaur, Brettrus, raced forward and attempted to dive under the HoldTech's arms. Its swirling limbs sent the fae flying.

Zelimir ran up, just out of the arms' reach. "We're going to get you out of there."

I shook my head, miming *just wait*, but he wiggly-vibrated my Cara. Bash stepped forward with his hands dramatically raised in front of him. He screwed up his face, and every tiny piece of metal in the HoldTech's arms froze in place.

"Stay back, Brettrus," Zel ordered.

The minotaur had already charged again. He hit the tube hard. My head cracked against the plastic and the edges of my vision darkened.

The reanimated SpiderTech surged forward and surrounded the minotaur. Their grotesque forms trembled under the necromancer's spell. Brettrus put his hands up, palms out, and scowled. I rubbed my head. The pain faded into a dull ache that matched the rest of my body. Even my thick skull hadn't cracked the plastic. Teyr stepped up next to Zel, and I gestured furiously at the hatch I'd entered through.

Teyr frowned. "Melting through the plastic will take time and could hurt him."

Zelimir cursed and disappeared underneath the Tech. Bash grunted. Sweat glistened on his bald head, and his body shook with the effort of holding the arms still.

Purple force magic seeped through the floor panel, and the metal gave way beneath me. I tumbled down into Zelimir's arms. He wrapped himself around me and launched us both backward, out of the Hold-Tech's reach, just as Bash's telekinesis gave way. A tornado of swirling metal death consumed the tube. Shade plucked me out of Zelimir's arms, and I yelped.

The necromancer's eyes dripped tears of blue-black power as he set my feet on the ground and tucked me protectively under his bony arm. I kept my injured ankle off the ground.

Shade whispered, "Destroy."

The world lit with green blaster fire. Soon, even the smallest piece of the HoldTech's metal stilled and became goo under the other Techs' assault.

Silence fell. Geminai and his Cara seemed mostly unhurt, though that could be because his little fairy already flitted around, covering his friends in sparkling magic that closed wounds and straightened broken limbs. A few of King Zephyr's guards lay on the ground, but one of them walked around to check on the others. Cordelia wiped a bit of blaster char fire off her face and leaned against a different guard next to a pile of boulders covered in purple runes that winked out one by one.

I looked at my fae, or whatever I should call them. Although Bash was drenched in sweat and oozed gray blood from a few thin cuts, he returned his axe to his back holster without wincing. Teyr cradled one hand to his chest, but he didn't even look dirty. Wine-colored blood ran down Zelimir's chin from a deep cut, but he stood strong as he assessed the situation. Shade....

Geminai, flanked by his Cara, stepped back into our path. At least he looked less thrilled this time. Shade sauntered forward, me limping alongside. His metal army scurried behind us until he stopped right in front of the troll. The sanity in his eyes looked questionable at best. He shifted, widening his stance and bringing it back together before going wide again, as if he didn't remember how to stand on two legs. His nostrils flared as he scented the air.

I clasped my hands together to hide my trembling as the reanimated SpiderTech stumbled to a stop. Teyr sent me a wave of calm, though his own uncertainty tinged its edges. True calm seeped through the Cara from Zel. The blood drained from Geminai's gray face, leaving him a sickly yellow.

"You may escort my pack." Shade's voice boomed above the hiss of mangled hydraulics. "But they will arrive armed. And if you put even a hair out of place on my Kitty's head, you'll not live through the night." Shade threw his head back and laughed maniacally.

The reanimated SpiderTech hissed and grated in an inhuman approximation of the sound. I almost pissed myself, and he hadn't even been threatening me.

Just as quickly, the laughter stopped. Shade released me and shrank back into his wolf form. The magic holding the SpiderTech together sank into the ground in a swirl of blue-black. The machines jerked and froze.

Shade pressed his dire wolf shoulder into my hip, and his tongue lolled out of his mouth. I swallowed and curled my trembling hand into his fur.

37

———

ZELIMIR

With Terris' wind magic pushing us along, the battlefield and my family soon lay far behind. Although Cordelia brought the guards and even the rune casting she'd inherited from our mother into the fight, I didn't labor under any delusion she'd helped in my defense.

She fought for her home. For my father's ambitions. For her own ambitions. And to see what happened if she did, just like she would have sat back and waited to see what happened with Geminai.

I took a deep breath. My mother died before I could truly form memories of her, and my father never spoke of her. Had she been just as calculating as my sister, or did I take after her? Could she have kept our family close?

My horse stumbled on a rock, jerking me. My sleek twists swung across my shoulder and into my vision. Stoneheim sat a scant few hours' ride from the Academy, an area of the wilds that the Upper Council had warded against rifts long ago. Perhaps my father and sister had a point. There were more rifts than before, and the Council didn't seem able to prevent them anymore.

I pushed my twists back and wound them into a quick bun before they could catch in the sticky blood on my face. Teyr rode on my left,

Declan behind us, and Bash behind him. Geminai's Cara surrounded us as if we were going to run, so we traveled in utter silence.

We hadn't been back to the Academy since Light's death. Councilor Drax, our tactician, had assigned us border patrol and only communicated through the bowls since then. Had things truly changed enough that my father could overthrow the Councils?

Doubtful. My father would use anything as justification to claim more power. And we disobeyed a direct order. Whatever might be wrong with the rifts, we could not waver in our allegiance now.

I brushed my fingers across the books in my saddlebag, drawing strength from the weight of history. Taking random guesses at the future never helped anyone.

Shade nipped at the heels of Exilis' pony, causing it to prance. Perhaps he thought he could frighten the little healer into fixing Declan's wounds. The human still had little enough control over the bond that my own ankle seared with his pain.

Even if the fairy wanted to heal Declan, which I very much doubted, Geminai had forbidden it, citing Council orders. I'd worried we were being rushed to the Academy to worsen our impression, and the troll certainly didn't do anything to dispel my concerns.

Shade barked, and Exilis' mount kicked at him. The wolf barely dodged. I *pulsed* an order to leave the animal alone and, to my surprise, Shade trotted quietly at Declan's side.

He'd turned back into a fae twice. Bash's dragon had emerged, and along with it, psychic powers he'd yet to begin exploring. Whether Teyr realized it or not, he'd spent five days in a castle full of young servants and not attempted to bed a single one.

I rubbed a hand over my face. My mates were changing.

Bash and Teyr had both asked me what our course of action would be when we arrived. I'd put them off because I didn't know. Now, a scant hour separated us from our destination. I couldn't remain indecisive. My Cara hummed as my mates pressed support from all sides. Declan made a confused sound, and I smiled. Declan made me smile. He made all of us smile.

I wanted the man in my Cara. And more, but what did one even do with a man sexually? I looked at Teyr, but I struggled to picture myself asking. I pushed that thought aside. One problem at a time.

I *pulsed* my intention to petition the Lower Council to keep our human. Bash sent back a clear affirmative, tinged with rare pleasure. Teyr *pulsed* ecstatically, bouncing up and down on his horse with questions and plans. Even Shade kicked up his heels, putting his nose to the sky and howling triumphantly.

Declan scrunched his face in confusion. It took everything in me not to drop back and sweep him into a kiss, but the tallest towers of the Academy rose into view over the horizon. The time for romance had passed. To face the Council, we needed to be strong. We needed to be warriors.

We needed Declan to be one of us.

38

KINNIA

"Declan!" Teyr jabbed a finger forward.

I glared at the ember and rubbed my ear. When we had crested the top of the volcanic ridge that encircled the town, I'd spotted a cluster of large dark, round buildings with the small town to one side, but I'd lost sight of the place as we descended through the valley.

The *thunk* of arrows into targets, the *crash* of swords, and the *whoosh* of magic filled the air. Geminai's Cara separated to ride more loosely around us as the trees cleared to reveal my first true sight of the Academy.

Little gardens overflowing with color and burnt-orange grass covered islands of various sizes, all separated by rushing canals. The larger islands held spacious training grounds where fae sparred and mounted strange, towering obstacle courses. The largest ones held the dark towers I'd spotted on the ridge. Nearly a dozen towers sprouted out of the dirt, making a patchwork compound almost as large as the small town we'd ridden past a few miles back. Round windows of all sizes studded their sides.

Geminai's Cara urged us toward the largest tower. Its enormous, rainbow-toned double doors sparkled in the sunlight. Training came to a halt as we passed. A troll that reminded me of a younger Geminai scowled before rushing in the opposite direction. What looked like a fat pig with a rainbow unicorn horn watched us from a patch of low, bright purple shrubs. I bit my lip to keep from laughing. Fae scanned our group and fell into step behind the horses. Our party of ten soon became a parade of more than fifty.

We all stopped in front of the massive double doors. I giggled as a comically small door opened in the center of one of the massive ones. A redheaded, freckle-spattered short elf stepped through.

"Welcome back, Anam Caras. I see the human amongst you." He waved at me, the sleeve of his diaphanous rainbow robe catching the light. In contrast to his wide-welcoming face, his pupils were slitted like Teyr's.

I leaned forward to wave back at the adorable little guy, but no one else reacted. I flushed and pulled my hand down.

Zelimir leaned over to me and whispered, "Councilor Odhrán. A friend of my father's and probable ally."

A second, bigger frame pushed open around the tiny door, and a taller fae, bent with age but dressed in the same robe, stepped through.

"Councilor Ambrocio," Zelimir hissed.

"Seize the human!" He pointed at me, his long, white beard quivering.

I froze. Zelimir wobbled my Cara unhelpfully. Bash filled our bond with calm readiness. I copied the dragon's relaxed posture and kept my expression impassive as best I could.

"You certainly took your time, Commander Zelimir." The angry councilor jabbed his wrinkled finger in my direction. "Get away from the filthy human. Its stink will not foul the sacred Anam Cara much longer."

I laid a hand on the hilt of my katana as my stomach sank. I didn't want my time with my Cara to end. The angry councilor whirled on his shorter counterpart and glared. Yet another door opened around the second. Though the fae who emerged didn't stand much taller than Councilor Ambrocio, he looked wider across than two of me. His purple skin swirled with softly glowing pink whorls. Councilor Drax! Zelimir had mentioned him by name. His hot-pink gaze caught mine, and he studied me with an intensity of focus that frightened me more than the other two fae combined.

"This isn't the place for this conversation." Councilor Drax's mellow voice floated on the breeze. "Come in. We'll see to your horses."

Bash placed a hand on my knee. I jumped in surprise, breaking eye contact with Councilor Drax. The dragon had already dismounted and stood next to me, his saddlebag draped over one shoulder. Gingerly, I removed the swollen ankle I'd bandaged as best I could with a strip of my tunic and some sticks from the stirrup. He didn't give me the chance to jump but grasped my waist and lifted me to the ground, holding me to his side so I couldn't put weight on the injured ankle.

I tried to push him away. "It's not that bad. I can stand on my own."

Bash just gripped me tighter.

I pursed my lips, but there were more important things. "Did you know the Council disagreed like this?"

The ember chuckled humorlessly. "Not a clue."

Shade pressed himself against my leg. Zelimir stepped next to him. Teyr sent a spike of excitement through our bond and came up on Bash's other side, so we made a single, united line. I swallowed. Although uncertainty filled my gut, my Cara bloomed with my mates' resolve.

Geminai's Cara escorted us through a small, round, red wood door that rolled aside, to reveal a circular room of dark stone. On the far side, a much larger, more decorative door stood closed. Someone had layered the ceiling with a fine, multicolored fabric, and the chairs in a ring along the walls looked plush and comfortable.

The smaller door rolled shut behind us, and we were alone for the first time since Cordelia caught us on the road. I leaned on Bash, and he helped me to a chair. Even that sent a lance of pain through my ankle. Teyr and Zelimir hovered. Shade whined at my side.

Bash knelt at my feet and unwrapped my hasty bandage. I winced. He grunted unhappily, then pulled the medical kit he'd picked up in Stoneheim from his saddlebag and began cleaning the wound. I hissed.

Zelimir sat heavily in the chair next to me. "You can't downplay your injuries anymore. We can feel them through the Cara."

I wrinkled my nose as Bash applied green goop to my ankle. "If you can feel them, why didn't you say anything?"

"I couldn't attend to you," Zel said. "We need you to look like a warrior."

My heart flip-flopped. What did that mean?

Zelimir inhaled as if to start a sentence but released the breath. Teyr paced a tight line in front of us. Bash handed me a waterskin, and I took a deep drink. The motion made my head ache. Once again, I needed patching up. Even with my *energy*, I couldn't compare to the fae. The round room spun. The vibrant ceiling and dark walls made a painful contrast. I focused on the stark line where they met.

Zelimir shook himself. "That new Tech went straight for you."

"HoldTech." I sank my fingers into Shade's fur. "And, yes, it did."

Shade wiggled under my hand.

Teyr stopped pacing. "Why?"

I shrugged.

"You do know." Zelimir placed a hand on my shoulder. "But I'll not push you to share your past now." He paused and looked at each of his mates before turning his purple gaze to me. "We've decided to keep you."

This was the second time he'd said that. And not just "I" this time, but "we."

Bash squeezed my calf while Teyr wiggled his eyebrows at me. I turned back to Zelimir. His powerful presence washed over me, lighting my core. Despite every doubt and logical I should be running. Instead, I grinned. My Cara danced with joy, and I fought not to jump to my feet and dance.

"Arrogant of you to think I'm 'keepable.'" I schooled my expression into a semblance of neutrality.

Teyr smirked. "Don't forget we can feel your emotions now. What is that, excitement and lust?"

I made a strangled noise. My cheeks grew so hot I could have single-handedly heated the waiting room. Shade growled at Teyr.

The ember held his hands up. "I just tell it like it is."

"I just need you to be honest with us." Zelimir brushed a finger across my cheek. "You've been asking questions about magic no human would. You blocked our bond while it grew. You've been through a rift and lived to tell the tale. Who and what are you?"

I stared at my pale hand against Shade's dark fur. Cordelia's warning echoed in my head. Alex—all my family—had trusted my *energy*. When the time came to use it, I'd failed. I may as well have killed them myself.

Bash tied off my new bandage and sat in the chair on my other side. He pulled my hurt leg onto his lap to elevate it, forcing me to turn and rest my back against Zel. The titan wrapped his arms around my waist as Bash leaned forward to cup my face with calloused hands. Bash kissed my forehead. Simple determination and comfort spilled into me before he released me. Teyr laced his fingers with mine. My experiences on Earth, my gender, my *energy*, I hid all of them to stay safe.

The room went gray around me. A memory of Alex's blood, bursting coppery over my tongue, hit me as real as the day he'd been beheaded in front of me. David's last accusing stare burned into me. Panic raced through my veins. It didn't matter what these fae wanted or needed, some secrets were best kept hidden.

Warm comfort pressed into me from all sides, and the room slowly regained its true color. I took a shaky breath. Rydel had asked me if I loved life. I loved it with my family at my side. Zelimir wasn't Alex. None of them were. And I wasn't Kinnia.

I could at least prepare them for what fighting at my side would mean.

"I have *energy* inside me." A single tear trailed down my cheek. "I don't know where it comes from or why, and it only affects me, but it's how I survived on Earth. Alone." My heart stuttered as I said the words out loud for the first time. "I should have been able to save my friends."

Zelimir slipped a hand around my shoulder and gently squeezed. "Whatever you fear, you're our mate now. We can feel your sorrow, your anger, your regret." He wiped away my tear. "Whatever lies in your past, we'll accept it. Cherish it. We are a culmination of our experiences."

Their support poured into me. My Anam Cara filled with wiggles again. I took a deep breath. Not wiggles, *pulses*.

"Do you want to become a part of our Cara?" Teyr asked when their *pulsing* ended.

I closed my eyes. Yes, so badly. Being with them, fighting at their side, it felt so right. But—

"Stop," Zelimir said. "We want you with us."

I opened my eyes.

The bigger of the two doors rolled slowly open. I pulled my feet off Bash's lap and straightened away from Zelimir's embrace. Then, we all stood. Whatever goop Bash applied to my ankle seemed to work miracles. Pain burned through me, but my ankle held my weight.

Zel *pulsed*. I had no idea what he said, but I could guess.

"Yes," I murmured.

The door disappeared into the wall with an anticlimactic *thud*. Murmuring voices and flashes of color on the other side made my stomach churn.

"They will test us." Zelimir stood next to me. "They will want to break us."

Bash stepped closer to my other side.

"They will question everything," our commander said.

Teyr draped an arm around Bash's shoulder.

Zel faced the open door. "But we're a Cara."

Shade padded in front of me and faced the door, his shoulders square in a way that reminded me of his filthy fae form. Bash surprised me by giving his rump an affectionate pat. The wolf glanced back at him, and a warm feeling I could only call love washed out of Shade's Cara. A picture abruptly flashed in my mind of fae-Shade kneeling, fingers splayed wide in the dirt, as neon red grass and bright blue trees dimmed. His blue-black magic injected the fading souls of the dead who had fallen in the battle that raged around him...and his army began to rise.

"We will fight to stay together," Zel said.

But I knew they already had.

Sneak Peek of the next Anam Cara romance
Behind Stone Walls

Fae dance with magic. Tech kill magic. Only she can walk between the two.

The most powerful Cara on Thrae must return to the Academy and face trials that tests each of their fae powers.

The prince who leads them.

An ember who can call up fire with a thought.

A dragon who fought in the civil war and was turned into an experiment.

And the wolf neckromancer who ended the war by killing his brother —the fifth in their Cara.

Fail even one of their trials, and their soul-bond will kill them. Succeed…. How can they succeed when someone is setting them up to fail…or worse, is out to kill the newest member of their Cara?

Only their bond with the newest member of their Cara can save them, and each of the fae linked to Kinnia must give themselves to her. But their prince and commander refuses. He is determined to keep his distance for he cannot risk destroying their Cara and the three fae he loves above all else—especially not for a human woman.

SNEAK PEEK AT BEHIND STONE WALLS

PROLOGUE
SHADE

I splayed my fingers wide in the dirt and wrenched magic from the beating heart of the fae wilds. The neon red grass and bright blue trees dimmed as I bent their power to my will. Clouds of billowing, blue-black magic injected the fading souls of the dead who had fallen in this fight. Innocent and warrior alike rose at my call. As one, my army turned toward the battle that still raged.

My Cara *pulsed* with my pack's strategies, but I filtered them out with practiced ease. Woven magic leant its wavering quality to the world around me, and I swayed with a wild grin.

A new Tech, fifty feet of cables, metal, and mutilated human ingenuity, loomed over the battlefield. Broken and bleeding corpses littered the ground around the mechanical legs that held the new Tech's metal body twenty feet off the ground. Tech of all sorts seethed around it, killing anything that breathed.

A crackle of my twin brother's golden lightning sparked at the edge of my vision. Fireballs, probably Teyr's, rocketed toward the horror's rectangular metal torso, then bounced off a clear shield and exploded midair, showering the battlefield in sparks. Zelimir's massive, two-handed purple sword flew through the air and lodged in the Tech's defenses, looking like a toothpick sticking out of a roast. I alone could destroy the untouchable monstrosity.

The reanimated body of a little gnome girl with a wooden toy still tucked under her arm lurched past me. EarthTech didn't care who they slaughtered. I sent a wispy thread of magic her way, a little extra power to make sure she had the chance to destroy what had destroyed her.

Two of the new Tech's massive, angled legs froze under Bash's control, but the abomination only dragged them along in its march across the battlefield. The elements of the world raged as fae pitted every aspect of Thrae's magic against the invading horde.

I took up the magic's song. The wild rhythm grew louder and louder. Everything but the massive monstrosity disappeared from my reality. Power gathered in my chest. The music of Thrae rose in my ears, and I swiveled my hips in time. As I reached the climax, the buildup of magic and tension released with orgasmic pleasure.

A surge of blue-black power shot from me into my nearest thrall. The magic took whatever energy the dead had left and folded it over itself before jumping to the next, and the next. As the magic left them, my thralls tumbled to the ground.

I trembled. Before my last thrall, the gnomish girl, fell, I took direct control of her body and pushed my vision into her eyes in order to behold my genius.

The condensed magic streaked toward the suddenly still monstrosity in the middle of the battlefield. My twin, Light, hovered beneath its body. Light's brilliant, golden magic spread out from his back like wings and held the massive Tech in place. Shimmering blood dripped from his chin, and he shook with effort.

"I love you." Light lifted his arms, trusting I could hear him.

My heart stuttered. The world's song fell silent. I caught myself as the gnomish girl faltered forward.

The spell hit Light, enveloping his golden magic in deep, dark blue. My magic used his as a focus. My face, his face, all the goodness in my world, contorted in pain. His arms trembled as magic ripped through him and raced upward. Pain filled my Cara. Swirling dark and light tore into the monstrosity's underbelly. With a shower of sparks and a metallic tearing sound, oil and metal exploded across the battlefield.

I fought to stay in my thrall as the gnome's dead body absorbed the impact. The Tech's legs shook under the uneven weight of its ruined carapace. For a moment, I thought the Tech would crush Light, but the thing went ruinously still. Celebration shouts and battle cries exploded over the clash of fighting.

My twin found my thrall's gaze, my gaze, as his knees gave way and he sank to the ground. Deep blue veins covered his skin and pulsed in time with my frantic heartbeat. His grimace twisted into something resembling a smile.

A total, desolate silence sank its teeth into our Cara.

I slammed back into my own body, screaming from a throat already raw. Light. I had to get to Light. I sprinted forward, dodging blasts of energy and wildly swinging swords.

At the feet of the monstrosity, I found a ring of clear burned dirt with Light at the center. My thrall's eyes had not lied. His face had gone blue, leached of all its gold, all the good.

My deadened legs wouldn't carry me. I dropped to my knees and crawled the final few feet to him. Maybe by the time I covered the short distance he would remember how to heal. Maybe then I could remember how to breathe.

Light lay motionless in a patch of darkly scorched soil. I'd been stabbed, burned, and briefly disemboweled in other battles. A pain beyond any of those wounds ripped through my chest.

My soft wolf paw pads met the ruined dirt at his side. My wolf ensnared my mind, quieting the roar of hurt. I curled around my brother's cooling body with a weak howl, my only accompaniment to the day's victory.

1

ZELIMIR

I GLANCED TO MY LEFT AND SLIGHTLY BEHIND ME AT SHADE as I led my Cara mates through the door and into the Lower Council's audience chamber. We four loosely surrounded Declan with me in front, Bash and Teyr behind and slightly to each side of him, and Shade, as always, at Declan's side. I detected something indefinable in Shade. His Cara? I couldn't be sure.

From the corner of my eye, I glimpsed Declan trying mightily to hide how he favored his wounded ankle. I faced forward and prayed the Council didn't notice.

The massive, round door rolled into place behind us, sealing us in the windowless room. Hundreds of fifs lit the cavernous space, reflecting light off the polished, bare stone that looked black at first glance, but showed rainbows of dark colors in the light. Bickering over what decorations should exist in this neutral chamber had long ago resulted in a ban on all ornamentation except for an intricately carved arch of the same stone over the dais ahead of us where the Lower Council sat. The effect quailed most fae who entered the room for the first time, but I took strength from the austerity. In this place, we had nothing to hide behind. We could only trust the Cara to be strong enough, as we had the first time we took the vows.

I stopped a scant five feet in front of the Lower Council's raised stone dais. *Presumptuous*, my father's voice nagged in my mind. Politeness meant little to me with Declan's red blood still damp on my tunic. I straightened and *pulsed* to my mates. We parted from the circle to create a line. Bash, my dragon second, stood to my right, lilac head held high. Teyr moved to Bash's right, with fire flickering in his golden, slit-pupiled eyes. Declan's dark, curly hair bounced as I nudged him to my left. Shade, happy once again in dire wolf form, plopped his ass down straight on Declan's booted feet.

"As requested, we present the part-fae, Declan." My voice echoed off the bare walls. "We do not believe a mistake has been made and would like to finalize the Anam Cara."

Silence filled the room. The five fae who held our fate in their hands stared down at us from chairs carved of the same dark stone as the walls. Councilor Ambrocio sat front and center, his diaphanous, rainbow Lower Council robes draped over an antique, formal Cara uniform that only accentuated the way the tall elf's frame bent with age. His long, white beard brushed the floor. I didn't know if I should put any stock in the rumors about his ailing mind, but I knew he wouldn't stand with us. As ambassador to the Upper Council, he stood on no side but theirs.

To his left sat Councilor Gnuq, Headmaster of the Academy, wearing only his open Council robes. The satyr's pot belly had grown in the six years since we'd last been here, probably full of convenient deals and edicts that supported his reign over the training of Caras and Seccas alike. He rested his hands on the curly, golden hair that crested the midsection where his human and animal halves met and offered me a satisfied smile. I repressed a grimace. The Lower Council had earned my loyalty time and again, but I didn't know if I could count on Councilor Gnuq alone.

Councilor Odhrán sat bolt-upright in the far-left chair, though he barely cleared the armrests, wearing Council robes buttoned up to his chin. The short elf brought his trademark exuberance to the Lower Council, often swaying votes, and he managed our understanding of Tech as Liaison to the Jalan. His warm smile, as open as Councilor

Ambrocio's suspicion, eased the foul taste Councilor Gnuq left in my mouth.

To the farthest right, sat Councilor Drax, our former mentor and friend. His deep purple skin, swirling with hot-pink magic, glowed under his robe around worn leathers decorated only by a tiny, yellow lava flower. Before our demotion to border patrol, the Master Tactician managed our movements, as he did the movements of all Caras and Seccas. I had been counting on his support, but he would not meet my eye.

Lastly, I faced Councilor Xerxes. The spymaster looked much like the bhelrian he could shift into, all sharp features and cropped, brownish-yellow hair. He wore a suit of unassuming cream linen under his robe, but I knew better than to underestimate him. I could only hope his love of information would urge him to keep Declan close.

Councilor Xerxes laced his long fingers together in front of his face as he leaned forward. "The human—or mostly human, as you claim—is only a piece of the problem. Shade remains a wolf, and a replacement for a dead mate remains unheard of." The spymaster locked eyes with me. "Your Cara is in shambles, Commander Zelimir."

Declan spluttered. I stood even straighter. We'd never corrected Teyr's early lie about new fifths being common, but the Council couldn't know that.

My father's voice echoed in my ears, and I resisted the urge to clench my jaw in defiance. "My Anam Cara is in better shape with Declan than it's been since the Battle of Light."

Councilor Drax nodded sharply. "Shade shifted. We read the reports."

The tension in my shoulders eased slightly. Councilor Drax might not have looked at us, but he at least he hadn't spoken against us either.

Councilor Ambrocio waved dismissively. "The same report stated this useless human got captured at a rift that opened closer to our academy than any since the school was established."

"There have been three reports of rifts opening near the human"—Councilor Drax frowned—"four, if we include the one near the Waltzing Willow." He balled his fists. "The quantity of EarthTech that came through the rift a few hours ago implies Earth was waiting for the rift to open."

I swallowed. Bash had *pulsed* a similar suspicion, and I hadn't missed his purple-and-white scales shifting to belie his worry on the ride here. I couldn't deny I found the Tech's behavior strange, as well—if Tech could be said to have behavior. But surely, the best place to solve the problem of the escalation in rifts and what the Tech were up to would be at the Academy with the brightest minds of a generation within walking distance.

Councilor Ambrocio narrowed his eyes. "Whatever Tech happens to be patrolling on the other side is what comes through."

Fear leaked into Declan's Cara, and I sent him a wave of calm. Confusion replaced the fear, and I gritted my teeth.

Councilor Xerxes hummed. "With the escalation of late, perhaps it was only a matter of time before a rift appeared so close to the Academy."

Councilor Ambrocio fluffed his beard. "Four extra rifts is odd, but not unreasonable. Don't create conspiracies out of coincidences."

"Should we consider the Battle of Light?" With a sparkle of magic in his palm, Councilor Odhrán conjured a sheaf of papers and studied them. "The battle predates the human, but Commander Zelimir and his Cara were, obviously, instrumental."

Teyr sent me a spike of frustration. I ignored the hotheaded ember. The facts of our world couldn't be avoided to spare our feelings.

Councilor Drax shook his head. "We established the Battle of Light was bad luck. The big Tech—ChargeTech, I believe—stumbled through the rift and the others followed."

Curiosity spun through Declan's Cara. I had come to know him piece by piece, and I wanted more. My mates wanted more. Declan wanted more, I thought. But it took true emotional vulnerability to live with the soul bond the four of us shared, and our human simply didn't have the practice. He needed the training we'd all received.

Councilor Gnuq clopped a cloven hoof against the stone floor. "The rifts may be concerning, but they're not why we're here."

I eyed the satyr. His balding head reflected the light of the fifs as he studied Declan and licked his lips. Only years of diplomatic training kept me from sliding over to shield Declan from his gaze.

"I welcome the Anam Cara for retraining." Councilor Gnuq grinned. "If they can work together and repass their trials, who are we to interfere?"

I took a measured breath. Many fae called Councilor Gnuq the most powerful satyr alive. The Council relied heavily on his ability to control crowds in the Academy. He would make an invaluable ally, if he really wanted the same thing we did.

Councilor Odhrán hopped to his feet on his chair. "You can't expect to treat a veteran Cara like trainees."

Councilor Drax sighed. "They are a promising Anam Cara, but they don't have their first century together yet. They're hardly veterans."

Councilor Xerxes cocked his head to one side. "I don't like the idea that, after six hundred years, our magic is making mistakes." He ran a thumb along his thin lower lip. "To brush Declan off may be short-sighted."

"Not you too." Councilor Ambrocio sneered. "This *human* makes a mockery of our traditions."

Councilor Xerxes narrowed his eyes at Declan. "Rifts appearing around Declan isn't enough to draw conclusions. We require more infor-mation. He may have fae in him somewhere." He pursed his lips. "Come closer, human."

Declan slid his feet out from under Shade and clasped his hands behind his back like I'd shown him. Despite the fear trembling through his Cara, he took three confident steps forward.

Bash snarled and lunged after him. I twitched my hands behind my back and shot out a thin layer of purple force to grab his collar. My second growled but didn't struggle. His newly awoken dragon still strained against his iron control. We needed as much retraining as we could get. It wasn't until Declan began pulling us back together that I noticed how out-of-sync my mates had gotten. Since we lost Light, we'd all fallen back toward the fae we had been before the bond.

Declan held his head high as Councilor Drax stepped down from the dais and circled him. After a few slow circuits, he returned to his seat, and Councilor Xerxes stepped down. The spymaster lacked our old mentor's discretion and began prodding Declan. When he discovered the ears, the seated Councilors murmured amongst themselves.

Councilor Xerxes eventually retook his chair and looked at Councilor Ambrocio, who scoffed. Councilor Gnuq slid down happily. Declan's fear spiked, and our human batted Councilor Gnuq's hand away from his chest when the satyr tried to touch him. Bash growled again. I committed the intrusion to memory and tightened my grip on my second, as much to keep myself rooted in place as the dragon.

Between the Council's orders and our own prejudices, I hadn't thought to balance our bond as we traveled. To manage a true Cara, we needed to trust and love each other equally. My mates needed a commander, not the romantic Declan brought out in me.

The Councilors finished their inspection, and Declan returned to stand to my left. Shade circled him and rubbed against his hips. Declan's fear eased, and Bash relaxed. I released my magic. My hand ached from how hard I'd had to maintain my grip on the dragon.

"If you intend to fly in the face of all tradition, I have no choice but to reveal what I have seen." Councilor Ambrocio stood, and his beard shifted to expose the navy skin of his throat, the only clue to his heritage as an auspex.

I took a deep breath. In addition to more mundane magic, the old Councilor received visions like others of his clan. Most of the rumors about him suggested his visions could no longer be trusted, but that said nothing of what his fellow Councilors might believe.

"If we accept this human, I see our academy destroyed." Ambrocio braced his thin arms on the sides of his chair like the vision still wracked him. "Our towers drained of color to an Earthen white, and many of us dying in pools of our own blood."

Councilor Odhrán offered him a tense grin. "Ambrocio, I think—"

Councilor Xerxes tugged on his ear, and Councilor Ambrocio sat. The Councilors fell into a discussion as a soft haze of nonexistent room noise blotted out their words. Teyr crossed his arms. Bash rolled his neck out. Declan fidgeted with the charm on his belt. My heart pounded in my ears. Councilor Xerxes might affect our ability to hear their conversation, but I doubted he'd stop his fellow Councilors from observing us.

Councilor Ambrocio turned back to us as the sensory magic faded away. "We shall take a vote."

The air in front of each Councilor glowed a soft green as they voted. Moments later, the glow condensed into a bright circle visible to all five of them.

Councilor Drax raised an eyebrow. "Two in favor, one against, two abstentions." He met my gaze. "Commander Zelimir's Anam Cara will be given the opportunity to prove the magic is correct with retraining." He looked at Declan. "You understand what this means?"

Declan bit his lip. Councilor Drax's gaze softened. Perhaps our old mentor still remained under the surface.

"Your Cara is fresh," he said. "Your minds still walk their own paths. By training, you merge those paths, tangling them together and solidifying what connections grow, until you become a single, streamlined unit. Everything but a true hive mind." Five strings of pink magic grew out of the pink lines on Councilor Drax's forehead, tangled together to form a knot, then turned into a solid, glowing ball. "If you don't merge correctly or if you fail one of your trials, your connections will shatter." The ball burst, leaving behind scraps of broken, pink magic.

Declan flinched.

Councilor Drax turned back to me. "Will the Anam Cara submit?"

Declan shifted and tugged on my arm. If we'd been anywhere else, I would've been charmed. Here, I gritted my teeth. He'd just shown the Council he couldn't understand our *pulses*.

"You don't have to do this," he whispered. "I don't want to be the reason you lose nearly a century of work."

I addressed the Council as if Declan hadn't spoken. "We will submit."

Shade howled. Councilor Ambrocio glared as the sound bounced around the chamber.

"So be it," Councilor Drax said. "I strip you of your rank as Anam Cara. Report to Bodmier for equipping. You will undergo the five trials—"

I stepped forward, perilously close to the base of the dais. "We request our first trial."

Caras completed trials in the order we arrived at the Academy, which put me first. Declan would be last.

Councilor Ambrocio stomped. "You haven't even begun training yet."

Teyr stepped up beside me. "Our rank doesn't change our experience." He gestured to Councilor Gnuq. "The rules state an Anam Cara may request their trials as they feel ready, don't they, Headmaster? That's what separate us from mere Anam Seccas, who are tested at regular intervals."

Councilor Gnuq grinned. "Why, yes, you're right. And as headmaster, I think it only fair our newest recruits follow the same rules as all the others."

"Three days hence." A deep voice boomed around us.

The Upper Council. I'd never heard them directly before. I took a step back and poured calm through my Cara, as much for myself as my mates. Only sheer will kept me from pulling Declan to my chest. Councilor Ambrocio existed to ferry messages between the Upper Council and the rest of us, but only they would reach into this chamber and make pronouncements. A tense silence fell as the whole room held its breath in anticipation of more.

Councilor Ambrocio stood. "The Upper Council has spoken."

Councilor Drax cleared his throat, his eyes fixed on Declan. "Three days hence. I hope for your sakes that your confidence matches your skills."

Declan grabbed my arm again, and I batted his hand away. The Upper Council, the remains of Varsina's Cara, fae so powerful they no longer considered our world their home, had taken an interest in us. I couldn't remember a time in the last century when they'd interfered with how the Lower Council ran the Academy or anything else. We had to excel now more than ever.

Anam Cara

A Flash of Silver
Behind Stone Walls
The Crystalline Heart

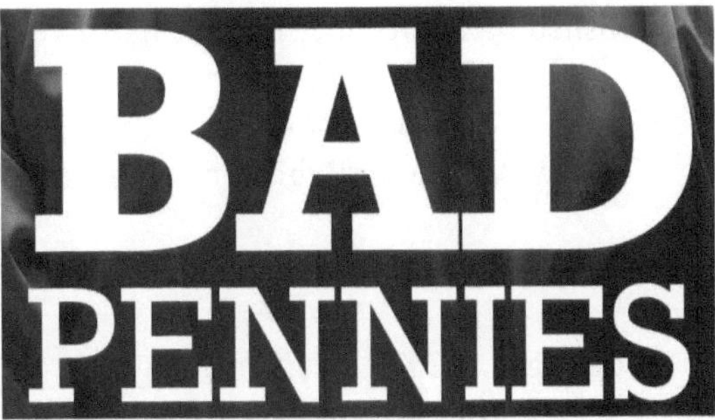

JOHN BUKOWSKI

A SEQUEL TO PROJECT SUICIDE

Published by PathBinder Publishing LLC
P.O. Box 2611
Columbus, IN 47202
www.PathBinderPublishing.com

Copyright © 2025 by John Bukowski
All rights reserved

Edited by Doug Showalter
Cover designed by Kassondra Hattabaugh
Cover photo by Pixabay

First published in 2025
Manufactured in the United States

ISBN: 978-1-955088-83-1
Library of Congress Control Number: 2024922419